MEAS

IN

FRIENDS

FRANKIE WILLIAMSON

For Leanne

CHAPTER 1

I step onto the 6.10am bus, which I lovingly refer to as a peasant wagon and do a small internal happy dance that there are empty seats. I park myself on one, put some music in my ears and look around at the rest of the blurry-eyed passengers wondering if they too would rather be anywhere else but here. I wonder the same thing every morning whilst vowing that things will change: I'll get a different job, win the lotto, marry a rich man etc. etc. All of which I have slim to no chance of doing. Partly as I never play the lottery, but mainly because I am already married to a not very rich man.

I met Will when I was young and impressionable. I was quite happy to marry him, deliriously so actually. It's just that sometimes, no occasionally, well almost never really, I wish that I had listened to my (very wise as it turns out) mother who often told me to marry for money the first time and for love the second. I didn't listen and now I am trapped in a moneyless marriage. I suppose it's better than being trapped in a loveless one and as we don't have kids it would be easy enough to trot off into the sunset alone, but I love him and he (mostly) makes me happy so stuck I am, I guess...

I'm jolted out of my daydream as the bus jerks to a stop. Reluctantly I climb off and make the short walk to the office. It's

Thursday— team meeting day. It's only a team meeting in the sense that the whole team tend to be in it. This is not by choice. We would all rather be doing something fun like trying to trap our nipples in car doors or trying to wax our fanny with gaffer tape. It is not a team meeting in any other sense. The 'team meeting' pretty much involves our rancid boss talking for an hour about how amazing she is and how shit the rest of us are. She uses the word *team* in at least every other sentence to reinforce how much of a team we are.

To further reinforce the mantra, she throws in her favourite phrase 'we all just need to get along.' We don't.

Not. At. All.

In fact, 90 per cent of us can't stand her or each other. The other 10 per cent have bonded like only the institutionalised can in our mutual hatred of the rest who are total, utter fucktards. Our great leader (OGL when we're being covert) being the Queen fucktard. She's like Cruella de Vil but with no sense of style and even less people skills. What's worse is the fact she has no idea how awful she is. She waltzes in with a fake smile plastered on her face screeching greetings to anyone unlucky enough to be in earshot while the rest of us imagine her dying a slow, horrible death.

I decided long ago that hers was a face I would never tire of hitting. Every time she talks to me through gritted teeth about a 't' I didn't cross or an 'i' that I didn't dot I feel my knuckles twitching. One day the twitching will turn into an upper cut and I'll be sent on the walk of shame down to HR. I would be a hero, though an unemployed one.

Today's meeting starts much the same as all the others. We go through the sales figures. Despite mine being the highest for the fifth week in a row, I don't get a mention (also for the fifth week in a row). The reason being, the delightful Bianca (B for short) hates me. She would never admit this and if anyone dared to suggest it to her she would gasp and howl and shake her head in a performance worthy of an Oscar. However, it's true. I'm punctual, I'm honest, I'm NEVER off ill, I work super hard AND more often than not I have the highest sales figures.

In a nutshell, if I left she would go down like the pilot of MH370. Despite this she has zero time for me, she smiles at me through gritted teeth and barely utters a word unless it's to tell me I haven't done something right. I cannot recall a single occasion in the last two years when she has thanked me for my hard efforts or said anything which could resemble a compliment. It wasn't always like this.

She was so excited at the prospect of what my amazing selling ability could bring her that she practically pissed her pants when I accepted the job. Her over-the-top enthusiasm during my interview regaling me with tales of team camping trips and visits to the ice-skating rink ought to have set alarm bells ringing that she was on the crazy side of crazy. But it didn't and the money being offered was good, so I jumped in. It wasn't long after my first week that I realised I had made a dreadful mistake and that B wasn't just crazy, she was bordering on psychotic. She was (is) also uber paranoid.

Despite her constant attestations about everyone getting on and being a team there is actually nothing B likes less than people getting along. She prefers conversations between colleagues to be kept to a minimum, only work must be discussed and only ever in a positive light. You must NEVER say anything negative, and woe betide anyone who dares speak the truth. There'll be none of that truth telling honesty here. No siree. If you can't say anything false and positive, then don't say anything at all. This is one of the reasons B hates me.

There are two people traits I hate, and both begin with the letter L: lying and laziness. These are the foundations upon which B has built her team. I refuse to lie and, rather than seeing this as a positive attribute, B sees it as the opposite. She actually told me that she thought I was negative. When I asked her to elaborate she said, and I'm not kidding, 'I see you talking to people.' That was it, her remarkable reason for deeming me negative. It's almost as profound as 'I see dead people' but not quite as spine tingling. What she actually meant is I don't talk bullshit to people. If something is going on and it stinks, I'll say so.

She thinks I'm on a one-woman mission to destroy her and her reputation, though she's done an incredible job of destroying that herself. She has me pegged as something akin to the leader of the Church of Scientology and I'm brainwashing all her staff into thinking she's useless and her department is shit. No brainwashing is required. She is useless and her department is shit. Any simpleton can see that.

She controls all in-office conversations with her stalking skills. I reckon she could pass a stealth test for the SAS with ease. She watches for signs that people might be daring to move away from their desks to have a quiet conversation. Then Ninja-like, she prowls until she spots her prey. This is where her stealth skills stop, and she sticks out like a white woman in a mosque. You spot her coming and quickly try to turn your conversation to a work (not work personnel) related topic. She isn't fooled. She stands within earshot until you have to admit the game is up and toddle back to your desk.

Some people may wonder why (a) I haven't left, and (b) I haven't been fired. I haven't left as I can't find another job that pays as well. I have literally sold my soul to the Devil. B doesn't sack me as B doesn't sack anyone, she prefers the 'push them out' method of employee cleansing. If she grew some balls and actually sacked me, she would have to explain to the powers that be why the person who earns the most money is gone—me 'talking to people' simply isn't going to wash. As a result, we are resigned to our toxic mutual loathing. Luckily, I have side-kicks who keep me sane. If not for them I would have thrown myself out of the sixth-floor window years ago.

Willow is thirty-one, she's married with two adorable kids (not so adorable that my ovaries have started twitching but adorable enough). I clocked her rapidly rolling her eyes during my first ever team meeting and made it my mission to befriend her. It wasn't that difficult, it seems she had been desperately waiting for a like-minded soul to save her from oppression. When I asked if she fancied going for a coffee to escape the fun house, I wasn't sure if she was going to kiss me, lick me, high-five me or just burst into tears on the spot. And so, our friendship blossomed over a weak almond latte and a caramel slice.

We recruited Charlotte when she joined the team six months later. She's a sweet girl of twenty-six, desperately seeking love and desperately wishing she had never fallen in love with her colleague Tim, who subsequently fell out of love with her (I don't think he was actually ever in it) so she had to find another job. She couldn't bear to see him every day. He wasn't going anywhere so she took the first job that came along (this one) falling for B's one big happy family interview act hook, line and sinker. It happens to the best of us. Despite the sweetness her astuteness eventually came through for her and she cottoned on to B's 'divide and conquer' game playing pretty early on.

So, there we are in the meeting, rolling our eyes at the act we've come to know and despise. Our great leader turns to one of our not very illustrious colleagues and says, 'Louise, despite the fact you're an arse-licking, brown-nosing, poisonous snake you have the most improved sales this week so well done, the rest of you could take a leaf out of her book.' Ok, so I made that first part up. She is all of those things and more, but our great leader didn't mention any of them.

Louise's improved sales mean she has gone from sixth out of eight to fifth. Woo freaking hoo, throw her a banana. This is the kind of crap we have become accustomed to. Not even a mention for Willow who despite only working four days a week is second on the list. I'm pretty sure there is steam coming out of my ears, and nose and possibly my arse. I feel I am going to spontaneously combust at any moment. Willow and Charlotte both see this and give a pitying shake of their head. Jess (who isn't part of our gang purely as she likes to stay neutral) looks at me and shrugs her shoulders. Am I in a parallel fucking universe?

Why don't one of you fucktards (who get shat on from a great height daily) open your fucking mouths and speak up, I scream inside my head. Willow and Charlotte have mastered the ability of not caring a jot about B or her mind games, but you only have to look at some of the others' faces to know that they haven't. God why don't they stand up for themselves? I am left in a state of shock when at that moment Charlotte (with a look of pure determination on her face) says, 'Excuse me B.' B looks up, the fake smile is firmly in place, but her eyes have turned almost black.

'Yes Charlie,' she says. She knows Charlotte hates being called that by her (just her, she says it's too familiar and they are not on those kinds of terms!) and I'm sure B's done it just to throw her and put her on the back foot.

'Err, well, I was just wondering…'

'What?' she replies.

'Why haven't you said anything about Hannah's or Willow's sales figures when they have been first and second for the last month or so? I mean, it seems a bit unfair for them to work so hard and get no recognition for it.' I swear she said it all without taking a breath. I also swear you could hear a fairy fart; the room went that quiet. B's grin stayed firmly in place as she carefully considered her response.

'I'm not sure your information is right, Charlie, and I don't recall the figures for the past month but if you are right, and I doubt you are, it is simply due to the fact that they have well-established clients with whom I am in regular contact. As you know, a call from me can make the difference between a sale and no sale, such is my influence. Everyone else's clients are all pretty new to this firm and I have yet to build the relationship with them that I have with Willow's and Hannah's.' She practically spits out my name. 'Moving forward those relationships will form and Hannah and Willow will have some real competition.'

Did I just fucking hear right?? Our sales figures aren't due to our hard work but are due to her making calls and building relationships with clients. Is she for bloody real?? I want to tell her to stick her job up her bony arse. From the look on Willow's face she wants to do the same but neither of us will. We need the money and sales jobs are few and far between at the minute. Everyone else in the room looks down. They all know it's bullshit but none of them dares say a thing. Poor Charlotte looks green. B looks super pleased with herself and says, 'Right, if no one else has any questions we'll get back to it.'

The second we are back at our desks I Skype Charlotte and Willow. 'Coffee?'

***

We head to our favourite coffee shop. The waitress nods to me in a 'your usual' fashion and I nod back. Then I let rip, filling the air with expletives, some of which I'm sure I have just made up on the spot, unless I missed twatinator being added to the dictionary.

'Why do you let her get to you so much? If you didn't, she wouldn't get any pleasure out of winding you up and she would focus on some other poor bastard,' says Willow.

'I've tried counting to ten, I've tried to take deep meditation-like breaths and I have tried imagining her naked. It wasn't pleasant. In my head she looked like an under-cooked chicken with a black brillo pad for a muff,' I say.

'She's just not worth the wrinkles the stress is giving you,' says Charlotte.

'I know you're both right, but she gets under my skin like a tick. I am sick of hearing myself say the same thing over and over and I'm sure it's only a matter of time before Will files for divorce. He keeps telling me to leave sales altogether and find something that makes me happy, but I know we can't afford for me to do that. Especially not if we want to have babies.'

'There's your get-out clause,' says Willow. 'Get preggers and have a year off. You have a different perspective when you've had children and your priorities change.'

'Cover your ears Charlotte, we're about to have another "my kids are the best thing that ever happened to me since Danny Wood fingered me in year ten" speech.'

Willow kicks me. 'Piss off. It was year eleven.'

We all burst out laughing and I feel some of the tension lift.

'God, how did I wind up here?'

CHAPTER 2

I get home and decide to go for a run. Running always makes me feel better.

I do a quick three miles which is enough to relax me a little bit and make me less likely to be sat in a crumpled, crying heap on the kitchen floor when Will gets in. Once upon a time he would bound through the front door, give me a kiss and ask, 'Have you had a day?' These days he slinks towards me with trepidation, gives me a quick peck on the lips, asks no questions then runs off to get a shower.

'Have I had a day, you ask? Have I! B was fabulous today. She walked, no floated into the office on what can only be described as a heavenly cloud. She gave us all a £1,000 bonus just because it was Thursday and said that as we were all so amazing we could take Friday off. I know, she is a splendid human being. So splendid in fact that I have nominated her for the Nobel "Best Boss That Ever Walked the Fucking Planet prize".'

I summon up a smile that reaches my eyes, I did get an A in GCSE drama, so this is not difficult to do. What is difficult is trying to keep at bay the tears that are welling up in my smiling eyes. They're not sad tears, they're obviously not happy tears either. Fuck no! They are tears of frustration.

Why do I let this woman dominate my every thought? I cannot stand her and yet I have let her take over a sizeable portion of my brain to the extent she is my first waking thought, my last thought and my only thought between the hours of 9am and 5pm. I have let the witch take over my life. I don't even know when exactly it happened. She just seeped in a little more each day and now I can't get rid of her. She's like a poisonous weed I can't control so she grows and grows and I fear one day will be my every thought. Ugh, I shudder at THAT thought.

Determined to not have another night ruined by bitterness and anger, I wipe my eyes and prepare to greet Will as he emerges from the shower. Towel wrapped around his waist, bronze skin glistening with water, his deep brown eyes penetrating mine. He really is a handsome bastard. 'What's for tea?' He asks.

'I was hoping you might have an idea,' I reply

'Pub it is then.'

This is never a good idea when I have had a day like today as a) I'm likely to drink too much and b) when I drink too much I cry. I will also miss not throwing on my pj's, which is my usual after work ritual. My feet are barely in the door before I race upstairs most days. Poor Will, I go to work looking half reasonable and by the time he comes home I look like Worzel Gummidge's older sister.

Will sees the look of fear on my face and knows instantly the reason.

'It's ok, we'll just have a main and one drink and be home by 9pm.' I like his optimism but I'm not at all convinced that we'll be home anywhere near 9pm.

I throw on some clothes, it's pretty cold so skinny jeans, jumper and long boots will do the trick. There's a hint of muffin top threatening to peep out from under the jumper and over my jeans so I carefully tuck it in. I really should have put the high waisted jeans on which I have discovered are the best hiders of muffins known to man. Even the muffiest of muffin tops can be made to disappear by a pair of high waisted jeans. The only thing the 80's got right.

Luckily, or unluckily depending on how I feel the morning after the night before— the pub is only a five minute walk away so there's no driving required. It's quiz night tonight but it starts at nine and as we will allegedly be home before then there is no chance of winning the thirty quid prize or the bottle of fizzy cat piss, they pass off as Champagne for the runners up.

We take our seats in the snug and peruse the menus. Will decides he is going to drink wine instead of lager, we elect to order a bottle rather than two glasses as it works out cheaper. We plump for a bottle of Marlborough Sauvignon Blanc and I head to the bar to order that and a couple of steak and chips. As I'm about to order I hear a familiar cackle and follow it to the familiar face across the bar, familiar as in one of my very best friends. There are two things I can do in this situation: one would be the sensible option of pretending I haven't noticed her and shuffle back to hide in the snug so as not to turn our early night into a late one and the other (not too sensible option) is to shout her name, wave my hands madly and get her to join our table.

Within seconds we're doing the squealing hugging thing. I drag her over to Will announcing, 'Look who I found'. He does the honourable thing and acts equally as excited as I did (with less squealing) but I am very aware that he is not excited at all for he knows exactly what happens when Nicky and I get together and it is never pretty. We are both at an age where we should know better but we rarely do. My day just got a million times better!

'You should have said you were coming,' I say to her. 'I could have seen if Charlotte and Willow wanted to join us, well Charlotte anyway. Willow doesn't play out on a school night.'

'We didn't know ourselves until half an hour ago,' she replies. 'James thought he would be working late but he got finished early and I couldn't be arsed cooking so here we are.'

Nicky's fella James emerges from the opposite side of the bar and after the obligatory air kissing and hand shaking, sits down. James is a nice guy, boring as frig but nice. Thankfully he does like a drink though and when he drinks he develops a bit of a personality. He is the polar opposite of Nicky. She is fabulously independent, loves adventure and has a wicked sense of humour. They say opposites attract and the two of them are as opposite as cream and crackers. They've been happily plodding along together for a few years now though so it's clearly working for them and who am I to Judge?

***

Meals devoured Will ditches the wine and turns to lager leaving Nicky and I to the mercy of the bottle. The quiz is about to start, our good intentions for an early night are clearly out of the window so Nicky and I decide we may as well order another bottle (surprise, surprise).

I'm not very good at pub quizzes. Don't get me wrong, I'm a master at the music and entertainment rounds. Anything to do with the Kardashians or *Real Housewives of* *insert pretentious city here* and I am your girl. I'm also pretty good with sport as long as that sport is Formula 1. But anything else is a mystery. This is where Will comes into his own and our teamwork shines.

He is a mountain of useless information. What he doesn't know about current affairs or history since 15,000 BC is not worth knowing. I'm unclear where he gained all of this knowledge as he was shit at school and never went to Uni. He would argue what I know is useless but I disagree. To me, knowing which of the Kardashian/Jenners is which and who is dating/married to/divorcing which rapper/sportsman is important in the social media led world we live in. You see EVERYONE has an opinion on the Kardashians so you can strike up a conversation with literally anyone in the world. Not everyone knows what global warming is or what it does (or can translate it into a different language) so you tell me which is the more useful of the two.

Exactly my point.

Round one is always 'the news today' and unless it's been on Facebook it's unlikely I'll know it so I leave it to Will and carry on chinwagging with Nicky. We have opted to be a team of four (technically at this precise moment we're still a team of two, Will and James) to increase our chances of winning and because Nicky can't be arsed trying to think.

Round two is sports, no F1 questions, so I'm not needed.

Turns out round three is my round. I gear up, even after five glasses of wine I know my encyclopaedic knowledge of all things reality will not let me down. I'm very wrong. I don't know if it was the wine, the questions, Nicky screeching in my ears or all three but I failed miserably. Only one of the questions was even about the Kardashians: 'Which of the Kardashian family recently walked in the famous Victoria's Secret fashion show?' Even Will knew the answer (I'm sure most blokes in there did).

I consider calling for the question to be re-asked as technically it wasn't a Kardashian it was a Jenner and I announce this loudly for all to hear. Will shoots daggers at me, I lower my voice. Nicky is pissing herself. When she laughs, I laugh and before long (much to Will and James' disgust) we are both cackling like demented witches. This might be acceptable in a busy city pub on a Saturday night but at the pensioner filled local on a Thursday night it does not go down too well. We are being stared at by everyone.

I'm not certain (as it's hard to hear over the cackle) but I think the quizmaster just called for us to keep the noise down while he announces the answers. Will and James are hissing at us to, 'shut the fuck up,' but we are gone. We've got to the point of hysterical laughter and we don't know what we're laughing about. All we know is that another bottle of vino is required.

'What a splendid idea, naughty Nicky.'

'I know, I'm full of them, Holy Hannah.'

We burst into hysterical laughter once more and Will and James snap. They grab each of us by an arm and march us out of the doors. We collapse on the footpath in a heap and they leave us while they go back inside and pay the bill.

Fuck, the concrete is cold. It brings me to my senses sharpish and I have an amazing idea.

'Why don't you come back to ours? I've got a bottle of Prosecco in the fridge with our name on it.'

'Sounds good to me,' Nicky answers.

We help each other up just as Will and James emerge (looking less than amused, I'm not sure they're about to get any happier when I tell them what has been decided while they've been gone).

'Nicky and James are coming back to ours for a drink.'

'Are we?' James asks.

'Yes, we are. Hannah kindly asked and I kindly accepted so you can drive us there,' Nicky informs him.

James is always the designated driver of the pair which comes in handy on nights like this when it is freezing cold and we're too pissed to walk. 'I'm not sure Nik, we've to be up for work in the morning,' pleads James.

At this point Will sticks his two penneth in.

'Yeah, James is right, Han. We've to be up too and you've already had too much, you'll regret it in the morning. Why don't we arrange something for the weekend instead?'

Will is trying to be assertive. I don't take kindly to his tone of voice so I put my arm through Nicky's.

'I'm a big girl, I think I'll decide when I've had too much so show us to the car please James.' And with that I start dragging Nicky down the street.

This is a tad unwise as I don't know if I am going in the right direction and I'm going to look a real tool if I have to do an about turn in my current state of huff. Thankfully James strides past. Confirmation I'm on the right track. As we stumble along I realise I probably am a little fresh and should just go home to bed but I won't give Will the satisfaction. I resolve to water down my Prosecco with soda.

We arrive home and I dart upstairs to the loo to empty my bladder leaving the other three mulling around downstairs. The men don't look happy and I'm sure I hear Will say he is going to put the kettle on. Our kitchen/dining area is open plan. If Will leads everyone in there I won't be able to meddle with my drinks. I really need Will to have them all sit in the living room.

'Will, it's bloody freezing. Put the fire on so we can sit in the living room,' I say as I make my way back downstairs.

'Ok boss,' he says.

Fabulous, I can sober up while having the pleasure of feeling like I've got one over Will. I manage to make it to the bottom of the stairs without falling and my heart sinks when I enter the room. Nicky has already poured us both a glass and the fizz is sat beside her ready to be re-poured. Oh shit, how am I going to get out of this one? I could take my glass into the kitchen while making toast (obligatory post skinful delicacy), pour the contents away and top up with the soda but I'm only going to get away with that once. It will have to do.

'Hey, who wants a snack? Cheese on toast, peanut butter on toast, jam on toast, plain toast,' I ask.

'I'm good thanks,' Will's reply is no surprise.

'Me too,' nor is James.'

'Ooh go on then I'll have cheese,' says Nicky.

I pick up my glass and head into the kitchen. I throw the contents into the sink just as Nicky walks in.

'Need some help?' she asks. Phew I got away with it.

'Chuffing nora that went down quick, let me bring the bottle in here.' It seems she has noticed my empty glass. 'I don't want to sit with those miserable twats anyway. They can enjoy their brew in peace.' I brace myself for another full glass. It might actually work out well, if I can keep pouring it away as quick as she fills my glass we should be done soon and I can get to bed.

Nicky returns with the bottle as I'm grating cheese onto a plate. Holding the cheese is actually far more difficult than I had imagined. My face is contorted in concentration as I try not to grate my knuckles. I'm blinking wildly trying to focus my eyes. It's like looking through a kaleidoscope and I'm beginning to feel a little sick. This is not helped by Nicky thrusting yet another full glass at me.

'Here you go, get that down yer neck.' I can't think of anything I'd like to do less but as it was my idea to carry the party on I feel guilty and take a sip. It's not half bad. I hope I feel the same way if it decides to leave my body in a most violent fashion in around six hours' time.

PMA (positive mental attitude) required. Sickness is not allowed. I'll get some carbs down me, pop a couple of paracetamols and possibly a Berocca, get a solid fiveish hours and be good to go.

'So what do you want to do with yourself, Han?' she asks.

Go to bed is what I think but what I say is, 'For now or for life?'

'For life, you know your whole life is still ahead of you.'

Oh crap. Nicky has a habit of insisting on these deep and meaningfuls when she's had a few and they tend to go on for a while. I try to think of an answer that will get the conversation over quickly. I'm dying for the loo again, my bladder is as weak as a fat kid around cake.

'Well, go on, where do you see yourself in five years? Not working for bitch face surely. My ears couldn't cope with your constant fucking whingeing.' She bursts into laughter. It's loud and the kitchen door slams shut. 'Oops my happiness seems to have upset the boys,' she says.

'I don't know what to do. I'm not good at anything and I don't know how to do anything else,' I answer.

'I'm going to rent my house and go travelling for a year. James isn't keen just yet but I'll work my magic,' she adds a wicked cackle for effect.

'Balls. Aren't you a bit old for backpacking? You'd be the oldest couple in the hostel. Unless they're all 18-30 you're screwed,' I say.

'Knob off, I'm not staying in a hostel. I am a sophisticationed lady and only the best will do,' she replies.

'You can't afford the best Nik; you're always moaning you're skint so you better lower your sights.'

'Well thanks awfully for shitting on my dreams Han, always the pessimist.'

'Realist, you mean. I'm just pointing out the obvious flaw in your plan.'

'Dream, Han. It's a dream not a plan. It will become a plan as soon as I convince James as he is the planner extraordinaire! Right, so now you've dismissed my dreams let's have a laugh at yours. Don't say shagging Channing Tatum cos that ain't never going to happen!'

I feign despair, 'What? Never? Now who's shitting on who?' We both piss ourselves (almost literally in my case). 'I've told you, I don't know. I've always quite fancied owning a coffee shop.'

Nicky convulses with laughter and spits a gob full of fizz into the sink. 'You? Working with the public? I almost pissed me pants. If there was ever a person who shouldn't work with the public that person would be you, no offence.'

'Oh, none fucking taken,' I say feeling somewhat aggrieved.

'Don't get me wrong, you're all smiley and that, but you're not very tolerated of people are you.'

'You mean tolerant and yes I am. I've worked for that mean bitch for long enough without beating the living shit out of her. I'd say that's very tolerant.'

'That's different though,' she says.

'How exactly?' I ask, intrigued.

'Because you work for her, dickhead. You react, you get sacked and as much as you hate her you can't risk that. Now imagine yourself in your little coffee shop making totally shit coffee as you're not a Barista and serving totally wank cakes cos you're shit at baking. Don't look at me like that, you know it's true. Anyway so you do all that and a perfectly lovely looking customer walks up to the counter and informs you it was the worst coffee/cake they've ever tasted and cat piss with a side of bird shit would have been nicer. What do you do?'

I ponder carefully, as carefully as anyone who has had a skinful can anyway and say, 'I tell them they've obviously ruined their taste buds by smoking too much crack and suggest they get the fuck out and don't come back. In my gaff the customer will not always be right,' I answer feeling pretty pleased with myself.

'I rest my case,' she says shaking her head.

We finish our drinks and Nicky tops us up with the last of the bottle. We eat our now clap cold cheese on toast in silence and slink back to the room in search of warmth. What we find is both men snoring on the sofa. Rock and Roll! Even Nicky is looking tired now. I suspect all that deep and meaningful has taken it out of her and tell her so.

'It's exhausting being a philanthropist,' she says.

'I think you probably mean philosophist but you're not one of those either.'

We finish our drinks in relative quiet as I muse over Nicky's 'philosophy'. As much as it pains me she is right. I know fuck all about running a coffee shop. I've never even worked in one. I also have zero patience and imagine my lack of customer service qualities would put me out of business in record time. I soooo want to do it though. It's been a dream/desire/wish/hope of mine for at least eight years. Ever since Will and I paid our first visit to Cornwall.

We stayed in a gorgeous B&B with super nice owners who, after the first night noticed we were wine drinkers (the empty bottles in the bin being the give-away) and put wine glasses in our room. You don't get that kind of attention to detail at the Travelodge. The B&B was close to the beach. I'm not really a beach person, besides the sand welding itself to everything there is the lack of toilets. The ones they do have look like they have been frequented by a group of delinquent toddlers who have not yet been potty trained. I hate that in order to have a 'nice' day on the beach you need to take at least 25kg of paraphernalia with you which takes three fucking hours to pack up when you've had enough (which in my case is usually an hour in).

But I do love looking at the beach, the colours of the sea against the sand and sky, the sheer peacefulness of it; the wondering of what is beyond the horizon fills my heart with hope. When I'm stood staring out I always feel inspired. Will and I found a fabulous café right on the seafront and our weekend was made. We spent many a happy hour drinking coffee, eating cake, musing over where we would moor our boat and it came to me, my perfect job; owning a coffee shop. Imagine coming to work every day, looking out at the crystal blue sea under a perfect blue sky, spending the day chit-chatting to all and sundry and everyone would be happy because they were either on holiday or lived surrounded by such beauty.

I remember telling Will. His response was pretty much the same as Nicky's but instead of spitting fizz into the sink he almost choked on his flat white. He said I was living in cloud cuckoo land and that it was cold at least 350 days of the year and rained for at least 300 so I'd most likely be looking out at a grey sky and no sea, talking to myself as customers would be few and far between when it was pissing it down. Bubble burst. I spent the next couple of hours sulking and only cheered up when he apologised and said he was all for me following my dreams but thought I should do more research before I make a life choice based on a couple of afternoons drinking coffee at the seaside.

I wake with a jolt. I must have nodded off and see that Nicky has done the same. She's also managed to spill the contents of her glass on the carpet. Either that or she's pissed herself. I elbow her and she slurs a few words before falling back into a deep sleep. I see that Will is no longer on the sofa. What a cock. He has taken himself to bed and left the rest of us to it. It's half-past midnight. Oh shit.

Less than five hours before I have to be up. It's barely worth going to bed but I am way too old to even consider pulling an all-nighter.

I peel myself off the sofa and retrieve some spare blankets from the cupboard. I throw one over Nicky and another over James and head upstairs. I spend thirty seconds scrubbing my face with a wet wipe and another thirty brushing my teeth (mainly my tongue in a vain attempt to prevent it furring overnight) and throw myself in bed giving Will a good elbow in the ribs to stop him snoring.

CHAPTER 3

God help me. I wake up four minutes before my alarm is due to sound. My head hurts, my mouth is dry and I think my breath could fell a bull at fifteen paces. I drag myself out of bed and pray a hot shower and a good teeth brushing will make me feel almost human.

It doesn't quite do the trick but it does make me feel slightly more awake. I quickly dress and head downstairs. For a second I'm confused. I distinctly remember leaving two sleeping people on the sofa and yet there is no one here. I check the kitchen and notice that I didn't put my phone on charge. Oh joy. Three per cent battery left and a text from Nicky: 'Gone him, ting you tmrw xc.'

I put the kettle on, perhaps a strong coffee and toast will do what the shower couldn't. I've started to feel dizzy and I've broken out into a sweat. I convince myself it's hunger. Breakfast made I sit down and tuck in. Two mouthfuls of toast is all that is needed for my stomach to decide it really is not happy with the contents and I run gagging and spill my guts into the toilet. Each time I wretch my head feels like it's going to explode and I have a hot flush. So this is what the menopause feels like. I'm not keen.

Confident I'm done I flush the toilet and see Will standing in the doorway.

'Don't say a fucking word,' I snap.

'Well you're chirpy this morning. Was it the cheese or the toast that did it?'

'You are not funny, dickhead. Maybe if you'd put me to bed last night instead of abandoning me I might have had enough sleep and be ok.'

Will shakes his head. 'Love, you were asleep when I went to bed and I don't think the reason you're chundering is due to you sleeping on the wrong furniture. I think it's probably got more to do with the three bottles of wine you necked.'

'Whatever it was, I don't feel at all well,' I say.

'Go back to bed and I'll bring you some water.'

'As fabulous as that sounds I can't, I have a little thing called work to go to.'

'Ring in sick, they don't have to know the reason,' he replies.

'I can't, I've got big meeting this morning and if I don't turn up I will be signing my own P45.'

'Fine, you better think of something to perk you up then.'

'Thanks for that,' I say. Like I hadn't thought of it myself. I brush my teeth again and try to disguise my grey pallor with make-up. It's not great but it will have to do. I take two ginger tablets, grab my lunch from the fridge and head out of the door. I'll do my hair when I get to work.

I ring Charlotte en route.

'Hello, what bleeding time do you call this?' she answers.

'Sorry, I thought you'd be up,' I say

'Well I'm not and wasn't due to be for another forty-five minutes so cheers'. Oops. There's only one thing Charlotte likes more than the thought of everlasting love and it's sleep.

'What time are you going to be in then?' I ask.

'8.59, like always,' she replies.

'Can't you come in a bit earlier?' I plead.

'No I chuffing can't. Why the hell would I want to spend a minute more than I have to in that hell hole? Why does it matter to you anyway?'

I decide to tell her the truth. It's not like she's going to grass. 'I'm hanging. We went to the pub last night, bumped into Nicky. She came back to ours and I didn't go to bed until after midnight. I feel and look as rough as a badger's arse.'

'How will me coming in earlier help you?' she asks.

'Well, I just thought you could maybe bring me a bacon butty. I'm already on my way and the shops don't open until later,' I answer.

'And what do I get out of it?'

'The pleasure of knowing you did a good deed.' It's the best I can come up with.

'Knob off, I do those all the time so don't need any extra pleasure there.'

'Ok, how about I buy you a coffee every day next week and lunch today,' I offer.

'Well I'm awake now with no chance of going back to sleep so I may as well. Red sauce or brown?' she asks.

'I can't believe you have to ask. Brown. See you soon and thank you.'

I arrive at work hoping to enjoy the two hours before OGL arrives and her darkness envelops all of those around her. I am mortified when I see her pointy face and bad hair already at her desk.

She barely looks up and does not acknowledge me. This is going to be uncomfortable. I hope Charlotte gets here sooner rather than later, safety in numbers and all that. Plus Charlotte has the ability to ignore any atmosphere and will rattle on regardless.

I duck into the kitchen hoping to hide out while Charlottes arrives and as I didn't ask her to get me a coffee I'll waste some time making one. I start pouring the milk when in walks B. Oh good god no. I feel so uncomfortable I would happily shrivel up and die. My head is pounding and my stomach is churning and I don't have the strength for this. I try and think of something, anything to say but my tongue will not unfold. B turns to me.

'I just wanted to let you know that I saw the e-mail you sent to Matt. He didn't show me it, I just happened to walk up behind him when it was open on his screen and I saw it.' I send Matt lots of e-mails (he's a funny guy who speaks his mind but has no filter) but by her tone I suspect she is talking about the one I sent him yesterday afternoon when I was fuming from the meeting and in which I may have said B was the most manipulative person I had ever had the misfortune of meeting and that with the ethics of a snake she would do well in the markets of Tunisia. My tongue curls up a touch more.

'Well everyone is entitled to their opinion, Hannah, so we're not going to fall out about it. You had a bad day yesterday so probably weren't thinking straight.' With that she waltzes back out of the kitchen. What an absolute BITCH. What the hell does she mean I had a bad day and wasn't thinking straight? The only bad bits of my day were the bits she was fucking in. I consider racing after her but I don't have the energy. Why the hell did Matt not give me the heads up? I could knock him out. He's a nice guy and the equivalent of the school class Clown but he has no sensor. I replay what she said in the meeting yesterday and what she has just said. She gets pleasure from making me feel as small and insignificant as a gnat. On occasion when I am ranting Willow suggests that I am paranoid and that B doesn't have the intelligence to play mind games but I know she is a master at them.

I can feel my bottom lip wobbling as Charlotte walks in announcing, 'There you go, Your Highness. Breakfast is served.' I take one look at her and the wobble turns into a sob.

'Oh bloody hell, you really are hungover, aren't you,' she says. She puts her arms around me and I convulse trying to cry silently so that B is none the wiser. 'What's the matter? If you feel this bad you should have stayed at home.'

'It's that evil witch,' I whisper between sobs. 'She's just made sure that I know that she knows I talk shit about her in e-mails. Basically she just wanted to make sure I knew she was a step ahead. I'm going to fucking stab Matt.'

'What's he done?'

'The gormless twat let her see an e-mail I sent him about her yesterday and then failed to tell me she had seen it so I was unprepared for her smug summary when she ambushed me.'

'Bleeding hell, what a dick head, do you want me to twat him for you?'

I laugh in spite of myself. 'I'd prefer you twatted her to be honest.'

'Look, we have told you a million times. Just ignore her. She's a miserable hag and this place is her life. Her life is devoid of happiness so she tries to make everyone as miserable as she is. She has no fella, no friends, no personality, no dress sense and no social skills. So why would you allow a person like that to grate on you so much? You have way more going for you than she does and that's why she hates you so much. People like you and they respect you and that's what gets under her skin. No one has any respect for her so she tries to force respect by being a manipulative bully, drawing people in one minute with cream cakes on a Friday and forced conversations about X Factor and then knocking them back down again. The retards hang on for the dangled carrot and get delirious when it's their turn to grab it so when she turns back into Cruella they don't think she's that bad really. Me and Willow know her games. I get that you are targeted more than the rest of us but you've got to learn to just shut her out,' Charlotte says.

'Well what do you suggest I do to stop that happening? Electric shock therapy, lobotomy, hitman? Unless she changes her ways I can't see me changing my feelings,' I reply.

'What about you just smile and pretend she's not bothering you? I don't like it when you're sad.'

'For you, I will try. So tell me what you're doing at the weekend,' I decide a subject change is the only way forward.

'I have a date!' she says, face beaming with excitement/anticipation/love for someone she probably hasn't even met yet.

'Eeek exciting! Where did you meet this one?' I ask.

'On the internet.'

'Please tell me it wasn't Tinder or POF,' I say screwing up my face.

'No actually, it was Match. I've been on there a couple of weeks and messaged this guy a few times and he seems really nice so we're meeting tomorrow night for a couple of drinks.'

'Show us a pic then' I say.

Charlotte starts flicking through her phone. 'There,' she says thrusting the phone under my nose.

'Mmmm, he looks pretty nice. Twenty-nine, an older man eh!' I say.

'I figured he might work out better than the pillocks my age that I've been meeting lately.'

She's not wrong. Over the last few months she has had numerous dates with numerous pillocks, one of whom was her mate's brother. I tried to warn her against it but she assured me there wouldn't be a problem. She had had a long discussion with her friend who was totally cool about her dating her brother and if things didn't work out they would still be friends and he would still be her brother and it wouldn't be at all awkward. Yeah right. What actually happened was they went on three wonderful dates where he acted like the perfect gentleman. Picking her up, opening doors, paying for their meals, talking about the amazing career he was going to have in architecture and basically acting far more mature than his twenty-one years. That changed the first time they went on a date and he wasn't driving. After a few drinks she stupidly agreed to go back to his house (the parents and sister were out for the night) and he turned all Traveller, practicing their courtship ritual of grabbing. For a teenage Traveller boy this involves chasing a girl you fancy and, well, grabbing her in the hope that she might allow you to steal a kiss. Well how could they refuse such a romantic gesture?

Unfortunately, he did it with even less finesse than they do and lunged at her telling her he had always wondered what it would be like to shag one of (yep one of) his sister's mates. She realised that perhaps he wasn't the man for her after all and escaped from under him while he was trying to wrestle his kit off. She left him stood knacker bare with his undies around his knees, manhood ready for action and his parents making their way through the front door. Thankfully her mate thought it was hilarious and exactly what her arsehole of a brother deserved so the friendship survived.

'I hope this one is the one, my lovely. Are you leaving early then to de-fuzz yourself? You don't want him sneaking his hand up your skirt and thinking you've trapped a ferret,' I say trying to stifle a giggle.

'I'll have you know I'm not easy and there will be none of that behaviour on a first date.'

'What? Shaving, or putting his hand in your knickers?' I inquire.

'You're not funny, so leave me alone and go get some work done. Don't be crying over your bacon butty either, It'll be soggy enough by now.'

'Suppose I better had actually before OGL comes looking for me. See you for that lunch I owe you.'

***

Mercifully the meeting isn't too painful, and OGL disappears not long after and is away for most of the day. I decide not to say anything to Matt. Technically it was my fault for sending the e-mail in the first place to someone who I know to be as discreet as Louis Spence after a date with David Beckham, so I have vowed instead to be a bit more careful about the subject matter of my e-mails and to whom I send them.

Usually on a Friday night the vino is cracked open almost as soon as I step in the front door but after last night I'm not really feeling it and opt for green tea instead. I'm sure my liver and my soul will be restored to full health and I'll have serene thoughts. We shall be having takeout in line with the law of Friday night and we might push the boat out, get wild and watch Graham Norton. If I'm really lucky Will won't fall asleep half way through, and if he does and he's lucky I won't smother him with a tea towel.

I have yet to fathom what it is about the clock striking nine on Friday night that turns Will into a narcolept. I get up earlier than him EVERY morning. We go to bed at the same time EVERY night and I manage to keep my eyes open. He on the other hand is knocking out the zeds by 9.30pm without fail. Sometimes he wakes briefly to take another sip of wine but mostly I just steal his lukewarm glass. His loss and all that.

It's as though his inner twat says, 'Right then Will, you've worked bloody hard for a good thirty hours this week (he's not part time, I just imagine that, like everyone, he spends at least seven and a half hours of his working week in the loo or reading the *Daily Mail* online) and as the man of the house you have a right to sleep anywhere at any time so get your head down son and have some well-earned rest.' I amuse myself as always by sticking him on Snapchat with various filters.

When I get bored of that I flick through Facebook. I do this most nights, usually at three minute intervals just in case I miss anything. Now this is what pisses Will off. He doesn't get how I can concentrate on watching something on tv while simultaneously scrolling through my phone. He gives me snide glances. Like it somehow affects his enjoyment of whatever we happen to be watching. It's not like I'm asking him to look at it. If I don't look, I might miss something really amazing like, 'Anything for Attention Angela *checked in at Leeds General Infirmary* 'Hope they can get me sorted.' Cue the comments, 'Oh no what's up babe?' 'Are u ok hun?' 'Let me no wot's happening.' All met with, 'I'll PM you.' So why bother fucking putting it on then?! Do you want people to know or not? Oh I see, you only want people to know enough to feel sorry for you but not enough to know that actually there's rock all wrong and you're just being a drama queen. Or, 'Carrying on Claire DhyllonandMhaddersonsmummy' with, 'OMFG I am so sick of that fat f***ing slag. So wot If I go out every weekend Im a single mum and I desurve a brek.' Usual comments, 'rise above it hun your 10 times beter than her,' and, 'tek no notice she's nowt but a scruffy get. U r a fab mum and them kids r luccy to have you.' Yep really lucky. You're an amazing mum because the hashtags attached to the twenty seven photos you take on the one day a week that you actually spend with your kids says so #onlythingsIneedinmylife #myworld. Except for fags, booze and men you've just met because you seem to need those too.

My favourite though is, 'Looking for likes Louise' who loves to post pics of her in various states of undress accompanied by, 'I will be this skinny again if it kills me.' Beneath are always the same comments, 'Babe you are perfect as you are.' 'You are so hot.' 'I would kill for your figure what are you talking about?' How about someone kills her and puts us all out of our misery. I can't believe I know these people and don't know why I don't just ditch them. Yes, I do know, it's called noseybitchyitis. Plus who would I get wound up about and slag off it I didn't have those nonentities in my friends list?

Will is still asleep and I have exhausted all of my usual social media outlets. Worse still the wine bottle is empty so I may as well drag my own arse to bed. I give Will a hefty shove and bellow, 'Bed'. He hauls himself up and I resist the urge to punch his poor weary face for sleeping through yet another Friday night. The best night of the week with the promise of a whole weekend ahead and he sleeps it away. I'll get my own back at seven in the morning when I force him to get up and assist with the cleaning. The excitement never ends.

CHAPTER 4

'Now then you little minx, how was the weekend and more importantly how was the date? Your texts weren't very informative!' I say with bated breath.

'In a word, fabulous! He was a perfect gentleman, even hotter in the flesh and we had so much in common. We're going out again on Wednesday night.' Charlotte says, her excitement spilling over.

'Wow, two dates in five days. Should we buy a hat?' Willow asks, always the voice of practicality.

The three of us are sat in our usual lunch haunt replaying our weekends and bemoaning the fact it's Monday again. It seems that Charlotte had the best weekend. Mine involved numerous trips to B&Q and Asda, Willow's consisted of cleaning puke from not one, but two sick kids.

'Where you off on Wednesday then and how come you're seeing him again so soon? Isn't the rule one date a weekend in the first few weeks so as not to seem too keen or peak too soon?' asks Willow.

'He said he isn't interested in rules and game playing. We enjoyed ourselves so why not see each other again sooner rather than later?' Charlotte replies sounding a little miffed.

'Ok, don't get your knickers in a twist. You know I never really dated. I have to live vicariously through you so I am not fully au fait with the current dating regulations,' Willow explains.

'Sorry it's just that you're like the third person to ask me the same question. I don't know what the big deal is. I didn't say I was moving in with him just that I was seeing him again.'

'Chill your boots I said it's fine,' Willow replies looking annoyed.

'So where are you going?' I ask trying to lighten the mood.

'Cinema and dinner. Nothing fancy. He just wanted us to have a more relaxed night so we're going to a 6pm movie and then for dinner after.'

'Back row Betty eh,' I add.

'No, I've already told you I don't do things like that,' Charlotte answers incredulously.

'Ah but you said on a first date and this will be your second,' I push.

'Well it won't be happening then either!' Charlotte says firmly.

'Totally changing the subject,' Willow offers. 'Did you hear that brown nosing cow speaking to OGL this morning?'

'I presume you're talking about Emma,' I say. Emma is a work colleague with more faces than the Town Hall clock. She'll smile to your face while sticking a knife in your back.

'In one! She slags OGL off whenever she's out of earshot but then whenever she's around she's got her head up her arse. She drives me insane. She took it to a whole other level this morning when she offered to take some clients off her hands. She spent all last week moaning she had too much work on. Maybe if she worked normal office hours like the rest of us rather than making up her own and barely working three on seven off she might get her fucking work done. She'll take on the extra work, get an intern to do it then take all the credit. Devious, two faced bitch she is.'

'I don't even know why she works,' Charlotte adds. 'She treats it like a hobby and never tires of making sure we all know that she doesn't need to be there.'

'Trust me, if Will was raking it in I wouldn't be working, not in that hell hole anyway.' I say stating the obvious.

'Where would you be working then?' Asks Willow.

'Like I've told you a billion times, I'd be in my coffee shop.'

'What, you'd do that even if you didn't have to work?' Charlotte asks sounding somewhat surprised.

'Yeah, it would be the first thing I'd do. There'd be less pressure to succeed then too. As long as it covered its own expenses I wouldn't even be bothered about a wage. It would be like volunteering to work for myself.'

Charlotte says, 'You're not normal.' Willow nods in agreement.

'Well what would you both do then?' I ask.

'Nothing!' they say in unison.

'You lazy cows,' I retort.

'Well why would we do anything if we didn't have to?' Charlotte asks.

'Yeah, I've got enough on looking after my little monsters. It would be nice doing nothing,' Willow says without hesitation. Her little monsters being Megan and Oscar, her gorgeous yet time-consuming children.

'Ok then, what about if you had to work but could do whatever the chuff you wanted?' I ask.

'Gift shop for me,' says Willow.

'Art Gallery for me,' adds Charlotte.

'Really?' Willow and I are equally shocked.

'Yeah, I love painting,' she says.

'Since when exactly?!' I ask.

'Since always. I haven't done any for ages and I need to get back to it but I've not found the time.'

'Well you learn something new every day,' Willow chimes in. Her dream of a gift shop is no surprise to me. She loves going in those cheesy little shops in market towns that sell little wooden signs bearing words of wisdom. She has a house full of them. She also has a very good eye for detail. Unfortunately, much like myself, she has no cash and no idea how to bring her idea to fruition so it will remain (as mine) a pipe dream to go to when real life sucks arse.

We head back to work in an upbeat mood having gone thread to needle on what our businesses would look like, where they would be etc. etc. Nothing like a trip to dream world to elevate mind, body and spirit. The mood is dampened upon entering the office. B is on the phone. Her face is red and she is whispering (or perhaps trying to whisper but purposely ensuring we hear certain words). 'When…how long do we have…why have we only just found out…of course I understand…no I'm not worried…' She ends the call and sits looking frazzled at her desk. Emma shuffles over.

'Hi B, everything ok?'

Emma is such a nosey bitch. She likes to know everything. She is one of those who likes to find out everything from everyone but refuses to tell anyone anything.

'Yes fine, why wouldn't it be?' B asks in a pretty terse manner.

I slump lower in my seat. When she's in this mood it's always a good idea to avoid eye contact.

'Oh, erm, I just thought you looked stressed that's all,' Emma mumbles.

'Well I'm not stressed and if I was you would be the last person I'd be discussing it with.'

'Right, ok then, yeah sorry to bother you.' Emma shuffles back to where she came from and I resist the urge to laugh. So B knows something and she wants us to know she knows something. That something is important (or B wants us to think It is) but for now she just wants us to wander/worry and isn't about to divulge it. She does have form for this. She likes to keep us on our toes by making out something big is going to happen and it always winds up being a massive let down that no one actually gives a shit about. The last time this happened we all debated her clipped bits of conversation which went a bit like, 'he's coming here…really…to see us…I can't believe it…we'll pull out all the stops…what an honour,' and came to the conclusion that Prince William was stopping by. He didn't but a client did, uber excitement.

It was actually 50/50 in the office between him and David Beckham. It was neither. It was one of our clients, not even a VIP one. He had been to the office several times before yet this time the visit was shrouded in mystery until the day before when we got an e-mail advising that a very important client was coming into the office and therefore we had to ensure that our desks were sparkling clean, we were wearing appropriate business dress and we were to act professional at all times. I was so glad she told us in advance because on that particular day I had been planning to come in dressed as

Wonder Woman and had arranged to give pole dancing lessons on the centre column in the kitchen. Bullet dodged.

I start typing a group message to Charlotte and Willow then remember the Matt situation and decide better of it. I'll text them instead when B disappears. We joke that she has spy cameras on us as even when she isn't in she seems to know everything that's happened. I say joke but to be honest it isn't one. Either she has spy cameras or she has a spy. She certainly has plenty of heads up her arse so it could be one of a few people. My money is on Emma or Sam. I can't really see what's in it for Emma. She's a slimy cow but she hasn't anything to gain by spying and she's all about what's in it for her. Sam on the other hand is desperate for a promotion.

She is part of the sales team but wants to be B's right-hand woman. The trouble is, she's not that good at her job. She's also a bit thick so hasn't yet realised that B is simply using her. B knows what she wants and knows that she's likely to do anything to get it and so she plays on it. B can't stand her. She has dangled the carrot cake for a good twelve months but Sam hasn't yet been able to nibble any of it. This is probably a good thing as she's a pretty big woman and the last thing she needs is more cake.

Her rather large frame is one of the reasons B doesn't like her. She seems to think you can catch obesity. She has no filter either so thinks nothing of questioning Sam's choices when she walks in with an apple turnover for breakfast every morning, well most mornings. Some mornings Sam has a change and gets an eclair instead. She is oblivious to the fact that this may be the root of her obesity issues. B is aware of this and tries most mornings (while trying to keep her own breakfast of a black coffee down) to educate Sam on better

43

nutritional choices. It's akin to Victoria Beckham giving classes on how to smile. B borders on the anorexic and Sam needs two seats on a plane.

CHAPTER 5

When Wednesday arrives Charlotte is happier than Sam in Greggs. Although she has spent the previous two days texting me with selfies of her in various outfits she still has no idea what to wear on her date and is starting to get frazzled.

We're now stood at the bus stop in the pissing down rain and neither of us has an umbrella. A perfect end to another horrible day at the office.

'You'll be in the cinema where it's dark so what does it matter what you wear?' I ask.

'I'll be going out for dinner afterwards though so I need to look good for that.'

'It will be dark and it's cold so you could wear anything under your coat and he'll never know,' I say, half joking.

'You're about as much use as a diabetic in a sweet shop,' she snaps. 'Just because it's twenty years since you last made an effort to look anywhere near presentable. Not all men like a woman in pyjamas you know.'

I deserved that.

'I really don't see what's so difficult,' I say in all seriousness. 'It's freezing cold out and you're going on a casual date. What's wrong with jeans, heels and a nice top?'

'Ok know-it-all, what kind of jeans? Boot cut, straight leg, skinny, high waist?' She asks sounding a little bit too hysterical.

'Denim,' I say. Charlotte is not amused and is getting more stressed by the second. 'Right Charl, enough is enough. Shall I just come home with you and help you get ready?' Willow is so much better than me at this kind of stuff but it's her day off and this girl clearly needs help plus stress levels for date two are at least a seven, bordering on an eight so when we hit 9/10 I'll be happy for Willow to take over. She has the patience of a saint and I have the patience of a very angry Frenchman who has just found out the deli has no cheese or croissants.

My kind offer of assistance accepted, we are now warm and dry and I'm sat cosied up on Charlotte's bed while she tries on every outfit she owns.

'I preferred the skinny ones with that top,' I say.

'They make my arse look fat though,' she replies.

'No, your fat makes your arse look fat,' I say, which results in me getting a face full of jeans when Charlotte throws them across the room in a fit of temper.

'You're supposed to be helping and you're stressing me out more,' she says looking like she may cry at any moment.

'Charl, I've seen more fat on a chicken wing, you looked amazing,' I say sincerely.

'But I didn't feel amazing though.' She has now slumped on the bed head in hands.

'Seriously, you're supposed to be leaving the house in twenty minutes and you still haven't done your hair. You really need to make a decision and get the fuck dressed!' I shout.

She puts on the first outfit she tried and says, 'perfect'. Thank fuck for that. I resist the urge to strangle her.

'Now get your barnet sorted, you look like you've just come off the set of Thriller,' I say.

Hair, make up and outfit perfect she checks her reflection for the billionth time.

'Are you sure you don't want me to drop you off anywhere?' I ask.

'No, I told you, he's picking me up so you need to get lost before he turns up. I don't want him thinking I've got you here to give him the once over,' she says.

'Charming, I'll just fuck off then, shall I?' I reply.

'It's not that I'm not grateful for all of your advice but yes, do one!'

I give her an obligatory hug, tell her if she can't be good to be careful, skip out of the house and out into the street just as a very new-looking white BMW pulls up. I hope it's not him. Only wide boys drive white BMs. I try to catch a glimpse but it's dark and difficult to see without the glare of the streetlight.

I look back a couple of times and note a guy get out of the car and walk up to Charlotte's door. Oh god, it is him! I'm going to have to ask her about his questionable taste in cars. Maybe he's just borrowing it from his pimp mate or drug dealer brother and really he drives a far more sophisticated vehicle.

I duck around the corner and jump into my old black VW Polo. I'm hoping Will has at least started dinner but I'm not too optimistic as I haven't yet had a call or a text asking what I would like or have planned. He is very cute when he tries to help out in the kitchen, as it's definitely not something that comes natural to him. I once left out two steaks and a bag of prepared salad and he rang to ask what I wanted doing with them. 'Well I don't know Will, you could pop to the shop for more steak and try and make a pants suit to go with Gaga's meat dress or you could try to build the Taj Mahal out of the salad croutons or you could try frying the fucking steaks and stick them on a plate with the salad (after opening the bag, let's be clear) and call it a meal.' I didn't say any of that to him as I know how lucky I am that he tries to help and his attempts do always brighten my day. The girls say he does it because I'm a control freak and he's scared of doing something wrong. What could he possibly do wrong with steak and salad?

Ten minutes later I walk into the house. I can smell cooked chicken which is a good sign. I can also smell boiled broccoli, which is not so good, unless he's parboiled it before frying. Maybe he's been doing some research. I walk into the kitchen. He hasn't been doing any research. I'm expecting stir fry but what I have is a (dry) cooked chicken breast with a side of vegetables three ways (boiled/fried/left raw depending on type). No sign of noodles. No sign of sauce.

'Da-dah! I bet you thought I hadn't bothered when I didn't text,' he says, looking thoroughly pleased with himself.

'I wish you hadn't,' I mutter under my breath.

'I thought I'd surprise you for a change, so dinner is served.'

I want to say, 'Whose dinner? Do we have a dog I don't know about that's keen to get in his five a day?' What I actually say is, 'Great, I'm hank.'

He looks so proud of himself, like a baby who's just found his toes. The trouble now is that as I haven't told him what I was expecting he might do the same thing again and it will be my fault for not telling him the error of his ways. Whilst trying to chew chicken with the consistency of an insole I decide I will wait until the weekend when we've had a couple of drinks and casually drop into conversation (through laughter so he thinks I'm being cute not controlling) what I would have done with the ingredients. That way there is less chance of him telling me where to shove them.

'Charlotte sorted then?' He asks.

'Well, she was washed and dressed so yes, I suppose she was sorted. I think her fella turned up just as I left, though, and he was in a white BM,' I say rolling my eyes.

'You're joking? What a knob. I hope you've told her we don't approve and therefore there won't be a 3rd date,' he says.

'I haven't had the chance yet, I didn't really want to muscle in on her evening of romance so I thought I'd tell her tomorrow if the date went well. No point telling her if it didn't, plus I'm hoping that maybe he was just borrowing it for the night,' I add.

'Who from, a Pimp?' Will asks. It's like he's actually in my mind.

'Exactly,' I say.

'Before I forget, I think I'm going out on Friday night,' he says, changing the subject.

'Who with?' I ask intrigued. He's not one for really going out.

'Just a few guys from work. Burger and a few games of pool.'

'Sounds riveting,' I say.

'You're right, I'd much rather sit in in my Pjs watching people watching people on tv like you do,' he replies.

'Actually I'll probably invite Nik round for wine and pizza,' I say.

'Oh great so I'll come home to you lushes pissed up on the sofa, awesome,' he sounds less than impressed.

'You love it! I'll see if she wants to stay over, saves her getting a taxi or poor James out of bed. Can you remember the last time she did that? I thought he was actually going to kill her.'

I honestly don't know how he kept his calm. I was pretty drunk but even I could tell he was annoyed. We'd been out to her works do. James wasn't going out or drinking because she had asked him to pick her up and he didn't want her winding up in a taxi alone at stupid o'clock. It was a couple of years ago. Nicky had driven to mine and we had gone into town by train and arranged for each of our fellas to collect us. I didn't want to stay at Nicky's as I had something on the next morning and she couldn't stay at ours as we had nowhere for her to sleep. Around 11.30ish we go outside and sit on a low wall. I ring Will to come and get me. She is supposed to ring James at the same time but as she's ratted she decides to abuse Will on the phone instead. When I hang up we're both in hysterics and fall backwards off the wall. Having consumed our body weight in wine we don't feel a thing and pull ourselves back onto the wall still pissing ourselves. It had been raining earlier so we're both filthy and cold. Nik is saying, 'Oh dear Jim is going to be very cross with me. He won't let me in the car looking like this.' At which point I realise she hasn't called him. By now it's almost midnight so she calls him and he sounds pleasantly surprised that it isn't too late and says he'll be there in twenty five minutes or so.

Five minutes later Will pulls up. 'Looking for business,' I ask.

'Not from two pissed up tramps I'm not, no. Get in dickhead, you're letting all the heat out of the car.'

'Soz boz,' I say clambering into the car followed by Nicky who wants to sit in the warmth and wait for James. Unfortunately, neither of us relay this to Will as we're both too busy laughing at my 'soz boz' which sets us off reminiscing about school days.

'Christ don't you two come up for breath? You're giving me bleeding headache.'

'Whatevs,' I reply which does nothing to dampen our hysterics. We're practically hyperventilating at just how totes hilare we are. Will is not amused. We arrive at ours and I pour a nightcap. Nicky's phone rings and it's James advising Nicky he is outside.

'Why doesn't he come in and have a drink?' I enquire.

'Cos he's a miserableist bastards,' Nicky slurs. 'He can wait til I finish my delish bino.' Her phone rings for the umpteenth time. It's James, again! This time Nicky puts him on speaker.

'Where the hell are you I've been sat here for twenty minutes?' He bellows.

'I am flinishing my bino, why don't you come in?' She asks.

'It's freezing cold and I'm wearing pyjamas so I'll stay put thanks. If you're not out in five minutes I'm driving home.' He hangs up.

'Ooh, he's so masterpull,' she says.

'Yes very Nik but you don't want to miss your lift so stop pissing about, get that down your neck and get your shoes on.' I bundle her stuff together and walk her outside. There is no car. The fresh air has hit Nicky and she begins wailing dramatically,

'Or my gosh he's left me, he's actually just left me.'

'Give me your phone,' I say and call James.

'What?' he barks.

'It's Han. Where are you? We're outside and can't see your car.'

'I'm parked right outside how can you not see my car?' He says sounding very annoyed.

'Cos I can't see your car,' I say scanning up and down the street.

'Just a second I'll get out and walk to the door,' he replies. 'Right, I'm at the door where the hell are you?'

'I'm at the door as well James and you're not here. We're freezing our tits off?' Nicky is still wailing like a banshee.

'You are at Bar 55 aren't you? He asks. It takes a few seconds but then the penny drops. Oh shit. She didn't tell him she was at mine. It's now 1am and he has been sat in the wrong place for the best part of forty minutes and that wrong place is a thirty minute drive from here.

'Erm, I'm really sorry James but we left the restaurant. Will picked us up and we're at mine now.'

The short silence is broken by his explosion;

'You have got to be fucking kidding me? Why the fuck didn't one of you morons tell me? Christ almighty, so now I've to drive all the way over to yours. In future she can fucking stay in or get some other bastard mug to pick her up.' I sense he isn't happy.

'Yep, ok we'll see you soon then,' I hang up.

'Is my James coming?' she asks totally oblivious to what just happened.

It is definitely my favourite Nicky story.

'Try not to do the same tomorrow. You know Nik goes from sober to pissed as a fart in thirty seconds flat, if she's staying over, she'll have no reason to take it steady. I'm not cleaning sick up after you both,' Will says.

'Well ok then chief of fun police. We shall be sure to keep our enjoyment to the bare minimum.'

***

The following day Charlotte skips into work with a very large smile on her face, which suggests the evening went well. I glance over at Willow and we both roll our eyes in mock exasperation. This is not the first time we have witnessed her unequivocal joy following a date so we will remain cautiously optimistic until at least the fifth happy date. The team meeting is at 9.30 so we're going to have to wait until lunchtime to get the goss. I pick up my phone to message Willow and as I do B walks in and the cloud of doom descends. I wonder what pearls of wisdom she has planned for us poor unfortunate souls today.

Yesterday I had the pleasure of approaching her to ask if she was happy with the presentation I had e-mailed her three weeks earlier. She had the nerve to ask why I hadn't sent it sooner (I did, she just didn't reply), why I had left it until the last minute (I didn't, she's had it three weeks), why I would want to put her under so much pressure when she is under enough already (I didn't, I sent it to her two days after she asked me to prepare it. In future I'll be sure to send it before I've written it) and why on earth I would use such a dreadful font for an important document (because that's the font she specified we should all use in a memo six months ago). The end result being that I have to re-do it in a font which doesn't offend her eyes and then send it back to her for review. I asked if she could just review the content now so I could make all the changes at the same time but she is way too busy and important so told me to change the font and send it back to her. I need to have it completed by Monday as that's when I am making the presentation. I hazard a guess that she will give it back to me with approximately 363 amendments at 4.59pm on Friday.

'It was even better than last time and I didn't think that was possible,' Charlotte gushes. 'He is just so much more mature than anyone I've ever dated before.'

'Even though he drives a white BM?' Willow kicks me under the table. 'I'm sorry but I've got to get this out before you go marrying him and become the wife of someone who drives a white BM,' I say.

'So what? It happens to be a very nice car, a damn sight better than yours anyway,' she says indignantly.

'I'm hurt,' I say, feigning distress. 'That cut like a knife.'

'Good,' Charlotte retorts.

'I just don't want you getting in deep then being surprised when he tries to sell you to the Serbian sex trade, that's all,' I say. Willow nods in agreement.

'You're too funny, said no one ever,' Charlotte replies.

'All right, let's get serious now shall we,' asks Willow, 'we know he's super good looking, a perfect gentleman, mature and has shit tastes in cars but what about all the other stuff? What does he do, where does he live, who does he live with, does he have any baggage? Dish.'

'Well he lives in Leeds and he's a solicitor.' That explains the car then. 'He lives alone in his own apartment,' she continues.

'A flat Charl, he lives in a flat,' I say.

'Well he called it an apartment so I am too,' she spits back somewhat defensively. 'He doesn't have any baggage as far as I know. We haven't actually talked about exes and that kind of stuff yet so I suppose I will find out tomorrow maybe.'

'Tomorrow! Bloody hell, you're not wasting any time are you?' Willow sounds shocked.

'Where you going this time?' I ask.

'He wants to take me to his favourite Thai restaurant.'

'But you don't like Thai,' I point out.

'Well Julian says once I try this place I will love Thai.'

I can see that Willow (like me) is trying not to laugh. Her face has contorted and has started to look a pinker shade of red, watching her try not to laugh makes it harder for me to keep a straight face and I have no choice but to allow the laughter to burst out rather than die from lack of oxygen. Willow follows suit and through cackles I manage to say, 'Julian?'

Charlotte is not seeing the funny side, 'What's matter with Julian? I think it's a very classy name.'

'For an 1830's artist maybe,' Willow snorts. Charlotte is becoming less amused by the second.

'You two never have anything nice to say, all you ever do is piss on my parade.'

'Oh Charl calm down, we're only winding you up. We're very happy for you and a bit jealous that you've got all the excitement of a new man and new experiences,' I say.

'Right then well I'll just keep rubbing your noses in it you jealous bitches,' Charlotte grins.

'Do you want me to come around and help style you then,' asks Willow, 'it's only fair as she did it last time,' she says nodding towards me.

'No, it's ok, Julian's going to do it,' Willow and I look at each other. 'He said he's really into fashion and I have the perfect figure for anything so he wants to have a go at styling me.'

I don't say anything but I think it's a bit weird. A guy she has met twice wants to choose what she wears. Perhaps he genuinely is interested in fashion and he's right, Charlotte has an amazing figure so maybe he does just wants to dress her in the way a fashion designer would their muse but it makes me feel uneasy. I don't want to add fuel to her fire by saying anything else negative about a guy I've never met so I shall wait and speak to Willow later. The styling plus taking her to a restaurant for food she doesn't like is just a bit weird but maybe that's what people do these days. After all, it's been a while since I had a date!

***

It's 4.54pm on Friday. I was wrong about OGL passing me 363 amendments at 4.59pm. She gave me 246 at 4.52pm. She was pleased with herself too.

'Hannah, I've had to make some changes I'm afraid but you've got time to do them before you leave, haven't you?'

It's a rhetorical question, I can tell. Nonetheless I say, 'I leave in eight minutes.'

'Some of us are too busy for clock watching but it must be lovely to have time to watch the minutes tick by and leave on the stroke of five,' she replies.

'That's not what I do, it's just today I have to be home and I'm not trying to be funny but you have had that document for three weeks. It's unfair giving me it back at literally the last minute and expecting me to do it.' I have no idea how those words went from being in my head to rolling off my tongue. I must have still been preoccupied with the Charlotte's date being weird thing because I was definitely not trying to say it out loud.

'You clearly are being funny and it's not the last minute. You just pointed out that you have eight minutes left or did until you decided to be petty and try to make a point? You now have six.'

'Well I'm sorry but I need to leave on time as I have plans,' I say, trying to have the last word. 'I'll take it home and do it at the weekend,' I offer, hating myself.

'Sorry, Hannah, but I need to have it approved before Monday morning and I don't want to work over the weekend. I don't take up your personal time - I don't expect you to take up mine.' With that she walks away.

What an absolute cock womble. She doesn't want to work at the weekend? She does nothing but work and delights in telling us all just how much she's had to do while we've all been enjoying time off. As for wasting her time, I don't know how the cheeky bitch dare. She has wasted my time for the best part of two years and now I am going to be stuck here making her unnecessary amendments only to reinforce that she is in charge and I am her minion.

Tears of frustration prick my eyes but I bite my lip and keep them at bay. I won't give her the satisfaction of thinking she's ruined my night. I'll do the amendments but put a delay on the e-mail to her so that she doesn't get them until later. I know that both Willow and Charlotte heard the exchange as my phone just pinged with messages from them. I'll reply later.

I say bye as they both leave and wish Charlotte good luck for her date. Something tells me she is going to need it. By 6.15pm I've done. B is still sat at her desk as I pack up my things. I stop at her desk and confirm the amendments are done and I have e-mailed them to her. Just as she's saying she hasn't had the e-mail her mobile rings. She answers it immediately and I seize the opportunity to run out before she sees that the e-mail still has not arrived. A small victory.

Three hours later Nicky and I have wolfed down a veg supreme pizza and some spicy wedges with sides of BBQ sauce and garlic mayo

'I'm stuffed,' I say

I have made a rather impressive food baby and am now struggling to force wine down. It's so weird how you can drink glasses of wine then eat a full loaf of bread but you can't eat the bread then drink the wine. It is without doubt, one of the great mysteries of life. Actually, it's probably not a mystery at all, I suspect it's down to science. I'll Google it later and find out. I do that all the time. Usually when watching a movie with Will. He gets so annoyed but I have to do it. If we're watching something and I see someone I recognise but I don't know where from I have to know at that precise moment. Sadly I cannot do that at this precise moment as my phone is out of battery and in my current stuffed state I can't move to get a charger.

'Let's just lay here while the pizza settles then I'll open that other bottle of wine,' Nicky says.

'Good plan Stan, though I can't see me being able to fit anymore in until about May,' I reply.

'You daft get, how has work been this week then?' She asks.

'Same old. That witch is still delighting in doing everything possible to piss me off and I'm falling for it every time. Do you know what she said to Sam today?'

'Enlighten me,' she says.

'The nasty cow sat staring at her while she ate her obligatory morning cream bun then announced that watching her eat was good for her own waist line as it made her feel sick and put her off food for the rest of the day. Can you believe she gets away with this shit?' I ask.

'What did Sam say?'

'Bugger-all as bloody usually. No one said anything and there was more than me that heard it cos I saw the looks on other people's faces,' I answer.

'Why don't you complain to HR or something? I would,' she says.

'Trust me Nik, it's not that easy. People have tried and failed. In fact when Jen and Andrew left last year they both cited her behaviour as the reason and yet she's still there, at the helm making lives miserable. I don't know what I would do if I didn't have them two there to sound off to. If they left I'd have to go on long term sick.'

'Or win the lotto and buy that coffee shop,' says Nicky.

'Yeah, or that,' I say wistfully.

'Speaking of them two how are they? Seems ages since I saw them both, we need to have a night out.' Now she's talking.

'Yeah we do, I'll crack on with arranging something but yeah they're good. Charlotte is in the throes of a new romance.' I say, raising an eyebrow.

'Oh, is she now, well do tell!'

'She's found herself some bloke on the internet called Julian,' I say with a giggle.

Nicky bursts out laughing 'Where exactly on the internet? Did she go back to 1836 or sommat?'

'You're not allowed to take the piss out of his name, she gets very defensive,' I say, 'but yes we did say he sounded like an artist from the 1800s. It went down like a fart in a lift. Anyway, he's a lawyer.'

'Course he is, he wouldn't be a plasterer with a name like that would he!' Nicky points out.

'He lives in his own apartment in Leeds, yes apartment not flat and he drives a white BM,' I say rolling my eyes.

'Dick,' is all Nicky has to say.

'She's on her third date since Saturday with him tonight. Willow offered her styling expertise but Charlotte refused'. I recount the conversation about Julian's desire for styling Charlotte's perfect figure. Nicky's response is similar to mine but for different reasons.

'He's called Julian and he wants to choose her clothes. Is she sure she's his type, cos it sounds to me like he might be more interested in Will.' Nicky says sniggering.

'I didn't think of that, I was more concerned that he was a bit of a control freak,' I say laughing.

'Well I didn't think of that. Maybe we're both wrong and he just is one of those guys that is into fashion and wants to make her look fabulous daaarling,' Nicky replies.

'Perhaps,' I say, 'but I'm going to be keeping my beady on him just in case.'

'What about Willow?' she asks

'She has her hands full with the kids but hasn't had a nervous breakdown yet so she's winning,' I say

'Good stuff and talking of kids I'm taking my niece to the theatre and wondered if you fancied it I bought three tickets just in case, safety in numbers and all that.' Nicky's niece is six and belongs to her younger, useless sister (US). Every now and again Nicky feels the need to prove her worth as an Aunt and takes her on various adventures. Generally she drags me along so the little shit doesn't run rings around her. The US lets her do what the hell she wants when she wants so as a result she's a spoilt brat. Think Verruca Salt meets Horrid Henry.

To Nicky's credit she does usually have her niece acting like a civilised human being by the time she takes her home but the hard work is rendered pointless about four seconds after she is back in the care of US. She spends too much time on her phone and not enough time on raising her kid. She jumps from one fella to the next following the same MO; they make risqué comments on her Facebook pics, she replies pretending to be offended, two weeks later there is a Facebook pic of her and commentator looking all loved up to confirm they are now a couple.

She has a status updating frenzy about her and her new man accompanied by numerous hashtags just to prove how serious they are. There's always #myone #hesakeeper #couple #cute. I always feel like adding #sloppyseconds #another2weektony #beoverbeforethesheetsneedchanging. Obviously I don't do this. Like clockwork, approximately two weeks after the great love affair begins it's all over bar the #allmenarebastards #singleforever updates and life returns to normal until she snares the next victim. There is little wonder her daughter is such a little shit, if she's not careful she'll be a slut too just like her mother and this is where Nicky's attentive Aunt bit comes in. She feels that if she removes her from the toxic environment and shows her that not all women have the morals of a *Love Island* contestant there is a chance she'll grow up not feeling like she is only as good as whoever is in her knickers.

'What you taking her to see?' I ask.

'Matilda,' is the reply.

'As in Roald Dahl's Matilda?' I wonder out loud.

'The very same. It's a very successful musical and the West End show is touring.'

'Oh god, a load of precocious brats singing and dancing, I'm not sure I fancy it Nik to be honest,' I say.

'Tim Minchin wrote the songs though so they might be good,' she says.

'That ginger comedian?' I enquire.

'The very same,' she says.

'So what's in it for me then if I have to spend a night with a brat watching a load of other brats sing and prance about?' I may as well get something for my troubles.

'I'll shout you a curry and a glass of wine,' she says.

'Make it all-I-can-drink wine and you're on,' I answer. Copious amounts of wine might make an evening in Daisy the devil's company bearable.

'Deal. It's the weekend after next so make sure you're available,' she says.

'Yes boss,' I reply.

'Shall I open that other bottle then?' she asks.

'Go on but I don't reckon I'll fit much in or stay awake to drink it. Shall I put a movie on for us to fall asleep to?'

'Why not, Will can turn it off when he comes in.' I put *Cry Baby* on. There is nothing better than Johnny Depp in a leather jacket. It's from back in the day when he looked like he smelt nice, before the fashion and lifestyle of Captain Jack Sparrow spilled over into his real life. I must have watched it 300 times and at least half of those times have been with Nicky. We know every single word but never get bored of it. We have been known to watch it twice in a row. I'm surprised the DVD still works it's that over played. I'm struggling to stay awake even as the opening credits come on.

CHAPTER 6

'Good night, girls?' Will asks.

We're in the kitchen. I'm making coffee and Nicky is supposed to be making bacon butties but has her face stuck in her phone as usual. We both fell asleep on the sofa missing most of the movie and dragged ourselves to bed at 1.30am. I had expected to walk into the bedroom and find Will but there was no sign of him. He climbed into bed just after 2am after banging into every piece of furniture we own so I was surprised when he walked into the kitchen pretty early looking slightly dishevelled but alive.

'Not as good as yours by the looks of you,' Nicky replies.

'I don't know what you mean, I feel pretty good considering,' he replies looking pretty pleased with himself. Considering what I wonder. I don't ask, if he wants me to know he'll tell me. I've long since got over any irrational jealousy I once harboured where if Will even breathed in the same direction as another female I was convinced he was going to dump me and I would give him the cold shoulder for three days at least.

Looking back I'm not sure why I thought not speaking to him would prevent him from screwing around. It was more likely to encourage him to do just that to give him a safe haven away from his psycho girlfriend. In my defence I had a rather large inferiority complex and believed that every other female in the world was funnier, prettier, slimmer etc etc than me and I couldn't understand why he would choose me when he could have someone else. I'm lucky that he stayed and put up with me. I would have dumped my arse and run for the hills. The turning point in our relationship/the mending of my psychotic tendencies was very much a light bulb moment sparked by (of all people) Liz Hurley.

Now I'm no Liz Hurley fan but if someone as stunning as she can be cheated on by someone as irrelevant looking as Hugh Grant with someone as facially challenged as that hooker then all us average folk have no chance. When I saw those news headlines a penny dropped. You don't have to be the best looking person in the world or the smartest person or the funniest person, if your other half wants to get their rocks off elsewhere then they will damn well do it and what you look like has little or nothing to do with it. That realisation changed my life and I started acting like a grown-up.

I didn't want Will to not cheat on me because he had never had the opportunity, I wanted him to not cheat on me because he didn't want to cheat on me. Talk about an epiphany. From then on I stopped breaking into a sweat anytime he mentioned going out somewhere without me and I stopped texting him fifteen times an hour to try and catch him out. Would he cheat? I'd like to think not but it's out of my control so I've stopped trying to control it. If he does he faces the consequences and it's as simple as that. He's a dreadful liar and the guilt would kill him, so if he ever cheated, I would know about it!

'Considering what?' asks Nicky. She's too nosey for her own good.

'Considering I drank the best part of a bottle of JD and at least six bottles of lager,' Will answers.

'You're probably still pissed then,' I pipe up.

'Quite likely, wife, so you best feed me quick smart. I need bacon and I need it now,' Will retorts.

Nicky has pulled her finger out and the bacon is sizzling away nicely, it smells delicious. I thickly butter some white bread cakes and get the HP on standby. Nicky has Ketchup. I have never understood this. Red sauce is for chips, brown sauce is for breakfast. It is the law of the land, or at least it was in the land where I grew up. You can't start throwing red sauce onto breakfasts. Before we know it folk will be having mayonnaise on their pork pies and the world as we know it will be no more.

'Bacon's ready. Are you having that brown muck as well, Will?' Nicky enquires.

'It's not muck, it is a delightfully tangy alternative to the sweetness of ketchup and a perfect accompaniment to bacon. It cuts through the saltiness perfectly,' Will replies.

'Have you been watching *Masterchef* again?' Nicky asks.

'How did you guess?' I reply on Will's behalf to prevent him from spraying a mouthful of bacon around the kitchen.

Breakfast eaten and hangovers prevented, we say bye to Nicky and make plans for the rest of the day which consist of cleaning, supermarket shopping and possibly searching for a holiday. I haven't told Will this bit yet as I know he won't agree. He's tighter than a gnat's arse, a stereotypical Yorkshire man. He doesn't like spending money and he likes me spending money even less. However, he does like a good holiday and with the weather being so crap I think I could convince him that it would be nice to have some sun to look forward to. Something cheap and cheerful that won't break the bank will do, Tenerife maybe or Gran Canaria.

Will wants us to save up for a new kitchen and extension. Ours is a tiny galley thing that is not conducive to entertaining. He wants to knock out the back wall and extend into the garden to turn the kitchen into an all singing, all dancing dining kitchen which I'm sure will look very nice but will take up half of our garden. I need to ban him from watching *Masterchef, Location Location* and *Homes Under the Hammer*. They all give him ideas of grandeur that our bank balance can't compete with. Not only that but with my OCD tendencies it will be me cleaning the bloody thing and the current one is done in less than half an hour.

I keep reminding him there are only two of us so we don't need the trouble or expense of renovating but he reminds me that we want to have kids so best do it beforehand or we'll have neither the time nor the money. I know he's right but the whole thing fills me with dread, I am trying to delay the inevitable as long as possible so spending some of our savings on a holiday should help.

'Skiathos it is then!' I dragged him against his will into the travel agent. I appreciate that's old fashioned in this technological age but if I had just opened the laptop up it would have been much more difficult to get him to partake in my search. Getting him sat in the travel agents on the premise of just looking was much easier. After initial grumbles and comments like, 'we're not booking anything though,' he soon came around to the idea of some summer sun and relaxed into the activity. Skiathos is a Greek Island and it looks pretty as a picture, the promise of boat trips sold it to Will. I knew it would, he can't resist a spot of holiday boating. 600 quid for the week so he was reasonably ok with being totally railroaded into it. Deposit paid we head for a celebratory coffee.

There aren't any seats inside our favourite café so we have the choice of going elsewhere and getting a bad coffee or sitting outside and freezing to death over a good one. We opt for the latter and sit next to the window in the hope that some of the heat from inside the building may escape through the glass and provide comfort. It doesn't. It's so cold I can see my breath and my feet have already succumbed to the pins and needles that precedes cold-induced numbness. I knew I should have worn two pairs of socks. Will has gone inside to order, in hindsight I should have offered so I could take refuge in the warmth.

I text Charlotte to ask about the date and Willow and to ask if she's heard from Charlotte in the hope it will keep my mind occupied and my hands busy, less chance of them developing frostbite if they're kept mobile.

Willow replies immediately, 'Not heard a thing, I've just messaged her myself.'

Interesting, it's 11.30am so she must be awake by now. Knowing she won't see us until Monday I thought she'd have been texting the second her eyes opened. Oh no, what if it was rubbish and that's why she hasn't been in touch? Maybe she's too upset, or too ashamed after sticking up for Julian so gallantly. Or maybe she had the night of her life and is still entwined in his arms oblivious to the world going on around her. I'll give her an hour to reply and if she doesn't I'll give her a call and jolt her back to reality. I am dying to know what he dressed her in. I imagine him turning up with a big white box containing a beautiful expensive gown like something off

Pretty Woman. For Charlotte's sake I hope he has better taste in clothes than he has in cars.

Will returns as I ponder and informs me he has secured a table inside.

'Thank Christ for that, my nipples are like bloody tent pegs!' I say, relieved. Inside is as warm as the outside is cold. I feel sweat building almost immediately. I'm wearing a hat, scarf, vest, long-sleeved top, jumper and coat. The sweat has welded my scarf to my neck and it's a relief to peel it off.

'I can feel a Primani sweep coming on,' I mutter. We have two months before we go away but there may be some bargains to be had and I wouldn't want to miss out.

'Seriously Han, you've just tricked me into spending 600 quid on a holiday, I'm not ready to part with any more cash just yet.'

'I didn't say now did I, just at some point between now and April,' I say to him. 'I didn't trick you either, you were a willing participant,' I point out.

'You know I can't resist the lure of a boat trip, in fact even a Pedalo would have swung it for me,' he says.

'You can knob off, I'm not going on another Pedalo. We were lucky to escape alive after the last voyage and I'm not doing it again.' We almost came a cropper two years ago in the Mediterranean Sea when Will insisted on a jaunt in a Pedalo despite the gale force winds. He wasn't even swayed by the guy hiring out vessels who asked in his broken English if we were 'cryzee' not that that prevented him from hiring us it, well forty euros is forty euros and he wasn't hiring to anyone else so why look a gift horse in the mouth?

Having heard nothing from Charlotte I ring her as soon as we get in. No answer. This is very unlike her. She has her phone with her at all times so I'm starting to see that meme 'never trust a person who always has their phone in their hand but never replies to your text messages'. I find it hard to believe that she would ignore me so maybe it is just out of charge and she's too hungover after her night out to re-charge it. I call Willow, she answers immediately.

'Hey, what's happening?' she asks in her best 'down with the kids' lingo.

'Have you heard from Charlotte? I've text and tried to ring and got nothing.'

'No, she hasn't replied to my texts either,' she answers.

'Do you think we should be worried?' I ask. I am starting to feel a little panicked. It's early afternoon and it's unheard of for her not to be in touch at the weekend or at least put some crap on Facebook, especially when she has been out on a date.

'We don't know this guy from Adam,' I add, 'what if he's done something to her?'

'I think you're overreacting just a little bit. She's either hungover or still getting her leg over and can't be bothered with us sad cases trying to liven up our own existence with her sordid tales.'

'Mmm, perhaps you're right but I've just got a funny feeling that's all. I might give it another hour and swing by hers to check it out,' I add.

'Well don't blame me if she goes ape at you spying on her. Let me know if you hear from her though.' And with that Willow hangs up. Three minutes later my phone bings. 'Hi, sorry I missed your call, was busy with Julian. I'll see you on Monday.' Seriously? She's been

MIA all day and that's all I get. WTF? I forward it to Willow adding, 'She's alive at least.'

Willow replies, 'You can call off the search party then.'

Will walks in and quips, 'What's up with your face? You look constipated.'

'Confused,' I say. 'Charlotte has finally replied to my text and phone call with the shortest text ever, in fact it's quite terse and could have come from B.' I read him the text.

'Well maybe she's just busy and hasn't got time to send you chapter and verse. You'll be seeing her soon enough,' he adds.

'I know, it's just unlike her that's all, she's usually bursting to fill us in on her shenanigans.'

There is nothing from Charlotte on Sunday either, not that I should be surprised when she clearly stated she would see me Monday. This Julian guy must be keeping her really busy. I think I'm going to have to insist on a meet and greet so I can see for myself if he really is a nice guy. I'll ask her tomorrow. Oh god, only nine hours before I have to be up and I'm nowhere near going to bed yet. Given the presentation tomorrow I decide to check my work e-mail. Big mistake, I have one from B, actually I have two from B but only one has any content, the other just has an attachment. I start to read, holding my breath.

'Hannah. I am not sure whether you deliberately tried to ruin my weekend or whether there was an IT problem but I did not receive your presentation until 9.25pm last night (Saturday). I have asked IT to check the system on Monday to see what went wrong. I cannot guarantee that I will have checked the presentation prior to

Monday morning so I suggest you are in the office early to ensure all my amendments are done.'

So she was expecting me to check my e-mails over the weekend then. What if I hadn't and I just rocked up at 8.55am tomorrow? The second e-mail contains the amended presentation. Oh my freaking god. I swear she has made more amendments than she made the first time AND pretty much changed all the previous amendments back to what they were before. She does it on fucking purpose. It is going to take me at least two hours to piss about with it and it's 10pm. I've had a couple of glasses of wine and I'm so tired I could sleep on a washing line. There is no way it is getting done tonight. I'm not e-mailing B back either. She can piss right off. It's the weekend and she's just managed to ruin the last few hours of it. Looks like I'm getting up extra early in the morning and spending even more hours in hell than I ordinarily do. Oh joy.

CHAPTER 7

As I slope into the office the next morning at 5.30am, I find myself once again thinking about where I'd rather be and why I'm not there. It's not like I lack ambition, I think it's more fear of the unknown and not having a scooby do how to set up my own business. I suppose if I wanted it that badly I could find out but then I don't really have time. By the time I get home at night, make dinner and do some exercise it's like 9pm and the last thing I want to do is business research with Google. There is also the small matter of lack of funds.

We have some savings but they're for Will's kitchen extension plans and nowhere near enough to set up a café, not even a small one. I'd struggle to buy a Nespresso with it.

Daydream over I turn my attention to the presentation that B has butchered. It's as though she wants me to fail which makes no sense as if I fail we don't get the new client and she doesn't get yet another pat on the back for taking all the credit for someone else's hard work. I cannot fathom her at all and I should stop trying to as I'm sure I'd be a million times happier.

I manage to make the amendments and have the presentation looking presentable long before I expect B to grace us with her presence. I e-mail it to her and await her reply which does not arrive before Charlotte. I practically pounce on the poor girl and she jumps out of her skin.

'What the bloody hell are you doing you muppet?!'

'Sorry Charl. I've been sat here over two hours by myself so the excitement of a friendly face arriving before the evil ones was almost too much to bear,' I say.

'Fair enough but you really should warn people before you jump on their back. I could have collapsed under the weight and caused us both a serious injury,' she replies.

'You cheeky cow,' I say, slapping her on the arm. 'I'm happy to see you after you made me go cold turkey over the weekend,' I add.

'What you on about?' she asks, sounding confused.

'You, not texting all weekend when usually your phone is surgically attached to your hand,' I explain.

'Get lost, it isn't and I was just trying to be present in the moment instead of being a slave to my phone,' she says dismissively.

'Present in the what now?!' I say, almost choking.

'That's what Julian says I should try to do more. I should pay attention to what I'm doing and who I'm with rather than constantly looking for entertainment and fulfilment in texts and social media. He says that when he's with me I get his full attention and he wants me to reciprocate so as I was with him most of Saturday I made the effort to do as he asked. It was quite liberating actually.'

I can't quite believe what I just heard. Charlotte, the queen of mobiles, the social media addict who can't breathe without Snap Chatting it gave up her online world for almost a whole weekend for a man she has met just three times. I find it seriously weird but refrain from saying anything negative about his Lord Almighty Julian.

'Really, well as long as you enjoyed it,' is all I manage to say. 'So how did Julian's styling go, did he manage to make a silk purse out of a sow's ear or were you mutton?' I ask.

'I'm not sure I actually know what any of that means but if you're asking did I look nice the answer is yes, Julian said I looked perfect.'

I bet he did I think, but I say, 'And what did you think?'

'Well it wasn't what I would normally go for but as Julian says, it's nice to be different sometimes and step out of your comfort zone.' And there she goes again with the 'Julian says', did I miss the third coming of Christ?

'So what were you wearing?' I venture.

When Charlotte is done filling me in on her 'Julian' look I retreat to my desk on the premise that I am super busy and need to work on my presentation. I just have to remove myself from the conversation before I say something I might regret and our friendship might not recover from. I think I managed to keep my true feelings hidden, just, but I genuinely can't believe that someone as confident and independent as Charlotte, someone who doesn't give a crap what anyone thinks and who is constantly on my back about how I shouldn't let B get to me or treat me the way she does is not seeing what I'm seeing and I don't like it, not one bit.

She showed me a picture of what she was wearing and I almost gasped. In essence it was a burka, parcelled up to look like a kimono i.e. it was red, but it was a burka. She was literally covered head to toe in a massive, red sack with only her head, hands and feet protruding. Her blonde hair was scraped back in what appeared to be a very tight bun and she looked like she was auditioning for a more colourful version of the Sound of Music. Given the reason Julian gave for wanting to style her i.e. her perfect figure, it's a bit strange that he proceeded to drown that same figure in twenty-seven metres of fabric. In the short time I was staring at the photograph I considered several reasons for this but came to the conclusion that the only reason he did it was to prevent anyone else looking at her figure, perfect or otherwise.

As the realisation hit me I felt the heat rise to my cheeks and a sickly feeling started rumbling in the pit of my stomach. I had to get away from Charlotte to catch my breath and to try and think rationally. I know that Willow and Nicky will say I'm being paranoid. It is, without doubt, a trait of my personality and I can blow things out of all proportion but just as with B I know that's not what I'm doing here. I've felt uneasy about this guy practically since day one and it's only been a week! If I'm right and he's trying to control what she wears this early in their relationship then what's he going to be controlling in a month or a year? I need to ring Willow; this conversation can't wait another minute.

I get up from my desk and start heading towards the toilets. Oh shit, will the hell never end? B is walking towards me. My throat tightens and my palms get sweaty, my mind playing out scenarios of what to do when I get closer to her. The stress is too much on top of the stress of Charlotte's conversion to Islam (in fashion at least). Oh god, she's right in front of me.

'I really thought you would have made more effort on such a big day, smart casual with the emphasis on smart when you have a pitch to make' she says as she strolls past. No good morning, no how are you, no how was your weekend. What a patronising, hypocritical bell end.

She wears the same two dresses week in, week out. They're the kind that probably cost 500 quid each but look like they were five quid in the Sally Army.

Focus, Hannah. Put the bitch to the back of your mind and make that call. Right, I dive into the small office across the corridor from the kitchen. It's supposed to be used as a 'thinking pod' but it's hard to do any thinking when there are half a dozen people in the kitchen making drinks and discussing what they did at the weekend. It consists of a small table, a chair and a telephone. It's the kind of room you see on movies used by negotiators trying to end hostage situations. All it needs is a set of earphones; I imagine it's already been bugged so that B can ensure it is being used as intended.

I call Willow. She doesn't answer so I call again, still no answer. I text her 'SOS. I need to speak to you NOW. Ring me. I'm waiting in the pod'. Thirty seconds later she calls,

'Are you ok, what's B done, is everything alright?'

'It's not me, it's Charlotte,' I whisper so as not to be overheard by anyone (Charlotte) in the kitchen.

'What? Is she ok? What's going on and…wait a minute if you're in the pod you must be at work and I'll be there in forty five minutes, couldn't it wait?' She asks.

'No it could not bloody wait, if it could I would have waited and not risked an interrogation from B as to why I am in here talking to you when I should be at home changing into my power suit,' I say.

'Changing into what…?!' Willow asks.

'Nothing, I'll tell you later, anyway Charlotte is fine, well I mean she isn't hurt or injured but she might be if we don't intervene and fast.'

'What are you going on about, you're really not making much sense and although you might have time on your hands I don't. I'm trying to pull Frosties out of Megan's hair because she thought it would be a good idea to turn her breakfast bowl into an Easter bonnet, prevent the mother of all tantrums from Oscar as I won't let him go to school in nothing but his Batman mask AND get ready for work aka respite so I don't really have time for your riddles,' she says exasperated.

'Ok, chill your boots. I'm really worried that this Julian guy is going to turn into, no already is, a fruit loop. Remember how he said Charl had an amazing figure that he really wanted to dress, well he dressed it alright. Head to toe, quite literally. He put her in a bloody burka.' I realise that isn't technically true but until she sees the photographic evidence for herself I need to embellish slightly so she gets the full gist of the horror we're dealing with.

'What? You mean he's a Muslim and he's trying to convert her?' Willow asks, a tinge of astonishment in her voice.

'Not exactly. It wasn't an actual Burka it just looked like one. He had her in this big sack with only her head, hands and feet poking out,' I say.

'Well maybe that's fashion,' Willow interjects, 'it's been a few years since I've been a follower of it so maybe burka chic has replaced boho chic.' She doesn't seem to be taking this very seriously and I tell her so.

'Willow, I'm really worried about where this is going and it's not a laughing matter. It wasn't just that he put her in those clothes, it was what she said too. It was all 'like Julian says' and I'm starting to feel like he might be a bit of a control freak. You read about it all the time don't you, guys who seem really nice and they're so attentive and pay compliments so you change your hair, your clothes etc. Then before you know it they've convinced you that your new hairdo needs new friends and dragged you away from everyone you know and love so that you're reliant on them. I think he's a control freak and we need to find out what he's playing at. I don't want Charl getting hurt.' I didn't intend to go on that long but once I got on a roll I couldn't stop.

'Han, I think you're getting a little bit ahead of yourself. Putting her in one outfit and saying a couple of things she repeats doesn't make him a control freak and I honestly think you need to rein it in a bit.. Shit, I have to go, Megan has poured her juice all over the floor and is paddling in it. FML. I'll see you in a bit.' Willow hangs up and I'm left pondering.

Back at my desk I'm relieved to see that B is not at hers. I want to stay as far as possible away from her today particularly after her none greeting this morning. I check e-mails, she hasn't yet replied to say whether she is happy with the presentation and my pitch is in less than an hour. I fully expect to hear from her around the same time that the potential clients arrive. I'm starting to feel nervous. I only got this pitch because B knows few other people have the experience to make it a success. I'm sure she would rather have anyone but me doing it as the thought of having to give me a pat on the back when it's all over will kill her. She might even have to give me a special mention in this week's team meeting. I can just see her now, gritted teeth painted on smile. I might actually look forward to Thursday for the first time in several years.

As I bask in the thought of future glory I spot Emma walking towards me. I hope she is going to walk straight past as I don't have the patience for her pretence this morning.

'Hey Hannah, are you all ready for the big pitch then, you must be a bit worried. I would be! They're a pretty big client so having them on board would be amazing for the business.'

It seems I've found B, Emma has swallowed her.

'Going forward with them on board will lead to even more business for us.'

Yep, definitely swallowed her.

'I'm feeling ok actually Emma but thanks for asking.'

'Really, so you're not worried that you might mess it up and lose us a potential BIG client.' She spreads her arms to emphasise just how big a client they are.

'Not really, I'm well prepared and have been giving pitches to clients of all sizes for several years so I think I'll be fine.'

'Right, well good luck anyway. Break a leg and all that.'

'Err, thanks', is all I can muster.

Emma is such a knob. She's clearly pissed off that she didn't get the opportunity to do the pitch; despite being pretty average at her job she thinks she's the dog's. Not a single person shares her high opinion of herself and I wish B would expend some of her venom on putting Emma in the loop. She might be less of a knob and more pleasant to be around then.

Fifteen minutes to show time and still no sign of B. I need to get the projector set up with my presentation and can't leave it any longer. If I do and the pitch is delayed it isn't going to give a very good first impression to the BIG clients. I head to the meeting room where Charlotte has already started to prep. Fresh glasses, jugs of water, note pads and pens and when the meeting starts Morning tea, which I always find very off putting. You can't present a pitch while feeding your face so I will have to watch while everyone else is gorging on pastries and mini bagels. This only becomes problematic if there is a noisy eater in the room. The only thing worse than a noisy eater is a noisy eater in an otherwise quiet room.

Just as I finish testing the projector my mobile rings and I am informed by reception that my 'guests' have arrived. I run to the ladies to ensure I look presentable with B's comments still ringing in my ears then await their arrival. Moments later in walk two middle aged, suited and booted men wearing too much aftershave. I smell it before I see them. It threatens to knock me out as I try not to take deep breaths in. I'm at risk of passing out and the presentation hasn't even begun. I decide to try panting breaths that women in labour are told to do in the hope it will allow enough oxygen to get to my brain without allowing any of the noxious smell to get into my mouth. Unfortunately, I don't account for the chest movement this entails and I realise I might look like I'm convulsing. I stop the panting immediately and move to the greetings.

This is by far the worst part of my job. Having to suck up to people I don't know or worse, who I don't know and can't stand. It is the only time in my life where I do bullshit and I hate myself for it. When I make small talk about a business I don't understand or give a crap about (and have to pretend it's the best thing in my life) I feel a tiny piece of my soul die. Some people get a thrill out of that stuff (B for instance), I do not. Plus, I'm pretty sure the people on the receiving end of my crap know it's crap but they have to play the game too.

Pleasantries over, coffee poured, I start the presentation. The first slide is exactly as it should be. I stumble when I get to slide number three. It doesn't belong there, in fact I'm certain it's one of the ones that B heavily edited, yet it looks exactly the same as the unedited version. I quickly flick to slide four and that's the same, then slide five. I'm starting to feel the panic rise, I didn't keep any of the old versions so I can't understand why that's what is now being projected all over the walls. I've totally lost my concentration and I'm trying to think of how to incorporate the final presentation into this one when the clients can see exactly the same as me and so will know I'm not following what's being presented to them.

'Is everything alright, Hannah?' one of them asks

'Oh yes, sorry, everything is absolutely fine, just a small technical issue I'm fighting with,' as I finish saying this the door bursts open and in walks B

'Sorry I'm late everyone, urgent meeting called without any notice, you know how these things can be. Gerrard, Paul, it's so lovely to see you again,' she says greeting them both with a firm handshake.

'Thank you for starting MY presentation Hannah, I can take it from here.'

I look from her to them and back again. What does she mean starting 'my' presentation? It isn't hers it's mine, it's always been mine and she wasn't even scheduled to be in it.

'I see you've got quite far in my absence but I'm sure you won't mind me re-capping to bring myself up to speed will you gentlemen.' She is not really asking them. Is she for real? Why does she need to re-cap anything? She never does pitches with anyone. That's how she passes the buck when clients aren't won. I really don't understand what's going on.

I lean in to her and whisper, 'there's a problem with the presentation, someone seems to have loaded an old version.'

'It looks perfectly fine to me; close the door on your way out.' Then it hits me, my chest starts to tighten, and I back up to the door and stumble as I try to open it without turning around. 'Do you need help there?' one of the clients asks,

'Err no, thank you I'm fine, sorry,' I mumble as I manage to extract myself from the room. The room has no windows and is tucked away down a corridor so once outside no one can see me. I flop with my back against the wall. I feel so humiliated. B has not been amending my presentation at all. It was perfect as it was. Well, she has been amending it but only to give me the run around. She has kept the original version to claim as her own and has now thrown me out of the pitch so that she can claim that too. She has purposely made me look an absolute fool knowing that I wouldn't dare say anything to her after the fact.

Tears start to form in the corner of my eyes and roll silently down my cheeks. How did I not see this coming? She has been out to get me for so long I should have known she would do something like this. If she hates me so much why not just sack me? Maybe that's her plan, claim I was too incompetent to do the pitch so she had to take over and therefore my services are no longer required. I can hear Willow and Charlotte's words of wisdom ringing in my ears 'don't let her get to you' but at the minute that is impossible. She has got to me and what makes it worse is that she knows it.

I manage to compose myself and walk slowly back to my desk hoping no one notices that my eyes are red and I haven't been gone anywhere near long enough.

CHAPTER 8

I have a good luck text from Will. Great. I can't respond now as that will just open the floodgates as although the despair has given way to anger I'm an angry cryer so more tears are likely to be shed than before and then everyone will know there's a problem.

Willow is in the office and she and Charlotte both look my way. I can tell by the concerned looks on their faces that they know something is wrong. They both send me text messages. I barely have chance to reply to one before another pops up. I shut them up with 'I'll fill you in at lunchtime, can't talk now as I'll start bawling'.

I go ring Nicky. B is going to be busy for a while so won't notice me gone and whether Nicky is at work or not she will answer her phone.

She works in the most laid-back place on the planet. Apparently everyone there walks around with mobiles in hand and not a single person bats an eyelid about it. They all use mobiles for work so no one has a clue whether you're taking a personal or professional call and even if it is a personal one no one cares as long as you get your work done and you don't take advantage. Imagine that, going to work and being treated like a grown-up. I fancy that's what heaven is like.

Nicky picks up on the first ring. I take a deep breath and launch into what just happened, impressing myself by not shedding a single tear. I do knock out a few expletives but that's understandable in the circumstances and Nicky is used to it.

'Right, so she's a mad bitch from hell. Tell me something I don't already know about her,' is Nicky's immediate response. 'Let's be honest Han, she behaves this way all the time, well maybe this particular way of screwing you over is a new one on her but screw you over is what she does on an almost daily basis so I don't really know why you're surprised. Angry yes, surprised not so much.'

'I don't know why I'm surprised but I do know I really need to find a way to get out of this place or find a way to get her out of it and I can't afford a hitman. If something doesn't give I am going to have a nervous bleeding breakdown,' I say through tears.

'So do something about it then instead of just talking about it all the time. You know what you are?'

I say, 'Enlighten me,' but get the impression it is a rhetorical question.

'You're a gonna doer. You're always going to do this or going to do that and then you never do it,' she replies.

'Well thanks for that, who needs enemies?!' I snap back.

'Alright it's not everything, in fact it's only one thing – leaving work, but you are always talking about doing it and then you never actually do it. You've got to grow some balls Han and just frigging do it.'

'I know but it's not that easy,' I answer.

'Well my lovely you better decide what the hell you do want to do cos if you don't know at your age you're never going to know and the clock is ticking. You're planning on having mini mes at some point so you haven't really got time for meditating in your undies and back packing around the African jungle until you find yourself,' she replies.

'Who mentioned anything about backpacking, you know very well that I only do luxury and you can't plug straighteners into the jungle, Giraffes don't have much call for them. Anyway I'm going now, I called for a cheer-up not a lecture so go get some work done, you skank,' I say, feeling slightly happier.

'You know I'm right though. Love ya.'

'Love you too,' I reply.

Nicky never minces her words and I'm never offended by them. She always knows how to make me feel better even though all she has done is tell me how useless I am. She is right, I do need to get my act together and decide what I want from life. I won't be pondering while backpacking though, I'm more likely to ponder while bathing on a beach in Skiathos. Although that is a couple of months away so perhaps I need to start pondering a little bit sooner. I know what my ultimate dream is but that's all it is, a dream. People's dreams seldom come true and dreams of owning a business in an industry that you've never worked in before are even less likely to come to fruition. I need to have a plan B, actually I need a plan A as current plan A i.e. the pipedream is no plan at all. That has to be plan B, or in fact, plan C behind the job I actually do and the job I'll have to go back to if plan A doesn't work out (whatever plan A is).

To my amazement B does not say a word to me for the rest of the day, I have been expecting to do the walk of shame since she turfed me out of the meeting room and yet she has barely even glanced in my direction. Perhaps this morning's debacle wasn't a precursor to sacking me at all and it really was just another way of her getting at me (which is what both Willow and Charlotte said when I filled them in).

Will is out tonight so when I get home I run a very hot bath with lots of bubbles and I settle down into it with a glass of wine for company. It is not my usual Monday night tipple but I feel like I deserve it after the day I've had. I'm trying to look on the bright side, the rest of the week can't possibly be any worse.

WRONG. The rest of the week is worse. Tuesday and Wednesday pass by uneventfully and then comes Thursday. At the beginning of the week I was open to the possibility that I might get a special mention in the team meeting. I should have known better and been careful what I wished for. I get a special mention alright just not in the way I had hoped. It all starts off innocuous enough with the reading out of the sales figures (just in case we're incapable of reading them ourselves from the six foot tall board in the office) she then announces she has 'fantastic news'. I am hoping it is going to be that she has won the lottery and was pissing off but sadly it isn't that. Oh no. The big news is that 'despite a certain person's best efforts to sabotage the potential acquisition of the biggest clients this firm has ever seen, I am delighted to say that acquire them we did. This of course would not have been possible had I not stepped in to save a truly dreadful attempt to get them on board by someone else who I ill-advisedly trusted to do the job given her experience and the fact that she is quite often the top of the sales chart. Not on this occasion though, the time when it really counted, no, on this occasion she was very much at the bottom of it'.

I am dumbfounded. She has finally given me credit for being the top sales person in this god-forsaken place but does so while throwing me under the bus for some fabricated corporate espionage. What a total crock of crap. The only sabotaging done was by her, the mad cow. While I sit boiling inside I look around the room and notice that for once I am not the only person squirming uncomfortably. Matt and Emma look a bit shifty but rather unexpectedly Charlotte and Willow look bemused. I have no idea what they could be finding so entertaining. I am hoping it is B's delusions and not what she is saying about me as it really is no laughing matter and as two of my best friends I expect better of them.

'So ladies and gentlemen we will be acting on behalf of Squires and Botts'. OGL looks thrilled with herself, everyone else looks awkward. Everyone, that is, apart from Sam, who to my surprise (and the surprise of everyone else, but most of whom reluctantly join in) starts to clap. Jesus wept, I have seen it all now. I know she is desperate to hit the big time but this is really taking the biscuit. I imagine she is one of those morons who claps when the plane lands.

NEWSFLASH dilberts. The pilots get paid thousands of twatting pounds a year to land that plane. It's kind of their job. Do you get clapped for doing yours (the obvious answer now if referring to B is of course yes but I mean in general)? No you don't, do doctors and nurses get clapped for doing theirs? No they don't, not even when they have saved someone's life. Ok so it's a pretty clever thing to do, not only keeping a piece of metal weighing thousands of tonnes in the air then bringing it down safely again but that is what they're trained to do. I think it's pretty clever being able to start someone's stopped heart again but I wouldn't feel the need to lead a round of applause if I ever witnessed someone doing it. Imagine if we all went around clapping every time someone did their job, it would be like living in a colony of seals but with fewer brain cells.

Half arsed clapping over, B dismisses her disciples. She is the first out of the room so I hang back and grab Willow and Charlotte.

'What the pissing hell were you two finding so bleeding amusing? Did you not just hear her slating me, no, libelling me, in front of EVERYONE?' I ask in my most serious voice.

'Yeah but no one believes her so calm yourself.'

'Thanks Willow for your amazing psychic insight, how do you know no one frigging believes her? You know how gullible and desperate for approval most of them are.' I am furious.

'Well yes that is true but the right info in the right ear changed that today.' Charlotte interjects.

'Please enlighten me because I'm confused as hell and the morning has been bad enough.' I say.

'We did a Snap Chat thing and sent pics of those e-mails you sent us straight after she ambushed you to Matt, Emma, Zoe and Gemma so they all saw exactly what happened from your point of view.' Charlotte says looking very pleased with herself.

'You did what? You have got to be kidding me?! B despises me as it is and you doing that will make it ten times worse when they run and tell her.' I say.

'They can tell her what they want but they can't show her any proof can they? Ten second view of an e-mail is all they got. We sent it while they were all here so that if they tried to screenshot it for any reason we would have known and confronted them. None of them did, so you see, in that meeting they knew B was talking a load of old bollocks.' Willow explains.

'And we were sure to send it to the few who do the most gossiping knowing full well they would be telling everyone else what happened. None of them are brave enough to say anything to B so you have nothing to worry about. Just enjoy having everyone on your side for once. Maybe they will all now see her for what she is.' Charlotte adds.

'I doubt it but thanks for the effort guys, I really appreciate you having my back. I know it's not easy when you have to work here and worry about putting food on the table but I'm grateful that you took a stand even if B is never likely to know, you do love me after all.' I say.

'No thanks necessary and don't get all mushy, we got sick of your miserable face that's all. We'd have done anything to not have to listen to you whining and plus you would do the same for us.' Charlotte's right I would and I am, well I'm trying with my intended intervention into this relationship of hers.

'Well I'm super grateful anyway you losers,' with that I change the subject. 'So when are we going to meet Prince Charming then?'

'I don't know, how about Sunday?' Charlotte asks. 'We could go for lunch to The Boat. Are you bringing your fellas?'

'Wasn't planning to,' I say.

'Me neither. I'd have to get a sitter then and It's too much hassle,' Willow adds.

'Ok well I'm sure Julian won't mind if it's just us girls, I'll tell him you'll be on your best behaviour.'

'Of course, we'll be very gentle with him,' I say convincingly. 'We need to sort a night out with Nik too, she was moaning she hadn't seen you both for ages. I would think that would be a thing to celebrate but apparently it isn't.'

'She spends half her life with you, we're a welcome frigging relief, I reckon. Willow interjects.

'Ok but I'll have to check when I'm free with Julian. He said he wanted to spend as much time as possible with me at weekends as he is going to be really busy with a big trial soon so week nights will be out of the question.'

'Well if you have no current plans, Charl, can't you just pick a weekend and tell him you won't be free on that one?' Willow suggests.

'S'pose. I'll speak to him first though. I want to be available when he needs me,' Charlotte says. She makes it sound like he's an invalid and she's his carer. I can't wait to meet this prick.

After work I give Nicky a quick call and fill her in on the day's shenanigans. She's her usual bullish self and I wish I could be as carefree as she is. She's quite a sensitive soul but she's also hard as nails, and if a hard decision has to be made she has no qualms about making it if it affects her for the better.

'You know what I think about the whole fucked-up mess, you can't stay in the same sorry situation and expect a different outcome or be shocked when the outcome is the same.'

Wise words indeed. No doubt Will has something similar to say when I fill him in. In fact, I might not bother. The less I talk about it at home the less it can affect my mood, right? It's not like he needs to know every bit of my pathetic working life so this evening I will grin and bear it. Maybe we'll go to quiz night and try and win a few quid to put towards our holiday or Will's new kitchen. Or a bottle of wine.

I need to make the most of this coming weekend as next is wasted on Daisy devil. Actually 'wasted' is a bit harsh but it's one of those occasions I wish I'd said no to, and now I'm wishing my life away until it's over. I will never learn to say no. Although, I have found that usually the things you dread are the things you enjoy the most. Nicky is aware of how I feel about it and has promised to give Daisy a talking to so she acts more like a little girl and less like Beelzebub. I might suggest that she picks Daisy up from school on Friday night, the longer she spends with 'Aunt Nik' the better behaved she is and having her from Friday afternoon will give her a good twenty hours in appropriate company.

Will doesn't want to go to quiz night. He's had a rubbish day at work and wants to stay in and get take out. It seems planning permission cannot be obtained for the building he's been working so hard to create for love nor money so his design is on the scrap heap. Four months of his life wasted. I try and lighten the mood with, 'It's not so bad, at least you got paid for it,' but he's not in the mood for being cheered up, particularly any that fail to acknowledge his creative genius. I suggest he tries to flog his design to another company somewhere but he points out it's under copyright of his current employers so he can't do that. Oh dear. I am pleased I decided not to regale him with the horror of my day. He can have the accolade of having the world's worst day for a change.

To his credit he does ask how my day was and whether the meeting was as eventful as always. I tell a big fat white lie and say work was ok, the meeting was boring as usual and inform him that he will have to fend for himself on Sunday as I am going to meet Charlotte's new fella.

'What new fella?' he asks.

'That Julian guy I told you about.'

'Oh, so he's actually her fella now, is he!' I haven't raised my concerns about Julian with Will as he will accuse me of being melodramatic. Even after all these years together he still won't admit that my first impressions of someone are pretty damn spot on!

'Yeah, well she's only been on three dates with him but it seems to be moving fast so Willow and I thought it might be nice to see what all the fuss is about.' I tell him enthusiastically.

He isn't fooled. 'You mean you want to give him the once over so you don't feel as bad for slagging him off.'

'No, that's not the case at all, we just want to share in her happiness, and I haven't slagged him off.' Another white lie.

'Pull the other one, you haven't had anything nice to say about any of Charlotte's blokes.'

'I haven't met any of them,' I say with indignation.

'Exactly! Never met them but always have plenty to say about them.'

'Whatever! She's my friend so I like to make sure she's with the right guy and not going to get hurt. Is that such a bad thing?' I ask, feeling dejected.

'No, of course it's not. I'm impressed that you've managed to stay quiet about him this long. Maybe you're mellowing,' he says giving me a friendly dig in the elbow.

I decide to forgive him for being so opinionated about me, after all it has taken his mind off work and he cheers me up so well when the boot is on the other foot.

'Mellow or not, you're still fending for yourself on Sunday. Now what we having for tea?' I ask.

CHAPTER 9

As is the norm we stayed up too late drinking wine on Saturday night and I was expecting the worst, yet despite not feeling brilliant when I woke this morning I have managed to clean the bathroom and am rewarding myself with coffee and cake. I sit down, phone in hand ready for some social media activity when I see there are messages from Charlotte (probably confirming the time for lunch this afternoon) and Willow (probably checking what I'm wearing for lunch this afternoon).

I'm wrong on both counts. Charlotte's cancelling our lunch and Willow's having a go at Charlotte for cancelling our lunch. Apparently Julian has had a really full on week and doesn't feel like he can give 100 per cent to meeting us so would rather do it at another time. He's very tired and can't face having to go out, 'he just wants to spend the afternoon at home, chilling out and having some alone time with me as he's barely seen me this week.'

He's barely seen her this week?! He's barely seen her this month as they've only known each other two minutes. I was willing (almost) to give him the benefit of the doubt until I met him but I am totally convinced that he is a total knob who isn't being cute and romantic wanting to spend time with her but is in fact being a psycho playing mind games in an effort to keep her away from people. I've been trying to convince Willow of this every chance I've had and am pleased when I see a text pop up from her which suggests she has come round to my way of thinking.

'OMG have you seen that message from Charl? Ring me when you're up. I'm starting to think you're right about this guy. He's either a control freak or an absolute drip of a mummy's boy. I'm leaning towards the former. Anyway, ring me when you drag your sorry, hungover arse out of bed xo.'

After a strong coffee and an hour's rant on the phone with Willow, during which we decide we'll just meet for lunch without them, I managed to wake Will up while shouting into the phone and he pretty much got the gist of what had happened without me having to repeat it all. He still thinks I'm being over-zealous and should be pleased that Charlotte has found herself an attentive man who wants to spend time with her. Attentive is one thing, controlling is another so I ask him to keep his opinions to himself.

'Have you decided what to do with yourself while I'm out?'

'It's Sunday afternoon, I'm going to watch the footy in my boxers and eat cereal from the box like any other self-respecting alpha male.'

He's talking rubbish, he doesn't even like football and we don't have cereal.

'Ok, and in real life you're going to…?'

'Meet James in the pub for a game of pool.'

'Well what's Nik doing if James is out with you?'

'How would I know? She's your mate not mine. You text her 350 times a day so I would have thought you knew her itinerary off by heart.'

'Don't be a smart arse. I'll message her and ask her if she wants to join me and Willow.'

'Why? So you have another witch for your coven? You can legitimately be the three Witches of Eastwick.'

'No one likes a smart arse, Will, and you're not even smart, you're just an arse. We will eat, drink and discuss what we have planned for our girls' night out. Do you have a problem with that?'

'Nope, no problem at all, my little ray of sunshine. I'm off to get a shower, I'm meeting James soon.'

I arrive at The Dove and Olive to meet Willow and Nicky, who had been planning a date with the oven cleaner but was easily persuaded to ditch it. The pub's a bit pricier than The Boat so doesn't tend to get quite as busy, which should mean we have no problems getting a table. I spot one in a corner that should be big enough for the three of us and claim it. If it gets any busier I'll be hidden from view so I message them both to tell them where I am just about at the same time as they walk in and clock me.

'Bottle and three glasses?' Nicky asks.

'Hello to you too,' I say giving her the obligatory friend hug and kiss on the cheek.

She shoots off to the bar leaving Willow and me to mull over every word of Charlotte's text. We gabble ten to the dozen, often at the same time and haven't come up for air by the time Nicky returns from the bar.

'So what's the crack with Romeo and Julian then?' Nicky giggles clearly enjoying her play on words and ignoring the fact that Romeo is a boy.

'How would we know? You know as much as we do, Nik. We were supposed to meet him today but he wants Charlotte all to himself without us meddling, so now we're not.'

'Yeah, but that's not exactly what Charlotte said though, is it? I thought she said he had been busy so wanted a quiet one with her,' Nicky points out.

'Well, yes, that's what her text said but that's not what it meant.' I say.

'I guess we'll never know, will we? Right, are we ordering? I'm bloody starving.' Nicky grabs menus from the next table.

Everyone's choice is Sunday lunch and we send Nicky off to the bar to order. She comes back looking sheepish and holding another bottle of wine.

'What's that face?' Willow enquires, though I too am curious. She looks like she just stole a tenner from her mum's purse and is reconsidering the error of her ways.

'Let me look at that text from Charlotte,' Nicky says. Her request is a bit weird given that she shut down the conversation before she went to the bar but I oblige anyway.

'Ok, well, I am pretty certain they are not having an afternoon of chilling out at home because I just saw Charlotte at the other side of the bar.' Nicky says.

'You what? Who with?' Willow asks. She sounds more intrigued than anything else.

'She's with a guy but I don't know who the guy is. She's with two guys actually, two guys and a woman...oh alright, she seems to be on a couples date.'

What the...?! She has ditched us to have a couples date with Julian. Why didn't she just say that instead of making up a lie? We would have been fine if she had said, 'Oh I'm sorry I've double booked and we're actually going out with Julian's friends so can we go out another day,' but to lie about it...

'I have a good mind to march over there and ask what the hell she is playing at,' Willow is furious.

'I'm with you there, the cheeky mare. I hate liars and she knows I do.'

'Hold your horses, you two. If it's any consolation she doesn't look particularly happy to be there. She looks really uncomfortable, although that might be as a result of the sack she's wearing, it looks itchy as hell,' Nicky says.

I'm intrigued. 'Why, what has she got on?'

'I told you, it's a sack. You know, like those sacks you use for the sack race at school only this one's got sleeves. It's most likely supposed to be a hessian coloured jumper dress but it definitely looks like a sack.'

'I see,' I reply, 'but back to the not looking happy bit, what do you mean she doesn't look happy?'

'The opposite of not looking sad, she doesn't look happy. She isn't smiling or joining in the conversation. She's just sat there looking a bit miserable.'

'Well maybe we should go over there to cheer her up then instead.' Willow suggests.

'No, I think you should both leave it. You two turning up when she has lied to you about going out is hardly likely to make her feel better, is it? She'll be miserable and embarrassed then. Just leave it until you see her and ask how her weekend was, see what she says about it.'

We spend another hour in the pub before sneaking out so as not to be seen by the little liar, liar pants on fire. She's the one in the wrong and we're the ones doing the sneaking, I'm not sure how that works. I'm also not sure how we're going to broach the subject with Charlotte. Although Nicky insisted that Charlotte looked miserable and like she would rather be in a Crocodile infested swamp than on that date I'm still annoyed that she lied about why she couldn't come for lunch. She knows us well enough to be able to tell us the truth, and if she really didn't want to go out with that pillock then why didn't she just tell him that?

When I tell Will he doesn't understand what the fuss is all about but then he never really gets fussed about anything. I'm just going to ask her straight out tomorrow and find out what the hell she was playing at. Speaking of hell, this weekend turned into a bit of a disappointment and I can't look forward to next weekend as we have Daisy Devil and the precocious brats to contend with. FML!

The following day I can't ask Charlotte anything as she doesn't turn up for work, and she doesn't turn up for the next couple of days either. She didn't bother to tell Willow or I that she wouldn't be in, we just go the same e-mail everyone else got from Reception advising she was ill. I messaged her and received a very short reply advising she was full of cold and felt like shit. As far as I can recall it's the first time she's been off sick yet I'm struggling to believe that's the reason she's off. Perhaps she saw us at the pub and doesn't want to have to face us.

I can't recall Charlotte ever lying to me, not even a little white one so I really ought to believe her but after the weekend's events I'm wondering if I know her as well as I thought I did. I raise my concerns with Willow on Wednesday evening when we have an impromptu drink in a pub close to work.

'Why would she lie about being sick, it's not like she's off all the time. In fact she's off none of the time,' I say. 'I can't explain it, but feel like over the last few weeks she's gradually developing into a person I don't really know.' Now the words are out I realise they sound foolish and irrational.

'Yes, she's been a little aloof but she's in the first throngs of a new relationship so that's to be expected.' Willow's wise words cement my foolishness.

'I suppose so, I think I've transferred all of my hoping B meets a sticky end energy into imagining Charlotte is a damsel in distress and maybe I've blown it all out of proportion.' I don't think I've blown it that far out of proportion but there is no denying that thoughts of Charlotte have engulfed my brain of late leaving no room to think about anything else.

'Are you and B mates now then?' Willow asks, knowing the question to be absurd.

'No, she hasn't spoken a single word to me since the presentation. She doesn't speak to me often so I only realised she wasn't speaking to me at all when I walked past her the other day and she looked down rather than giving me the usual "we're best mates, I hate you really" grimace.'

'Well they say silence is golden.'

'It's actually not. Silence is extremely passive aggressive and I know she's biding her time before torturing me again. I'm trying not to think about it. Perhaps that's why I've built the Charlotte thing up, it's more pleasant than building the B thing up since that only ever ends up one way, with me in a crumpled, crying heap.'

Perfect, now I've thought about it I won't stop thinking about it and the dread I've come to know and hate will once again envelop my every thought. In fact, now that I am thinking about it I realise that not only has B not spoken to me she also hasn't given me any new clients or assignments. I've been busy, but busy with existing stuff that is going to start dwindling very soon. B knows this, B knows everything. There are always lulls in sales, the lulls are filled by new selling campaigns for new clients. Products are seasonal and we always sell one season ahead. I'm finishing up on a sales drive for spring even though it's still winter. I have no summer products so I need new clients. No new clients means no new work, which means nothing to do, which means no job.

Oh fuck, I knew I shouldn't have thought about it. Is that what B is up to? Give me no work and then she can get rid of me by making me redundant? While I'd love nothing more than to leave the godforsaken place, I haven't been there long enough to get a good pay-off. The sneaky bitch. How did I not realise before? If she isn't going to give me more work, I'll have to ask for it and that means speaking to her. I don't want to speak to her, I'd be quite happy to never speak to her again. I could e-mail her, not very grown up or professional but at least it leaves a paper trail if she does try and do me over. Right, that's what I'll do. I'll send her an e-mail advising that my campaigns will be coming to an end in the next couple of weeks so pretty please can I have some more work. I'm already dreading her reply.

***

On Thursday Charlotte returns to work. She doesn't skip over to mine or Willow's desk as she usually does. Rather, she scurries to her own and hides behind her screen.

'Morning, you ok? I missed you.' I message to her. She replies advising she's fine, sorry she didn't get in touch but she was really rough and now she's going to have her head down all day as she's got a mountain of work to catch up on.

'Lunch tomorrow then?' I ask. She says she'll see how she goes.

She isn't in the meeting and I presume she's had a free pass due to her absence and workload. The meeting goes the same way they all do but B does announce that we have a couple of new summer products coming our way. Willow slyly gives me the thumbs up. I e-mailed B yesterday afternoon, she hasn't replied yet so I expect when the meeting is over I will hear from her and she will confirm that I have one of the products. I wonder what they are, I hope it's something good like skin care. I'm awesome at selling that, I'm shit at useful stuff like garden tools, I had my worst ever sales figures from a lawnmower.

Contrary to my assumption B did not reply to my e-mail. In all fairness she was out of the office for most of the day so probably didn't have time. Charlotte was quiet too. She didn't emerge from behind her screen until 5pm and shouted bye as she headed out the door. She must have been mega busy, or still feeling mega shit. She should have just had the whole week off. I feel bad now for questioning the validity of her illness. I'll buy her lunch and a treat tomorrow to apologise. Not that she knows I was questioning her but it will make me feel better.

Only two more sleeps until theatre time. I message Nicky to ask if it's still on (hoping she says it's not). Sadly she confirms it is and says she'll pick me up at lunchtime on Saturday. I've looked at some reviews for the show and everyone seems to love it so it might not be as bad as I'm expecting. If I drink enough wine beforehand I might even manage to sleep the whole way through it.

Friday lunchtime and still no e-mail from B, I was sure I would have heard from her by now. I don't want to have to speak to her —the thought alone is traumatic enough. I'll wait a bit then e-mail her again. I'm meeting Charlotte for lunch so I slope off to the café. For some reason Charlotte insisted on meeting me despite the fact we sit twenty metres away from each other. She said she needed to grab something from Boots first. I said I was happy to wander there with her too but she didn't seem keen so I'm now sat like Billy no mates waiting for her to arrive.

B is in today so we can't take the piss and have an extra-long lunch but I've already been waiting twenty minutes. I've ordered both of our coffees and my food. I messaged Charlotte to ask what she wants but she has yet to reply, just as I am about to call her she turns up. She half smiles at me, sits down and puts the menu in front of her face. The waitress sidles over. 'I'll have Caesar salad please.' Charlotte says without looking up.

'Caesar salad! Since when do you eat salad? What's happened to fat Friday and a burger with the lot?' I ask.

'I'm not that hungry today and I'm having a big dinner.' Maybe it's the tail end of her illness affecting her appetite as she can ordinarily eat two taties more than a pig no matter what she's having for dinner.

'Fair enough. What did you get from Boots?' I ask, noticing that our conversation is unusually stilted and Charlotte still has the menu in her hand.

'Oh, just some foundation I read about.' she answers, her face still covered.

'Char, as much as I like the menu in here I'm not that keen on talking to it so would you mind moving it the fuck from your face.' Charlotte slowly lowers the menu and I see her face for the first time this week. There's something odd about it, she appears to be wearing all of the foundation that Boots sell plus all of their concealer and a good amount of their eye shadow.

'What the fudge is with all the make-up? You're usually miss au naturel.'

'Err, they gave me a quick make over while I was in Boots.'

'Explains what took you so long I suppose, you might want to wash some of it off before you go back in the office though, you look like you're going clubbing.'

'Yeah, I will do.'

The stilted conversation carries on throughout lunch and I feel like I am interrogating Charlotte rather than conversing with her. She answers my questions but offers nothing in between. I refrain from saying anything about seeing her in the pub on Sunday as I don't think confrontation is going to help matters and when I ask what she is doing this weekend she says she doesn't know as Julian is organising it. Despite telling me she is fine now and over her illness I can't help but think she must still be feeling unwell as she isn't herself at all.

Back at the office I bump into Sam in the kitchen. After a bit of small talk she tells me how excited she is to have been given one of the new jobs B mentioned in the meeting. It can't have been a big one as while Sam is desperate for promotion she has very little experience so I can't see B trusting her with anything too taxing. Explains why she hasn't given it to me I guess

'Great news Sam, well done,' I say.

'Thanks, I couldn't believe it when she told me yesterday, I've started work on it already.'

It's a bit weird that she told Sam about this yesterday but still hasn't replied to me. I race off to my desk to e-mail her again.

No need, she's replied.

CHAPTER 10

'I'm starting to think you're right and she actually just does hate you. I suppose you can't please all of the people all of the time and you have to agree you are a bit Marmite'.

It's Saturday afternoon, Nicky and I are making our way into town with Daisy Devil who thankfully is plugged into her tablet so can't hear all the expletives being thrown around, mainly by me. I have just informed Nicky of recent work shenanigans which resulted in me being royally shafted in favour of the arse-licking twat Emma who is now responsible for selling the latest, greatest lip stain on the market. B felt I wasn't the right person for the job as it needed someone 'fresh and enthusiastic' both of which I apparently am not.

Why let a little fact like the previous two beauty items I was responsible for being the top selling products of the year get in the way of her favoured new sport, Hannah baiting? Not content with practically bringing me to my knees she added a good kick for extra measure and requested I let Emma have the presentations used for said products in order to 'get a feel for what the client is looking for'. I thought they wanted fresh and fucking enthusiastic? I told her that unfortunately as I liked to make each presentation unique I got rid of them once the marketing was finished so no longer had them. Then I pressed delete, and purge to make sure they were gone. Not before I saved them to a USB stick though. I was pissed off, not senseless.

The wonky-toothed, goggled-eyed bitch can figure it out for herself and woe betide her if she dares ask me for help.

'Do you think? Cos it's not like I've been saying the same thing for the last two years or anything is it. Nice of you to finally jump on my train.'

'Well mate, you do go on about it so I zone out most of the time but even I have to admit it does seem to be getting pretty personal.' Finally, Nicky is on board.

'Seems to be getting?? It's long since been got so I know I've said it a million times before but I seriously need to get my shit together and get the hell out of there.'

'What does Will think to this course of action then? I can't see Mr Sensible wanting you to do anything but a full-time stable job.'

Nicky is right; he doesn't want me to do anything but a nice stable job. But he would like a nice stable wife and currently he has one who's teetering on the edge of madness with only a bottle of sav blanc keeping her from falling over.

'He just wants me to be sane, so at this point he'd be ok with me working in Maccy D.'

'Daisy, take those earphones off we're here.' Nicky says not turning around or increasing the volume of her voice so Daisy carries on regardless.

'Yo, DD. Auntie Nicky said we're here so take the earphones off.' I say.

'I heard her the first time and my name isn't DD so stop calling me it, you're not cool so stop pretending you are.'

I want to batter the little shit but I stay calm. Nicky responds so I don't have to.

'Well if you heard me why didn't you take them off? And stop being rude to Hannah or you won't get anything from the stalls inside.

'I don't even want anything, so I don't care.'

Bribery doesn't work on her because she knows that Auntie Nicky will get her anything she wants provided she wobbles her lip and slags her mum off. Nicky is a sucker for her sob stories.

'Well don't have anything then but can you still move your butt out of the car so we can get inside? I'm dying for a drink and Auntie Nicky is paying.'

'My mum says you two drink too much and your livers will shrivel up and you'll be sad old women hanging around in pubs pretending you're twenty when really you're waaaay too old'.

I refrain from saying, 'Is that the same mum who can't keep her knickers up and who would sell you for half a bottle of Wkd and five fags,' and instead say, 'Your mum needs to stop sniffing glue.' Nicky kicks me. 'It's better than what I was going to say.' I shrug.

We manage to prise the tablet from Daisy's hands and get seated in the restaurant. There is nothing like the smell of a good curry to make the stomach rumble. Drinks delivered we peruse the food menu.

'I hate Paki food,' Daisy announces.

Nicky and I both choke and simultaneously cry, 'You can't say that.'

'That's what mum calls it.' Says the devil.

Nicky's face is bright red, she talks in a low growl her face twisted in anger. 'Your mother is a bloody idiot. How many times do I have to tell you not to listen to or repeat any of the nonsense that comes out of her mouth? Do you want to end up like her? Well, do you?'

DD shakes her head.

'Right then, that is an evil word and I don't ever want to hear you say it ever. Do you understand? If you say anything like that again you will stop coming to see me, ok?'

DD's eyes cloud over and her lip starts to tremble. I don't even think she is putting it on this time. I have never heard Nicky tell her off properly before and I'm a little scared.

'Sorry Auntie Nicky, I didn't know it was a bad word. I'll tell mum off when I get home if you want.'

'It's ok, I'll tell her myself. Now, what do you want to eat?'

We eat in relative silence. I realise Nicky has had more than her fair share of wine and she's supposed to be driving. This does not bode well as she's now in a foul mood so I'm scared to say anything. Thankfully I don't have to as she informs me we can walk to the theatre and James has offered to drive us home. It seems he thought we would both need lots of wine to get through the evening, he thought right! By the time mains are done Nicky has perked up, the devil had the good sense to stay quiet and eat all of her chicken nuggets before summoning up the courage to ask for ice cream.

'Of course you can, sweet pea,' replies Nicky and normality resumes.

'I'm really excited now, are you?' She asks me.

'Not really, Nik. Well I'm excited about the wine and chocolates I'm just not quite as excited about the whining kids.'

'Don't be a party pooper. It's going to be a right laugh, you'll love it. I've been listening to some of the songs and they're awesome.'

'Christ, it's a good job you're not driving.'

'Why?' asks Nicky.

'Because you've clearly had way too much already, you plank.'

We enter the theatre foyer and as I suspected DD's eyes light up at the stalls full of merchandise: t-shirts, drink bottles, Matilda bracelets, mini chalkboards, CD soundtrack (in case our ears don't get enough torture during the live performance). After going around every stall and determining they all sell exactly the same crap, DD decides on a chalkboard and a bracelet. £30 later and she's happy. When we finally make it to the bar I'm delighted to discover I can pre order interval drinks. If only I could do that in a normal bar. 'Yes please, barman. I'll have one now and one at thirty minute intervals for the next two hours.'

I do feel a bit guilty letting Nicky pay when she's not even driving now but she did offer it as a sweetener for me accompanying them. My guilt wears off quickly when the barman requests £36. Sweet mother of Jesus, nine quid for a mini bottle of wine! We won't be getting pissed at these prices. I send a picture of me looking sad and the price as a snapchat to Willow and Charlotte. I'm practically hyperventilating at the cost but Nicky appears nonplussed. 'God Nik, you must be pissed, you didn't even flinch when he said how much that round was.'

'I've been here before haven't I, so it wasn't a shock to me. Enjoy them though, cos I ain't buying any more.'

'Fair do's, I'll shout us a round to take in after the interval. I reckon I'm going to need it.'

DD is beside herself with excitement. She's eaten approximately two kilos of Minstrels and drank three pints of cold water. She now needs a wee and the queue is four miles long as the show starts in ten minutes. Not being too bothered about missing any of it I offer to take her to the loo while Nik checks in with James re pick-up time. Whilst we shuffle along like OAP's in M & S the midget takes the opportunity to ask me eleventy bastard questions a minute. It's like being on The Chase but without any cash to look forward to.

'Why don't you have a baby? When are you going to have a baby? What kind of baby would you like? (One not like fucking you.) Why don't you like my mum? Why do you like my Auntie? Why do you drink wine? What does it taste like? I think you're nicer to me when you have wine.'

I don't need the loo but opt to go into cubicle on my own just to give my ears a rest. We manage to get out and to our seats just as the lights go down. Oh balls, I was hoping to miss a few minutes at least.

***

I buy the soundtrack on the way out ignoring Nicky's laughter. 'I thought you were going to hate every minute and your ears were going to be bleeding from listening to precocious brats singing for two hours?'

'I never said that,' I exclaim knowing full well that I said something very similar.

'Whatever you knob, I knew you'd like it.'

When James arrives I hand him the CD and the devil and I sit in the back trying to sing along. Nicky sits bemused in the front taking videos which I have no doubt she is posting on every social media outlet she can think of. Upon arrival at my house I retrieve MY CD and the devils starts crying. I know the most appropriate course of action would be to let her keep it and just download it for myself on Spotify but it's mine and I like having an actual CD, it's more satisfying than a digital download, so instead I promise to copy it and deliver it to her the following day. She isn't best pleased but stops crying and I feel like we've bonded slightly over our newly formed love of *Matilda*. I say my goodbyes and bound into the house.

'You look happy or pissed, perhaps both,' Will says as I almost knock him over attempting to kiss him and race past him at the same time to get to the CD player. 'Blimey where's the fire?'

'I just want to put this on,' I say, waving the case in front of his face.

'What the chuff is it?'

'This is a life changer. A piece of inspiration that no person should ignore.'

'It looks more like a CD case to me, I didn't realise people actually sold them anymore. You haven't been sucked in by those bloody goranga shouting Monks have you?' Will asks in all seriousness.

'Have I balls. It's the soundtrack for the musical I've just been to, dickhead!'

'You've spent our hard-earned money on singing kids. Have you lost your mind? I thought you said it was an inspirational life changer or did I miss-hear?'

'No, you did not and in answer to your first question I am not pissed. I have just had the most amazing night ever. Oh my god, I could just go back again now and watch it all over again. In fact I think I could go back every day and watch it, including the matinee and still not get bored.' I'm so exhilarated I feel like I could walk on air.

'Are you winding me up here or what? You've been to see a kids' musical that you didn't want to see and you've come back rambling like a lunatic. Do you need a doctor?'

'Honestly Will, let me put some of the songs on so you can hear for yourself. It was like some of them were actually written for me and my life. Obviously they weren't because Tim Minchin doesn't know me and he wrote them ages ago but he is a bloody genius. A genius, I tell you. There I am feeling miserable after another week in my shit job with my evil boss wondering how the hell I am going to do anything about it and then I watch this show and boom; it's like a lightning bolt. It hits me square between the eyes and I feel high as a kite.'

'What hit you? Don't tell me, you've decided to write a musical?' He asks looking perplexed.

'What? No I am not writing a musical, have you not been listening to a word I said?'

'Han, I'm listening, but I'm not really understanding. You're talking like a motivational speaker, saying a lot of words enthusiastically but making zero sense.'

'Right, listen to this song and you'll get it.' I play *Naughty* and my heart sings. My mouth tries to sing but I haven't quite mastered the words yet and Will hates it when I say listen to this and then sing over it so I try to keep it to a low hum. With every word my heart swells, I don't think my smile can get any bigger and I feel like I'm going to burst. It finishes.

'Well?' I ask.

'It's no *Angels*, is it!' Will responds. I am not in the mood to have my bubble burst.

'No *Angels*, are you frigging kidding me? It's a trillion times better. Did you not hear the message? Can you not think of someone other than yourself for one minute and consider how those words resonate with me. Did you even listen to them?' I'm upset that he doesn't seem to be getting it.

'Ok love, calm down. Which words in particular are resonating with you? Reading between the lines given it's a kid singing I heard a lot about not putting up with stuff you don't like. Is that what you're getting at?'

'Yes, exactly,' I say, relieved that he does get it. 'You see, I talk a lot and I complain a lot and I feel sorry for myself even more but none of that is actually going to change where I am or what I'm doing is it? No, it's not.' I feel like I'm talking to myself now and Will just happens to be in the vicinity. 'Actions speak louder than words, right? So I need to act. I've got to take a leap of faith and do something, apply for another job, stand up to B. Anything. I just need to do it'. I feel exhausted all of a sudden and have to sit down.

'Ok, I'm glad you've had an epiphany so what's the plan?'

'God Will! I don't know, do I? I only came to my senses two hours ago, give me chance.' With that I decide to take myself off to bed. I don't imagine I'll get much sleep as my mind is whirring and I have a *Naughty* earworm.

CHAPTER 11

I'm still in an enthused mood when I arrive at work on Monday. I've informed Charlotte and Willow of my lightbulb moment. Willow showed more interest than Charlotte although both appeared sceptical. I spoke to Nicky several times over the weekend and she still finds my 180 on the whole *Matilda* thing hilarious.

Now the trouble with enthusiasm is that it can wain when not in the right environment, and I'm not in the right environment. I refrained from checking e-mails all weekend and I'm glad I did. I have one from Emma. She wants to have a 'brainstorming' session with me so we can 'throw around ideas' of how she goes about selling the products she has.

I don't want to brainstorm or throw around ideas. I want to throw her round. Her and B, in fact. I don't want to be here anymore. I haven't wanted to be here for ages and I am tempted to walk out. However, although Will is fully supportive of my new-found enthusiasm for story changing a la *Matilda*, he wouldn't be too supportive of me doing it while sat on the sofa in my pjs. He has made it quite clear that any plan has to involve me receiving a regular income and apparently being a Facebook sales pest isn't acceptable. It's a shame as I reckon I could totally nail the inspirational 'Going straight to the top' posts in my current frame of mind.

'What's with the face? I thought you were on the path to enlightenment and nothing was going to bring you down.' Willow has sauntered over for a chat.

'I'm still on the path but it has been temporarily blocked by the brown nosed bitch face.' I say.

'Oh, you mean Emma. What's she done?' I fill Willow in.

'If you wanted to be a bitch you could do it but give her loads of shit ideas. She's not that bright so if you say them with enough excitement she'll believe you and use them, then you can watch her die on her arse'.

I'm very tempted but I know my inner good self wouldn't allow me to do that. I've got more pride than to sabotage her just because I feel pissed off. I'd much rather give her my good ideas and watch her die on her arse because she has no idea how to execute any of them.

'No, I am going to be the bigger person and help her, I've got nothing else to do anyway and it's bad enough being in this place when you're busy and time flies by. I don't fancy sitting with nothing to do for eight hours a day.'

'I suppose so. Good for you. Have you heard anything from Charlotte? She was quiet again this weekend.' Willow asks beating me to it.

'Not much, she did reply to my *Matilda* text but it was short and sweet, I was thinking we maybe should try and re-arrange the meeting with the oracle that is Julian. Show some interest, you know? It might make Charlotte more accessible again if we appear interested. What do you think?'

'Ok, sounds good and I haven't got anything on over the next few weekends. The brats haven't been invited to any parties, which is understandable cos they're both obnoxious little shits at the minute. Even I don't want to spend time with them.' Willow says rolling her eyes.

'And that justifies my reason for not having kids yet, I couldn't cope with them being little bastards. I don't have the patience.' I have very little patience at the best of times and what I do have is halved whenever I am stressed due to work (most of the time) so I fear if I had a little person pushing my buttons they would wind up in a box on someone's doorstep.

'Trust me mate, you find patience you never knew you had when you spawn tiny devils, I usually find all I need at the bottom of a very large glass of wine and if I could afford it I suspect I'd find even more in a joint or two.'

My giggles at Willow's window into motherhood stop abruptly when I see Charlotte. At least I think it's Charlotte. It's a person who resembles Charlotte but only after a massive make under. She looks different but not in a good way. She looks drab and downbeat. She isn't wearing a scarp of make-up and she has her hair scraped back in a dowdy pony tail. Rather than her usual Primani chic she is sporting a bland navy polyester suit. She looks more like my mother.

I nod in her direction for Willow's benefit. She follows my gaze and the look on her face says she has the same thoughts as I. For reasons unknown Willow directs an awkward wave in Charlotte's direction and she in turn half smiles then scurries to her desk. I have no idea what this latest look is about but I'm willing to bet it has something to do with Julian.

At lunchtime I saunter over to her desk. She lifts her head up and I swear the look on her face is one of embarrassment.

'Hi stranger.' I say in a voice as chirpy as I can muster.

'Oh, hi,' says Charlotte, 'I didn't see you walking over.'

'I thought I'd come over and say hello as you seem to be ignoring me. Have I done something to upset you?' I ask.

'Oh no, I've just got lots of work on that's all and I don't want to be in B's bad books. You know what that's like.'

'Yes I do,' I reply. 'Were you busy working at the weekend as well? I didn't hear much from you then either.'

'Err no, I was just spending time with Julian, that's all, and he gets cross. Err … I mean he doesn't like it when I'm on my phone all the time. I've told you that before.' She speaks in a rather terse tone as though she's chastising me for daring to forget everything Julian has ever said to her.

Despite her agitation I press on. 'So what's with the new look? Is that something to do with Julian as well, I know how he fancies himself as a fashionista. Is he trying out minimal chic on you?'

'Actually he was just talking about the Kardashians and other celebs and the irony of how they mask their faces with make-up yet flaunt their bodies in revealing clothes and I realised that's exactly what I do. And so do you and most other women I know, come to that matter.'

If I didn't know better I'd say she was being patronising. I'm exasperated and don't believe for a second that Charlotte has had such an epiphany at all, I suspect Julian more than simply 'mentioned' the Kardashians fashion sense.

121

'I'm sorry, Charl, but I find that a little nonsensical. I could understand if you walked about looking like Eddie Izzard dressed as Kylie K but you wear very little make-up and dress smart and trendy for work. As do I and most other people here, with the exception of Olivia, obviously. She dresses like a right slag.'

Charlotte doesn't see the funny side of my last comment and simply says, 'We'll agree to disagree, I really need to get on with this now so I'll see you later.'

Over dinner that evening I give Will the gory details, 'I'm telling you, Will, she's like a different person. The old Charlotte was funny and dry and up for a laugh. This Charlotte has a stick up her arse and looks like she has a bad smell under her nose and I don't like her very much at all. She thinks she's better than me because she's dating a Lawyer with a fancy pad in Leeds.'

'Maybe she's just growing up now she's in a relationship. It happens, you know. She's finding out who she is and that might just be somebody a little different to who you thought she was. There's no point stressing over it or investing time in her if she isn't interested. Accept it and move on, you have lots of other friends.'

I know he means well but I don't accept that at twenty-six Charlotte has had a full personality bypass and morphed into a drab stuck-up cow. That kind of shit takes years to perfect and she seems to have changed overnight. I don't want to move on either. I love Charlotte (the old one) and I miss her. It seems ages since we had a laugh. I don't even know if the new not improved Charlotte knows how to laugh. We were supposed to be arranging a girly night out or weekend away and I'd still like to do that. I'll arrange a meeting with Nicky and Willow and see if they're still up for it then I'll see if

Charlotte is. I don't fancy my chances but I'd rather ask and her say no than not ask and hurt her feelings.

Perhaps thinking his last comment has upset me Will continues, 'You sounded a bit mental but I think I preferred the exuberant *Matilda*-loving Hannah of the weekend to the maudlin Hannah of Monday.'

'Well I'm still *Matilda* loving and beneath this maudlin exterior the exuberance is simmering. I just need to get to the bottom of this Charlotte shit and I'll be back with a vengeance.' That's the trouble with epiphanies; life always gets in the way of making the realisation a reality.

I meet with Willow and Nicky for the pub quiz and we agree a girly pampering weekend is just what the doctor ordered. We can go out and get pissed any time, what we need is quality relaxation and prosecco drinking time. Surely Charlotte can't say no to that? It will be a very sophisticated affair and she is, after all, very sophisticated these days. Or so she thinks anyway. We have a place in mind but it gets pretty booked up so it's unlikely we will be able to go until next month at the earliest unless we went midweek, and there's no way B would allow two or three of us to be off on the same day. That gives us plenty of time to convince Charlotte to join us. We can go ahead and book a two-bedroom apartment at the spa, tell her when we're going and hope that she's available. Will is going to flip when he finds out I'm spending more of our money but it will be worth it if it gets us back on track with Charlotte. As I haven't really spoken with her since our exchange at the start of the week I suggest Willow be the one to invite her.

'I'm not sure she's anymore enamoured with me than she is with you at the minute,' is her reply.

'What makes you say that?' I ask.

'Well I bumped into her in the kitchen this morning and noticed that despite her "make-up being a mask" sermon she seemed to be wearing rather a lot of foundation. She had her hair down as well and I'm sure she was trying to conceal the fact she had it on. I happened to say I thought she was done with wearing make-up and she scurried away like I'd just told her I had herpes.'

'I really don't know what is with her at the minute. Will thinks she's just "finding herself" but there's something else going on. I've had reservations about that now practically since day one and I keep going back to that every time something else happens.'

'I don't know Charlotte as well as you two but even I think it all sounds suspicious,' says Nicky. 'She hasn't really known this guy long and she seems to have changed completely. The Charlotte I know would have told you to get fucked if you suggested she wore too much make-up. In fact, she'd have put more on just to spite you.'

Nicky is right. That is exactly what the Charlotte of two months ago would have done.

'Hopefully a weekend away will show her what she's missing out on and the old Charlotte will make a come-back,' Willow says.

'I hope you're right cos in the paraphrased words of Rizzo, this one is a drag,' I say.

'Enough intervention chat ladies, I'm off to the bar and then let's crack on and try and win that twenty-five quid. We can put it in the spa kitty.'

With that Nicky swans off to the bar to purchase another bottle of wine while I ponder the headache I'm no doubt going to have in the morning.

CHAPTER 12

Charlotte didn't seem quite as enthusiastic as the rest of us about the spa date and told Willow she'd think about it and let us know. She needs to think fast as we managed to get a cancellation so will be going in a few weeks with or without her. Her response to my suggestion that we re-arrange our meeting with Julian was pretty much the same. Will is sick of hearing me rattle on about her and would be happy if I returned to bitching about work. That could easily be arranged as there's lots to bitch about.

Not content with humiliating me by giving what should have been my products away, B has decided that not only should I give my mountain of knowledge to Emma I should give it to Sam as well. I am not stupid, I realise that once I do this and they both finally grasp what the fuck they need to do, B will drop me like a hot potato. She has made it clear I'm not getting any new work and she is fully aware that my old work is done with.

I'll end up being made redundant having passed on everything I know to the two most incompetent people in the place. The only saving grace is the fact the pair of them couldn't grasp a fucking straw. I knew they weren't great but I didn't realise how useless they were until I had to work closely with them. It's like trying to train goldfish. They remember nothing. They don't write anything down and they have zero ideas of their own. I get why Sam is still here, B can push her around and she'll never stab her in the back. Emma, though, is a mystery. I realise that far from B getting one up on me, I'm getting one up on her as she's paying three people to do what I alone could do. B is all about the margins and her margins are suffering, big time. At their current rate of learning I expect B will be retired before she has the chance to get rid of me.

I've been keeping a record of what I go through with them each day and I estimate that I have had to repeat each section at least 16,320 times. By the time they get it, someone else will have brought out a better product. If that happens B will find herself in a heap of shit with the clients to whom Emma and Sam have to demonstrate their sales pitch in three weeks. There is more chance of me walking on water.

After spending another week of my life attempting to mould the retards into far less competent versions of me, I am not surprised when I receive a meeting invite from B titled 'Training catch-up'. No doubt she will take the opportunity to admit she was wrong and advise that I am the lead on both products. It's about time. She has sauntered past the three of us on enough occasions now to have heard how painful training the pair of them is. There is no time to waste. I could do the sales pitches tomorrow with my eyes closed but the quicker she hands them to me the more polished my performance will be.

'I may as well have trained them myself for all the use you've been,' B says as I stare dumbfounded. 'I'm appalled that you would try and sabotage them like this out of pure spite. We are a team Hannah, we do not throw our team mates under a bus. One fail all fail, you've heard my motto enough now.'

I am practically speechless, firstly I have never heard that fucking motto in my life (not from her anyway), she must be getting confused between that and 'moving forward', easy mistake to make. Secondly, what goddamn sabotage? I have spent the last few weeks of my life trying and failing to train a pair of incompetent chimps, which is a fucking insult to chimps everywhere. I have cajoled, I have bullet pointed, and I have drawn diagrams on the fucking whiteboard. How is it my fault if they are useless?

'I spoke with Emma and she was quite clear that your training style and lack of any direction is putting us and them in jeopardy. I expected more after all I have done for you.' She's loving this.

I feel my face redden, it takes a lot to piss me off but once I blow, I blow. 'Are you kidding me, B? You have seen me with them for hours on end, you must have heard me talking to them and telling them the same thing over and over again. They are totally inept. Precisely what training style would Emma like?'

'I would very much rather you didn't raise your voice or use that tone with me, Hannah. This is exactly what Emma was referring to. She said you get very defensive when she questions your way of doing something, such that she is wary of doing so and therefore feels that she isn't getting the best of your sessions at all.'

Defensive? How bloody dare she? She has yet to question a single thing I've said. She just sits and nods moronically. There is precious little dialogue at all, it's pretty much me talking to myself while they listen in.

'They haven't asked me a single thing. They let me talk, they don't write anything down and then they forget everything I've said,' I say.

'Yes, Emma said you would blame her for your inadequacies. So far everything she has said about you is right.'

I am furious and can feel the same tears of frustration stinging at my eyes. It's like being in a parallel universe. There is no point saying anything else as it's clear Emma has pretty much covered every angle in blaming me for her shortcomings.

'I am afraid I cannot allow this to continue.'

As B talks it dawns on me that I may not be in her company again as this might be the moment of my sacking. Oh god, I want to leave. I want to leave so bad but I want it to be on my terms. I want the pleasure of saying stick your job up your arse. Getting fired would be the most humiliating thing EVER.

'So this is your official warning. Either do as you have been instructed or there will be no job here for you. I have very high standards and expect a lot from my employees and you are falling far short. I will be speaking with Emma again next week and if nothing has changed you will be asked to leave. Do I make myself clear?'

'Yes, B.'

I hate myself. Yes B, no B, three bags fucking full B. I had the perfect opportunity right there to stick up for myself and say all the things that have been whirring around my mind for months and all I come up with is 'Yes B'. I am pathetic. Plus I now have to continue to train the muppets and do so in a most enthusiastic manner in order to prevent Emma running to B. I bet she's extremely proud of herself and what a clever girl she has been. She's planted the seed so that if the demonstration doesn't go well, I will get the blame and her incompetence will once again go unnoticed. Genius, when you think about it.

I have got to leave but I have nowhere to go. I have to give four weeks' notice so that gives me a bit of time. We're going on holiday at the end of next month and we have some savings so it might not be worth moving anywhere until after that.

Lightbulb moment.

I'll hand in my notice three weeks before our holiday. I am sure there is nothing in my contract that says I can't use holiday leave in my notice and even if there is what's she going to do, sack me?! I'll work at Aldi if I have to. Until I hand in my notice I'll remain professional and do as I am told. Six weeks isn't that long.

I'm so excited, I feel free. Like a weight has been lifted off my shoulders. I text Will 'I have made a decision. I am done with this shit. I am going to hand my notice in next month so I have two months to find a new job (it sounds better than six weeks). I'll start it straight after our holiday xx'. Then immediately after 'Is that ok???'

Unusually Will responds instantly. 'Good, it's about time you stopped talking about it and actually did it. My ears are tired of listening.' The cheeky bastard.

Having regaled Nicky with the turn of events she sets about trying to think of a plan to get me out of my current mess in order to make my last couple of months as pleasant as possible. I might be leaving but that doesn't mean I went to spend the next six weeks at the mercy of B. I'm sure she will be practically kissing my shoes for the last four weeks when she finds out I am leaving so I need to make the first couple at least bearable. We have already discounted a hitman (too expensive), staging a serious car crash (too high a chance of me being hospitalised), pushing one of them down the stairs (too risky if the CCTV cameras we believe are in situ are in fact, in situ). It dawns on me that all of Nicky's suggestions could also result in me being imprisoned and I'm starting to wonder whether I need to rethink our friendship.

'Well your input has been invaluable Nik but I really need to get back to work.'

'Anytime matey, just let me know if Plan A is a go as I know just the person.'

'As tempting as your offer is I think I'll run it by Willow and see if she can come up with something that isn't going to result in me being incarcerated or seriously injured, not to mention bankrupt!'

'Suit yourself, no skin off my nose.' Nicky hangs up.

I send a code red to Willow (code red being a text asking if she wants to go for lunch) and she responds in the affirmative. An hour later, clutching our lukewarm coffees we muse over my options. Unsurprisingly she isn't too keen on any of Nicky's ideas, though is rather tempted for the stairs as she thinks doing it myself will give rise to the greatest satisfaction.

'I've got it!' Willow exclaims.

'Hit me with it,' I reply.

'Video it!' This is not the response I was expecting,

'Video what exactly?' I ask almost afraid of the answer.

'Video the training sessions. Well, not all of them but at least one. If you have video evidence of what is happening in reality then Emma has nothing. If she was stupid enough to go to B again you could just produce your video evidence to show that she is lying. She is lying, right?'

'Of course she's fucking lying!' I say offended.

'Just checking. There you go then. Just video it, you could always make a reason up and say you want to practice the presentation on camera to help them make improvements.'

The more I think about it the more the idea grows on me. 'So, I don't do it secretly then?' It's wise to check as although I am liking the idea, I'm not entirely sure how to execute it.

'No you daft bint, if you do it secretly Emma won't know you've got one up on her, will she, and where would the fun in that be?!'

Willow's elaboration hasn't helped my confusion. 'One up, what do you mean?' I ask.

Willow's face says she wishes she hadn't said anything but her mouth says, 'She might act stupid but she's far from it. Alright, she sucks where work is concerned but in matters of all things devious she's a master. B will have told her about your little tête á tête so Emma will feel safe and smug in the knowledge that she's got one up on you. She will expect you to turn up at the next training sessions fawning all over her and not stepping one foot out of line. If out of the blue you announce you're going to be taping the sessions she is going to twig straight away why you're really doing it and victory will be yours. Imagine the luck on her daft face when the penny drops that she no longer has the upper hand or can hide behind the blame game. She'll be shown up for the useless tart she is and B is off your back. Winner, winner, chicken dinner.' Willow sighs in as if to say my work here is done. She remains silent while I ponder her splendid plan.

I put on my best Michael Caine and say, 'I like it a lot'.

***

The following morning I virtually skip into our next training session. Emma eyes me suspiciously and she's right to be wary as I wheel in the tripod with recorder already attached. I am not risking doing this on my phone and having the battery or memory fail. I have instead charged up the all-singing, all-dancing office video camera and checked it at least seventeen times to ensure it records and plays back.

'Hi ladies,' I say in my most enthusiastic manner.

'What's that for?'

It seems Emma is not quite as enthusiastic. Rude. It's a shame I wasn't recording her greeting.

'This?' I ask, nodding towards the camera like it might be something else she's confused about. 'This is a video camera,' I reply.

'I can see it's a camera, Hannah. What the hell have you got it for, though?'

Well now, Emma sweet pea, that wasn't actually what your question was, now was it? You specifically asked me what it was and I specifically answered you. There's no wonder you're especially shit at your job when you can't get a simple thing like asking the question you actually want the answer to right, is there? What an idiot. I am trying my bestest, hardest to remain sparky and jovial.

'I'm going to record our training. I thought it would be a really good idea so that you and Sam can watch yourselves and get a good feel for how you're coming across and then make changes where necessary.'

I feel so goddamn pleased with myself but don't let it show. My face remains neutral yet enthusiastic. The same cannot be said for Emma's. A look of disbelief starts to creep onto her face followed by the look of, well... the look of someone who has been caught with their knickers down. She gets it, she totally gets it, and Willow was right. I would not have missed this for the world. It was worth the bollocking just to see Emma's usual haughty look replaced by a look that simply says 'you bitch'. I'd call that one–all.

I arrive home still feeling euphoric. The rest of the training session wasn't bad once Emma got over her initial shock and accepted that I was the victor in this particular little battle. Sam was as nonplussed as ever about the whole thing. She just wanted to 'do whatever would make B happy'. She makes me want to puke.

My euphoria is short-lived when I set eyes on Will. He looks downright miserable. This is a turn-up for the books and I'm momentarily stunned. Will never looks miserable, that's my job. Will is always Mr fair to middling. Never knowingly thrilled and never, ever miserable. He doesn't see the point. In Will's opinion no problem, whether big or small, was ever solved with misery. He is right, of course, but sometimes misery is as good for the soul as ecstasy— the feeling, not the 80's party tab. My immediate thought is that someone has died.

He looks up as I walk in and attempts a smile. 'Everything ok?' I ask with trepidation.

'Not really, Han. It seems I'm in the redundancy pool,' he tells me with a look of dejection on his face.

Not a death then, so that's good. Redundancy I can deal with, death I haven't yet had to face so I'm relieved not to have to face it now. Oh shit though, if he's at risk of being jobless bang goes my chance of escape. I can't risk not having a job if Will doesn't have a job. I try to look and sound positive even though I feel like my numbers came out on the lottery and I haven't bought a ticket.

'Well what are the chances of you being made redundant?' I ask. 'Not high surely, you're a great employee. Punctual, knowledgeable, never off sick. Isn't that the kind of stuff they score you on?' I don't actually know what they score you on as I've ever been in a redundancy pool but I imagine it's not based on looks and dress sense.

'When the other person in the pool is Ted's (the boss) son I'd say the chances of me going are pretty high, wouldn't you?' Will has resorted to sarcasm, which is very unlike him. Now I'm worried. Will doesn't worry, I worry. If Will is worried then it must be worth worrying about. I'm searching the depths of my mind for the right thing to say.

'Well surely there's someone you can report that kind of nepotism to, make a claim or something,' is the best I come up with and the look on Will's face tells me it wasn't the right thing to say.

'Sure Han, I'll just go and call 0800 dob a job and see if they can take my case on. God you really are ridiculous when you want to be.'

'There's no need to act like a total knob. I'm only trying to help. Worse things happen at sea, and you're the one who says misery doesn't solve problems so practice what you preach,' I say.

'I'm not being miserable, I'm just digesting the information. I only found out a couple of hours ago and I'm trying to think through my options, which would be easier without you standing there grinning inanely at me like Little Mary Sunshine.'

'Well pardon me for breathing, you ungrateful pillock.' With that I stomp off upstairs to get ready for a night out. I probably should stay in and support my husband but as my presence is offending him he can piss off. I'm going out with the girls. Willow, Nicky and somewhat surprisingly, Charlotte. We're checking out a new cocktail place in town and will probably find somewhere for a little boogie. I'm not sure who was most surprised when Charlotte accepted the invite, me or her. It was as though her mouth said yes whilst her mind was screaming no. Willow thinks she'll be a no-show but I really hope she turns up and that when she does it's the real Charlotte, not Julian's modified version.

Dressed to impress in a little black dress and sparkly silver heels I head back downstairs. I'll probably die of pneumonia as soon as I step outside but at least I'll look good doing it.

'Are you going out?' Will asks.

'No, I just fancied getting poshed up to eat beans and toast on the sofa. Thought it would make a nice change.'

'Now who's being sarcastic?'

'Touché. Yes, I'm going out with the girls. I did tell you about it, remember? We had a whole conversation around my shock that Charlotte had said yes.'

'Oh right, yeah, we did. I just forgot it was today, that's all.'

'Well, don't worry, you won't starve. I bought you a steak and there's some chips in the freezer so knock yourself out. I even put some beers in the fridge before I went to work this morning. I know, I'm awesome.'

Will grins then moves over to give me a kiss. 'Sorry for being a pillock,' he says, planting a kiss on my lips.

'I forgive you, how do I look?'

'Gorgeous. Should I be worried?'

'Only if you keep acting like an arse,' I reply then head out the door telling him not to wait up and I'll text him later.

CHAPTER 13

We agreed to meet at the new bar and I'm the first to arrive so I order four Mojitos. May as well start the night as we mean to go on. The bar is pretty swish so I'm glad I frocked up. It's all dark wood with plush looking brown leather chairs and high backed bar stools. The bar itself looks like polished oak and there are crystal downlights hanging above it. It's very Manhattan. The music is coming from a piano in the corner and as pleasant as it is, I'm hoping the piano spins around later in the night and turns into a DJ booth. Piano music is fine for the first hour or so but once we've had a few cocktails we'll be ready to bounce our booties to some Beyoncé.

I'm halfway down my drink when Willow walks in with Charlotte. Well this is a turn up for the books indeed. Charlotte is dressed more demurely than is her norm but after the events of the last month this does not surprise me.

I greet them both but Charlotte's hug feels forced and uncomfortable. 'I bought us all a Mojito,' I say, trying to break the ice. 'I had to sign over one of my lungs to pay for them but it tastes amazing so it was worth the sacrifice.'

'I'm not drinking tonight,' Charlotte informs us. I should have known her joining us was too good to be true.

'Really?' I ask, trying not to sound too annoyed given the air feels thick enough.

'I'm trying to cut down, it doesn't agree with me and Julian doesn't like it when I drink too much.'

'Well, Julian isn't here and no one is asking you to drink too much, just to drink something. Anyhow these are cocktails so they're half fruit juice anyway. A couple isn't going to hurt you, is it?' Willow says, trying to sound convincing.

I'm sold and drink the rest of mine. Willow joins me and starts making her way down hers just as Nicky arrives. She picks up her glass, takes a large sip and says, 'Cheers.' She gives each of us a hug then turns to Charlotte, 'What's up with yours, you don't look like you've touched it?'

'Nothing, I'm just not drinking that's all,' Charlotte gives Nicky the bad news.

'Eh, you've accepted an invite for a night out to try the new cocktail bar and you're not going to try the new cocktail bar. That makes perfect sense.' Nicky is not quite as diplomatic as Willow.

'I'm just trying to cut down, that's all, because Julian doesn't like me drinking too much,' Charlotte says defensively.

'Well Julian isn't here and I'm not asking you to binge drink just try a bloody cocktail. I can tell you want to. You're a grown woman, you can do what you like, you know. Anyway, everyone knows there's hardly any alcohol in a cocktail, they're mostly fruit juice.' Nicky reiterates what Willow said three minutes earlier and Willow and I stifle giggles.

I can see that Charlotte is very tempted so to tip her over the edge I say, 'Why not just have that one and see how you feel, if you don't fancy anymore after it then just have mocktails but you can't go to the trouble of coming here and then not sample what they're all about.'

I know for a fact that if she has one she'll want another. Hesitantly she picks up the glass and takes a sip.

'See, didn't kill you did it,' adds Nicky.

In no time at all we're on our third round. As suspected Charlotte did not request a mocktail and is instead working her way down the menu in alphabetical order. She has finally relaxed and the Charlotte we know and love has arrived. I message Will to advise him of Charlotte's resurrection but he hasn't replied. Hardly surprising as not only is it 9pm but it's 9pm on a Friday so he'll be fast asleep on the sofa. He's probably got fed up with replying as I have sent him approximately thirty-six since I left the house. I suspect the more I drink the more he'll get. He'll be thrilled.

Unfortunately, the piano does not spin around and turn into a DJ booth. However, a DJ has appeared in another corner of the bar and the piano music has stopped. We are now listening to a heady mix of R n B and pop. It's not at all bad. I wonder if he takes requests. The night just won't be the same if we don't get to shake what our mamas gave us to *Crazy in Love*. Ok it's an old one but it's also a good one.

'I wonder if he takes requests?' Charlotte asks.

'Great minds, I was just thinking the exact same thing. We've got to get our song played,' I add. 'We don't want to look like sad acts bothering him though so let's wait a bit and see if anyone else does and then we'll pick straws for which one of us gets to go.'

'Well I am not going again,' it is Nicky's turn to speak, 'last time I asked a DJ to play a song I almost got barred so I'm not risking it, especially when this place has only just opened.'

'Nik, are you trying to do a bit of history re-writing there?' asks Willow. 'As I recall you didn't almost get barred for asking for a song. You almost got barred for calling the DJ a tone deaf twat who wouldn't know a decent tune if it bit him on the knob. I'm pretty sure you called him a few other choice words as well as trying to prise the microphone out of his hand.'

'Well he was tone deaf, what was that shit he was playing? He was playing for an audience of fourteen years olds when the room was full of twenty somethings. Who the fuck wants to listen to remixed Justin Bieber? Unmixed Bieber is bad enough.' Nicky is unrepentant. It was a hilarious night, in fact it might have been the same night that Charlotte convinced a very drunk, very amorous young man who took a shine to her to remove his trousers and wait for her in the men's toilets. Approximately three minutes later we saw him being frogmarched out by a couple of unamused-looking bouncers. I'm pretty sure *he* got barred.

'Another round ladies?' It's Charlotte's round. Her 'drinking doesn't agree with me' attitude of two hours ago has well and truly worn off. I wonder if she's relaxed enough to talk about Julian without getting her knickers in a knot. She heads off to the bar, menu in hand.

'Do you reckon we should ask her how it's going with the knob or should we just leave it as she seems to be enjoying herself?' I try to say in a whisper but it's more of a shout given the volume of the music.

'I reckon you should leave it, Han,' says Willow. 'She's having a good time and you don't want to spoil the mood. It was touch and go for a while when she first got here but it's like being with the old Charlotte so I don't want to risk pissing her off and having the new Charlotte return.'

'I agree,' says Nicky. 'In fact, she seems to be having a bit of extra fun over there without us.' I turn towards the bar and see Charlotte giggling at whatever a rather attractive man is saying to her. Despite her very conservative frock and barely there make-up she is still head and shoulders above most of the woman in here looks wise, including us, which makes her current choice of fella even more perplexing.

'You've still got it I see!'

Charlotte is back sporting drinks and a massive grin.

'What you on about?' she replies to Nicky's observation.

'You know damn well I'm talking about that hunk of spunk at the bar, so spill.' Nicky persists.

'There's nothing to spill, he was just asking what I thought of the place, that's all.'

'Oh yeah, pull the other one. He had right goo-goo eyes for you.' Nicky does not give up easily.

'Did he balls. You've had too much to drink. Anyway even if he did I'm taken so he can goo-goo off,' Charlotte replies.

'No need to be so touchy, I was simply making an observation and there's no harm in looking now is there!' Nicky responds.

'Hey, someone is talking to the DJ and it doesn't look like a member of staff.' I am desperately trying to lighten the mood which has grown a little heavy following Nicky's 'observation'. Two songs later the DJ starts playing *Despacito* and the girl who was previously talking to him starts bouncing about like Zebedee. 'I guess he does take requests then,' I note out loud.

'Not more fucking Bieber,' is Nicky's response.

Charlotte bursts out laughing mid suck (on her straw) sending cocktail flying everywhere and the mood lifts. Thank fuck for that. I'm not sure how much egg-shell-walking I can do.

The night ambles on very nicely indeed, arses are shook, drinks are downed and we all throw ourselves heartily into letting our hair down. The mood turns tense on a couple of occasions (generally Charlotte induced) which are thankfully short-lived mainly due to the fact that the more we drink the less we (Charlotte) give a shit. I had almost forgotten how much fun Charlotte was having barely seen her for the past few weeks. I really hope fun Charlotte is back for good. We end the night in the usual manner— telling each other how much they are loved and I spend the whole taxi ride home texting Charlotte telling her how much I've missed her and how happy I am to have her back. She replies with the same sentiment.

I don't actually remember sending any of the texts, I just read them when I woke up this morning. I barely remember getting home. I do remember Will pretending to be asleep while attempting to keep the annoyance out of his pretend deep sleep breathing but failing miserably. Usually he is fast on when I come in and I am pretty sure I was quiet as a mouse so I suspect he fell asleep at 9pm then woke at 11pm and watched medieval porn (aka *Game of Thrones*) all night. I did text him just before 2am to say I was on my way home. He didn't reply and I presume he raced to bed in the hope he would be asleep before I came home so that I wouldn't 'talk inane bollocks', which is what he accuses me of when I've had a few.

***

Monday morning swings around and I'm looking quite forward to getting into work and seeing the girls. I haven't heard from Charlotte since our post-night out messages but she's probably just been busy. We managed to get her to commit to coming to the spa, so we now have that to look forward to in a couple of weeks too. Thankfully it's mostly paid for so Will's not so great news won't mean I have to cancel. He wasn't his usual happy self about going to work this morning and me saying he should be grateful he has a job to get up to go to didn't really help matters. He was less than impressed with my attempts at cheering him up all weekend. I even bought him (myself) new underwear with matching everything rather than climbing into bed on Saturday night with grey baggy knickers and a black bra that's three sizes too big after being washed at least 14,000 times. It didn't raise much of a smile, it raised something else which was all over in a few minutes. It took me longer to get the damn stockings fastened. I guess all this redundancy stuff really is playing on his mind. Not that it ordinarily takes much longer than a few minutes but he usually shows some enthusiasm, especially for new knickers.

No sign of either Willow or Charlotte in the office. I am a bit early, as is B. She actually looks up at me. This is perturbing as she never acknowledges me when I walk in, she much rather favours

144

ignorance where I'm concerned. Not only does she look up she stops what she's doing and calls my name. Gulp.

'Morning,' I say in response hoping I sound cheery and engaging but knowing I sound more like a strangled goat.

'The presentation has been brought forward, there is a similar product being launched by a rival company next month so the Bensons need us to be one step ahead.'

Oh well, that shouldn't be too much of a problem, it's getting much better so I'm confident that by next week we should be ready to go.

'Not a problem. When is it?' I ask.

'This afternoon,' she replies.

This afternoon?! She has got to be freaking kidding me? Emma and Sam are almost there but they're not actually there. Emma could probably style it out but Sam gets way too flustered and the thought of a rival product being launched will give her palpitations for a week.

'Does it have to be today?' I think I say in my head but it turns out to be out loud.

'No, we can make it three weeks on Tuesday if that suits you better,' B says, her voice dripping with sarcasm. 'Of course it has to be today.'

'But I don't think they're ready,' I mumble.

'Well you better get them ready, hadn't you. You've had ample time and if you spent less time bitching and more time training they'd be up to speed already. I dread to think what state the whole thing would be in had I not intervened. I want a run through in one hour.'

I get the impression this is B's final word, nonetheless I try and make a final plea 'But...'

'No buts, one hour,' are definitely her final words.

Almost half an hour after this conversation Sam and Emma turn up. I summon both of them and tell them the news. 'Yeah we know,' Emma says, 'B told me on Friday.'

Why I am not surprised. It's just me she wants to drop in the shit.

'We've been working on it this weekend,' Sam pipes up.

Well bully for fucking you, don't need me then, do you?

'Great, well we need to do a run-through for B in an hour so you should be more than ready, see you in the Board room at ten.' I'm not even sure why I 'm still involved. I'm not doing the presentation and I won't be running the sales campaign so B could just leave me the freak out of it now. It's not as though I am going to get any credit if they happen to pull it off. If they're shit I'll get the blame for not training them properly, it's a lose–lose situation. I may as well pack up and go home now.

Just as I'm thinking this I see Charlotte walking in. She's late, which is very unlike her. I stroll over and as I get closer I notice that she isn't smiling and is once again wearing at least twelve layers of foundation. I know instantly that the old Charlotte has gone again. I try to hide the disappointment from my face as I bid her good morning. She doesn't look up, she says morning back to me but keeps walking to her desk. I feel sick.

The run-through is a train wreck. Emma comes across as pretentious as she is and Sam is like a deer caught in headlights. It's disingenuous meets twee and it's awful. I cringe all the way through, scared to catch B's eye. She cannot blame me for this. They have all the material, they just have no idea how to deliver it. I'm surprised at

Emma, not at her being pretentious but at her being dreadful. I thought this would be right up her alley, but it's clearly not. I can tell by the look on her face that she knows it too. Mercifully it is over, B is silent for a few minutes, then, 'bravo, the hard work has paid off. We'll have quick de-brief then you can prepare for the main event. Hannah you can leave now.'

What the …?! I cannot believe she is being serious. The hard work has paid off?? Only if the hard work was training on how to come across like the world's biggest snob or the world's most startled person. B can't have been watching what I was. Why on earth would she want to put that before a client? It will be a big nail in her coffin. Wait a minute, why am I bothered? She treats me like shit so I hope it's fifty nails in her coffin. They can chuck Emma in it too, not Sam, she's nice but dim but doesn't have a nasty bone in her body so she can remain coffinless. The others can rot.

I have filled Willow in on the situation (both B and Charlotte) and she is equally mystified. She is also super busy so can't join me for a bitching session over lunch. I'm beyond bored. Now that my work with tweedle dee and tweedle dum is finished I have nothing at all to do. It has felt like the longest day in the world. I was going to get lunch at twelve then realised I would have more of the day left than I had already endured so managed to drag it out until one while sneakily reading the Daily Mail. I've been out and bought the biggest sarnie I could fine, it's dripping with mayo and is so fat I'm struggling to hold it with two hands. So far I have managed not to spill any down my front but there is a large puddle developing on my desk. I am mid chew when I spot B from the corner of my eye. At first I think she's coming over to my desk, I look at the clock 1.36pm the big presentation is at two. She's probably going to get the tweedles for a final run-through. Oh shit no, right in the first place, she's at my desk.

'Hi B,' I stutter trying not to spit chicken mayo at her.

'You seem to have something…just…,' B points to her chin. I instinctively reach up and rub mine and a big blob of mayo smears across my hand.

'Oops, sorry about that.' I don't know what else to say. I wasn't expecting company, certainly not hers.

'I'll see you in the conference room in ten minutes for a final run-through.'

'A final run-through of what?' I'm intrigued. Perhaps she has lost it and forgotten I'm not the 'it' for this one.

'Of the presentation, what else you silly girl?' she replies exasperated.

'But I'm not doing the presentation B, tweed…I mean Emma and Sam are.'

'Not anymore. I'll see you in ten.'

I am left dumbfounded. Three hours ago the hard work had paid off. Now I'm 'it'. I have to hand it to her, she is a fabulous liar. I would never have guessed this morning that she didn't mean every word she said. She didn't though. She had no intention of letting those two do the actual presentation. She has just made me squirm to get it. She has a win–win situation. If I succeed, we get the green light and she can bask in the glory of not only that but the hoops she made me jump through to get it. If we fail it's all my fault and she can get rid of me in humiliating fashion. Clever, very clever.

I underestimated her and actually believed she was going to let those two clowns loose on clients. I can see her giving them the bad news. Emma looks over and scowls at me. I give her a big grin and wave.

Unsurprisingly my presentation is perfect, the clients love it and B is like a bitch on heat, as opposed to just being like a bitch as she is most days. She hasn't said thank you, though. Oh no, that would be a step too far and we don't want me getting ideas of grandeur, now do we. Emma has done nothing but scowl at me all afternoon. Sam was gracious enough, came and thanked me for the training and wished me good luck. I think she was relieved at not having to do it. Maybe she was bad on purpose, who knows. All I know is I have proved my worth yet again and although B thinks she is one up, we both know it's me. I suppose my job is safe for a little while longer then. Yippee.

I tried to talk to Charlotte again this afternoon but she wouldn't engage me at all. She mumbled a few one word answers without looking up. The only time she looked animated was when I pointed out she looked like she had a black mark on her face. She told me it was probably printing ink from reading the paper then kept her hand on her cheek. This blowing hot and cold is becoming hard to bear. Treating me with absolute disdain without any good reason is going to end our friendship if it continues. I can't keep putting 100 per cent effort in and getting zero back. To think I was actively encouraging her to find a fella and now she has I wish she'd never met him. She can support him all she wants, I know it's him controlling her. She would never treat her friends like this if she wasn't with him and as I have yet to meet him I fail to see how I can come to any other conclusion than that he is bad news.

CHAPTER 14

It's the weekend of our spa trip and it could not come soon enough. B has barely said a word to me in the two weeks since my amazing pitch. She has drip-fed me a bit of work here and there, none of it for the new clients and the days have dragged on interminably. Will managed to make it through the first round of redundancies mostly unscathed and still has a job for now so I feel less guilty about going away. It was pretty hairy for a while and there was even talk of cancelling our trip to the sun which would have been a stupid thing to do given it is now paid for and we would lose all the money as we have yet to buy holiday insurance. I need to add that to my list of things to do. I should be resigning on Monday but that is on the back burner until we know that Will's job is safe.

Unsurprisingly, Charlotte isn't joining us for our weekend of rest and relaxation. She claims she can't afford it yet comes to work in a new outfit every day and they're no longer from Primani. They look expensive and old fashioned. She dresses like a sixty-year-old woman who believes that looking professional requires a box suit and comfy loafers. She's Miss Trunchbowl without the moles. Despite Charlotte's clear reluctance to join us I cannot wait to get my relaxing on.

The spa is AMAZING. The apartment is huge with views across the countryside. It has wooden floors and a massive multi-coloured rug in the middle of the room. The kitchen is all white and very sleek (and won't be getting used) with a ginormous Smeg fridge. I open it and see that it doubles as a not-so mini-bar. It contains full bottles of champagne, white wine and beer. They're not those miniature things or half bottles they give you in the fancy London hotels. The ones they charge you the same price as a full one for knowing that you'll be sorely tempted when you return from a night out eager to keep the party going.

The bathroom has the biggest bath I have ever seen, it could probably fit us all in. There's a double sink and a bidet. I've never used one, they scare me. I have visions of it either shooting up the wrong hole giving me the shock of my life or firing clinkers all over the bathroom. I'll give it a miss. The bedrooms both have queen-sized beds and the mattresses are sooo comfy. I've been laid down for a good five minutes now and don't want to move. Nicky is laid at the side of me and Willow is in the other bedroom most likely doing exactly the same. It's the kind of place you wish you were staying longer.

Our first treatments are booked for 2pm so we have almost three hours to sample all the facilities. I've no real desire to go in the pool but there's a gym and several saunas and steam rooms so I'm keen to give them a whirl. I suspect the girls will give the gym a miss and opt for swimming. We unpack our leisure wear of choice plus robes. There's no better place to be than somewhere you can wear a dressing gown all day and not be judged. As I thought, Nicky and Willow are going to the pool so I've said I will meet them in the steam rooms in an hour.

'You know we came here to relax don't you?' Nicky isn't impressed at me coming fully gym equipped.

'Going to the gym is relaxing for me, makes me stress less about my middle aged spread and wobbly thighs. You should try it,' I retort.

'You should knob off, I like my wobbly thighs and middle-aged spread thanks very much. Anyway swimming is the best form of exercise so I'll be a lean machine in an hour.'

'Good point, well made Nik,' Willow chimes in.

'Who asked you? That can't be true anyway. Whales are fat and they swim about all day,' I reply.

'They're fat to keep them warm,' Willow says.

'So what's your excuse then?' I ask, nudging her arm.

'Now now ladies, it's a bit early for the banter. We haven't even had a drink yet.' Nicky has been desperate to crack open the champagne since we arrived. Ordinarily I would be all for that course of action but didn't think it wise to drink then go sampling the facilities. We can do without injuries.

Once the exercise is done we make our way for our massages. Willow has gone for a hot stone job and Nicky and I have gone for the fully body massage incorporating an 'invigorating salt scrub'. God knows I could do with some invigorating. They couldn't accommodate all three of us at the same time, in the same room as I requested so Willow is on her own. Serves her right for choosing a hippy treatment. Although I expect she will get more relaxing done than I at the side of motor mouth.

We strip down and put on the paper knickers, those one size fits no one monstrosities where if you haven't recently been waxed everyone can see whether your collar matches your cuffs. Not a single living person could pull them off and look sexy, though Nicky is trying – shimmying around the room giving her best alluring eyes.

I stifle the laughter as two masseurs walk in. They don't look like they're going to be much fun. They have super-serious expressions and I'm not convinced that either can speak English. Perhaps that's why their expressions are so serious, they're trying to work out what to say. They gesture to us both to turn over onto our front and we do as instructed. Ooh now they might look serious but they have gentle hands, at least mine does. As she glides them up and down my back changing the pressure I start to drift off. I have no idea why we tried to book ourselves into the same room as I'm on my way to the land of nod and Nicky is already there, gently snoring away.

I feel my whole body relax and then I start thinking, this has always been my problem. Relaxed body always equals a fervent mind. Charlotte pops into my head and I'm thinking about the change in her and trying to make sense of it. I know that it's because of him, I just don't know why. I'm intent on discovering what it is. I see her as she was when I spoke to her last week, caked in make-up and reluctant to look me in the eye.

Oh my god! I bolt upright. 'Nik, Nik!' I shout.

She jolts awake. 'What? Where's the fire?'

'He's abusing her,' I say firmly, my mind totally clear. Clarity has hit me like a tonne of bricks.

'Who is doing what to whom?' She asks, still half asleep.

'Julian. The bastard is hitting her. I knew there was something. God how stupid am I! She's supposed to be one of my best friends and I've been so wrapped up in how her relationship was affecting me I didn't see it. I see it now. We've got to do something to help her.'

My heart feels like it is going to beat out of my chest and I am on the verge of tears. Nicky recognises the signs and sends the masseurs away. I'm not sure they understand what's going on but they back out of the room.

'What makes you think he's hitting her and what has changed since you last saw her to make you suddenly think he's a wife beater?'

It's a fair question to ask and simply makes me feel even guiltier for not realising sooner. 'It all makes sense,' I say, 'the sudden change in personality, her reluctance to do anything remotely fun, the fact she is so inaccessible, the clothes she wears and the fact that two minutes after denouncing make-up she twice turns up to work covered in it. She's covering the bruises and she's frightened to death of him. We should have seen the signs sooner. I need to speak to Willow.' I grab at my robe and throw it on then run along the hallway shouting Willow's name.

I feel sick to my stomach. We need to get Charlotte away from that monster. We need to head home now and drag her away from him.

I'm going to kill him. I am going to hit him so hard he won't know what day it is. Give him a taste of his own medicine. Poor Charlotte, poor innocent sweet Charlotte. She could have any man she wants and she's chosen that absolute sack of shit. I wonder what he's doing to her right at this moment, terrorising her probably. Frightening her half to death.

'What's all the bloody racket, I was trying to relax?' Willow emerges from one of the side rooms looking sleepy. I feel like I'm speaking in tongues as I reel off what I've just said to Nicky. I stop to take a deep breath.

'I think we will have the drink after all,' Willow says as she takes my arm and starts guiding me back to our room.

Willow pops the champagne, which seems wholly inappropriate in the circumstances but I need a drink so I down it. 'Right,' she says. 'Do you want to tell me how the hell you've gone from a relaxing massage to deciding Charlotte is a victim of domestic violence. Slower this time so that I can actually understand.'

I start to talk but it's like an out of body experience. I go back to the very beginning of when Charlotte met him and the things he said (or she said he'd said) and the changes in her and end with two weeks ago in the office. It's only when I speak of this again that I remember thinking Charlotte had something on her face. It was a bruise, a goddamn bruise. Why didn't I realise at the time?

'We've got to go home and rescue her, we can't stay here and leave her to his mercy,' I say resolutely.

'Whilst I admire your passion I don't think we should be storming anywhere accusing anyone of anything when we have no proof,' Nicky says.

'You mean you don't believe me?' I ask, affronted.

'It's not that I don't believe you, in fact, the more I think about it the more sense it actually makes. I just don't think it's wise to go storming around there like the cavalry she hasn't requested. If he is doing those things to her and she is frightened of him she isn't going to be in a hurry to piss him off by running into the night with us, is she? I think the sensible thing to do is talk to her and see if there is any truth in it. Then we can try and help her.'

I can't believe what I'm hearing. She wants to just leave Charlotte in that bastard's hands. I feel so responsible and wonder how long it's been going on. I think back to when she first met him and he started to dress her, was that when he started abusing her as well or was that just the start of him trying to gain her trust? Charlotte isn't stupid, she wouldn't stay with a man who beat her; she's smart and streetwise and she would have seen this coming and run a mile, so why then am I so convinced that she's being mistreated? How did he turn a sassy smart arse into a submissive robot? Compliments alone wouldn't have done it, she's nobody's fool. She WAS nobody's fool.

I don't know what she is now but I do know that we need to help her. She isn't going to escape from him by herself, if she was, she would have done it long before now. The trouble is how do we get her alone to talk to us? She's reverted back to snubbing us, she barely looks us in the eye so I can't imagine she is going to accept an invitation to dinner particularly when the last time she came out with us it concluded with her being used as a punching bag.

I have so many questions and scenarios running around my mind. Were the signs all there and we missed them? Could we, SHOULD we have done something sooner before she fell so far into his clutches. I've never known anyone in this situation before so I have no idea how to go about it. I feel like I want to run from here straight to her house but the more thought I give it the more I understand where Nicky is coming from. If we turn up on the door making accusations it's unlikely to end well for Charlotte. We need to be smarter than that and bide our time. We can't wait too long though, as there's no knowing how far he'll go.

The rest of the weekend falls flat. Lounging about being pampered feels wrong while Charlotte is stuck at home, god knows what happening to her. I have sent her a couple of texts but she's sent the usual short and not particularly sweet replies, at least I know why now; he is watching her every move, controlling her every action. He is carefully and cleverly distancing her from all those who know and love her the most so that he's the only one she has. At least he thinks that's what he's done. He thinks wrong. We won't abandon her, we won't allow that bastard to win.

With the weekend ruined we leave the spa early. We talk of nothing else all the way home and the more we talk about it the more we all reach the same conclusion. We've discussed what might have happened that day at the pub had I gone storming over and confronted Charlotte. There is little wonder she looked so miserable, she didn't want to be there but had no choice. It seems as though bits of her soul have been torn out so that what remains of her is a shell that he can control. It's going to stop. We're going to make it stop. We don't know how yet but we have to do something.

We've decided I should speak with Charlotte's mum. I know her pretty well. She and Charlotte have always had a really close relationship so if anyone knows what the hell is happening it's her. I am a little worried that if she doesn't know I run the risk of worrying her to death but it's a risk I have to take to try and help Charlotte. I have no proof that Charlotte's being abused but every fibre of my being tells me I'm right, and for once in my life I hope I'm not.

Will is surprised to see me walk in several hours earlier than planned. He knew something was wrong as soon as I stepped in the door looking red eyed and dishevelled (probably as a result of staying up until 3am drinking champagne and crying) rather than polished and sleepy from a weekend of relaxation. He made a wisecrack about getting a refund and I burst into tears.

He is supportive of my plan to go and see Charlotte's mum although he tries to persuade me to wait a few days until I have had more time to think about it. I tell him I've thought about nothing else all weekend and have no desire to sit around thinking about it any longer. I'm going this afternoon and that is that.

***

I arrive at Charlotte's parents' home with a knot in my stomach. It's a large detached house on the edge of a cul de sac with a manicured garden and gleaming white window frames. The house should be inviting but seems more foreboding at this particular moment and I walk up the driveway with trepidation.

I haven't decided how I am going to word what I have to say. Do I just blurt it out on the doorstep or do I make small talk over a cuppa and then ask if she's noticed anything different about Charlotte lately?

I ring the doorbell, my heart pounding so loudly it's like having a drum in my ears. Charlotte's mum answers almost immediately and I am taken aback at the sight of her. Ordinarily she always has a smile on her face and her skin is glowing. She's an Oil of Olay gal according to Charlotte and a pretty good advert for them. At least she was. Today she stands before me with dull, grey skin and eyes that no longer shine with happiness. If eyes are the window to your soul then these eyes are very troubled.

'Hello lovely, to what do I owe this pleasure? Charlotte's not here, if that's who you've come to see.'

'I'm not here to see Charlotte, I'm here to see you, Jean. Do you mind if I come in?'

Without saying a word Jean steps aside and lets me in the house. She leads me into the living room and gestures for me to sit down on the brown leather sofa. I do as instructed. The house is immaculate and I say so then feel shallow for engaging in such trivial small talk with a woman who looks like she has the weight of the world on her shoulders. She thanks me and goes off to make tea.

There are photos of Charlotte and her brother everywhere. I don't recognise this Charlotte now. She is happy and care free, beaming at the camera in every shot and pulling daft faces. Tears prick at my eyes. I wipe them swiftly away as Jean walks back in with a tray containing the tea things and a plate of biscuits. We sit in silence for a few minutes until she pours the tea. She offers me a biscuit but I don't take one. My mouth is so dry I wouldn't be able to swallow it and in any event sitting munching on hobnobs doesn't seem very appropriate. We sip our tea and talk about work, her house, her son, the weather and any other topic that springs to mind as we skirt around why I'm here. I keep trying to say what I want to say but the words won't form. They get stuck in my throat. I excuse myself and go to the bathroom.

As I make my way down the hallway I pass more photos of happy Charlotte, spirited Charlotte, the Charlotte who took no shit and sent a bloke packing in his pants when he got too amorous. That does it. I turn around and march back into the living room.

'I think Julian is abusing Charlotte,' the words tumble out surprising me as much as they surprise Jean.

Time appears to stand still for a second before silent tears start falling down Jean's face. The tears turn into sobs and I realise they are not just tears of sorrow, they are tears of relief. Relief that someone else suspects what she does, she is not going mad, and she is not imagining things because here I am saying exactly what she thinks.

I sit down beside her and take her hand in mine. It feels cold and fragile and I swallow down tears of my own. She doesn't say a word as I recount as gently as possible every incident, conversation, message that has led me to this conclusion.

'I thought I was going mad,' she says. 'It was little things at first like the change in clothes and not wearing make-up but she seemed happy so I put it down to a phase. She's had a lot of those in her life and they usually pass by swiftly. It was when she stopped calling as much or making excuses as to why we couldn't meet him that I started to worry. No one works as much as she claims to do. I knew I was right when we saw her a few days ago having not clapped eyes on her for weeks. I didn't want to be right, I so wanted to be an over-protective mother who just couldn't accept that her little girl didn't need her anymore but that's not it. I know it's not. The light had gone from her eyes. She looked like a watered down version of herself.

'I asked her what was wrong, pleaded with her to tell me if there was anything bothering her and she said she was just tired and not to fuss. I've always been able to tell when she's lying though and I knew that wasn't it at all. I asked about him and whether he was looking after her but that made her angry and she questioned why I would ask that and wanted to know what I was trying to get at. She didn't stay much more than five minutes and when she left I felt like I was saying goodbye to a ghost. I don't know where we've gone wrong. She grew up in a loving family, her dad has never raised his voice let alone a finger to me. She's never been a shrinking wallflower either she could make her brother cry with one look when she was younger. How could we let this happen? Why didn't we see the signs sooner and help her?'

She starts sobbing again and my heart breaks a little bit more. I'm questioning what I thought I could gain by coming here. Was I looking for someone to tell me I was wrong and everything was absolutely fine? Or was I looking for validation and someone to tell me I had been right all along? Whatever I was thinking then I sure as hell don't know what I'm thinking now. I feel foolish and ashamed, sat in front of this shattered women without any answers. I certainly don't feel any better for having my suspicions confirmed. If anything, I feel worse like someone has put a knife in my heart and twisted it. What wouldn't I give now for Willow to have been right when she said Charlotte was in love and didn't want to spend as much time with us anymore. I couldn't accept that though and so here we are and I don't have the answers.

'What can we do?' Jean asks in a barely audible whisper.

'I don't know,' I say. It's the only answer I have.

CHAPTER 15

I spend the next few days in a daze. Work doesn't help to keep my mind occupied at all, with little or no work to do I have far too much thinking time. I should be excited with our holiday only a few weeks away but I'm anything but. I keep my head down and I come home again, all the while trying to come up with a plan to 'save' Charlotte. She, in turn seems to spend her days trying to avoid me. She barely moves from her desk and I feel like her stalker. I sit staring at the back of her computer screen all day trying to catch her eye.

Neither Willow nor Nicky have thought of anything and Jean has been in contact every day since our meeting so I am under constant pressure. In all fairness, Jean simply asks whether Charlotte has been at work. She doesn't enquire as to her health or wellbeing and I suspect she feels that if Charlotte's at work she must be alright and she can't bear to think of anything beyond that. Charlotte isn't responding to her texts and hasn't called her. I don't know how she is keeping it as together as she is. I feel like I am responsible for her and I want to fix everything and make her feel better but I just don't know how. The holiday Will and I booked is in a couple of weeks but at this point I don't want to go. I'm scared to leave in case something happens.

My phone rings and I'm jolted from my thoughts. It's Willow.

'I've been thinking, we just need to ask her outright,' she says. 'Skirting around the issue isn't going to get us anywhere and she isn't going to volunteer the information, so short of stalking her and spying through her curtains in the hope of catching him in the act I don't see that we have any other choice.'

I ponder her suggestion. I have considered merely asking the question however I don't know where we would ask it. It is not the kind of thing I can blurt out while she is at her desk and she isn't going to accept the offer of a night out from me anytime soon. The only option would be to see if she wanted to go out for lunch but the chances of her saying yes to that are pretty slim.

'Ok, well we can't do it in the office and she isn't going to come on a night out so shall we just try and arrange a lunch? Do you think both of us should be there for support or do you think she'll feel like she's being ambushed and act all defensive?' I hope Willow will agree to safety in numbers as I feel like I'll need the moral support.

'We'll both go,' Willow says. 'You know what you're like. You'll get wound up and starting making accusations and she'll just leave.'

She's right, that is exactly what would happen and I am relieved to have her company no matter what the reason.

'I'll leave you to ask her though, she seems to respond better to you,' I say.

'Perhaps she realised early doors that you had suspicions and has just been keeping you at arm's length. We don't know what she's been going through or what that piece of shit has been filling her head with so don't feel too bad that you're not top of her Christmas card list anymore.'

'I don't. I'm ashamed of the way I was acting and the things I said about her when they first got together. Now I know why she was doing those things I just want to give her a massive hug and tell her I'm sorry,' I say and tears well in my eyes as I realise how much I miss her friendship.

'Well hang on in there and if lunch goes well that chance might come sooner than you think. I'll try to call her and arrange something but I won't hold my breath for her answering, she's not exactly sociable these days.'

To my surprise and relief, Willow messages later that evening to say that Charlotte is up for lunch later in the week so I call Jean to let her know. She is very emotional and thanks me for 'everything' and once again I'm left with a feeling of insignificance and shame. I'm not doing anything. I should have been doing something weeks, months ago even and I didn't and now she and Charlotte are paying the price. Some friend I am. I am overwhelmed with a sense of sadness and need to talk to Nicky, she knows me better than anyone and will understand how I'm feeling. I call her but she isn't being as empathetic as I'd hoped. Instead she tells me to get over myself and stop wallowing.

'You're not going to be any use to Charlotte if you stick with this woe is me attitude, so suck it up, buttercup. You need to put your game face and your hard heart on. You've got to understand that Charlotte might not want to hear what you've got to say and you need to prepare yourself for the rejection. If you go in there thinking you're going to be her knight in shining armour and that after a few wise words from you the spell will be broken and you'll be hugging it out by the end of your lunch break you might be very disappointed.'

Her words hit me like a thunderbolt. I hadn't considered for a second that Charlotte might not listen. I was worried that she might be upset with me for not speaking up for her sooner, not that she might be upset with me speaking up at all—that she'd be so under his control that she wouldn't want to get away, even with an offer of help. What if I can't save her? What if her mum and dad and brother and everyone else is relying on me and I fail them? What if we can't ever save her?

I'd been pacing the kitchen while we talked but now I reach back and grab a stool. I need to sit down.

'Han, Han are you listening?' she asks. For a moment I forget she's hanging on the other end of the phone. 'Han, are you ok? Sorry if you weren't expecting that but you need to be realistic and know what you might be letting yourself in for. I've been there before, remember?'

I do remember. I take a deep breath. 'Well no, I hadn't thought of that but now you've made me feel even worse about talking to her. What am I going to do if she won't listen? How do we help her then?' I plead.

'You can't. You just have to be there to pick up the pieces and be present enough that he knows you're not just going to leave her at his mercy. That's what he wants. He wants everyone to abandon her so he's free to be the master to her puppet. Your preventing him having the control that he wants. Even if she doesn't answer your calls or texts you're at work with her every day so he'll be worried that you still have some influence over her. That's what you've got to cling onto if she doesn't listen. At least you can keep an eye on her between nine and five.'

Nicky's right. He might be able to control who and what she sees on an evening or on a weekend but he cannot do that quite as easily during the week. There are at least eight hours a day between Monday and Friday where the only person with control is B, so for once I am going to focus on that being a positive.

'Thanks, Nik. I'll let you know how we get on at lunch. Keep everything crossed.'

'I will, good luck. Love ya.'

***

I lie awake for hours going over what I'm going to say and how I'm going to say it. When the alarm goes off I don't want to get out of bed. I've come to terms with the fact that Charlotte may not want to be helped or feel she needs any help, what I haven't come to terms with is how I will relay that information to Jean.

I don't believe she will be as accepting of the fact that Julian's control is such that Charlotte would rather live every day facing his fists than dare to defy and leave him. Nicky mentioned the Stockholm syndrome. It's a phrase used for victims of kidnappings who grow to trust and feel affection for their captors. I don't know how Charlotte feels towards Julian but I suspect there is a sense of loyalty and affection towards the Julian who doesn't knock her around; the Julian who says sorry after every incident; the Julian who is a good-looking lawyer with a fancy flat. Is that why she stays, or is it just because she's frightened to death to leave him?

Sat at my desk the hours have ticked by in a sloth-like manner, I have looked at the clock at least 6,000 times and each time I do hardly a minute has passed. I have butterflies in my stomach and I ask Willow if she feels the same. I am comforted when she replies that she does. To try and keep my mind busy I practically begged B for work, an action I now regret as I haven't been able to concentrate on it for days and it is building at a rate of knots. If Charlotte doesn't react well I don't imagine me ever getting through it.

I look at the clock again, it's one minute since I last looked and still over an hour until lunch. I haven't spoken to Charlotte today. She didn't acknowledge me when she walked in, she did her usual scuttle to her desk with her head down and I wonder what the hair hanging around her shoulders is hiding. She usually wears her hair up, as I recall that's the way Julian liked it, so wearing it down is out of the ordinary.

I realise that I am way ahead of myself and that despite what Jean said I still have no actual proof that he is doing anything but every little thing out of the norm feeds my suspicion and today it is amplified beyond all that is rational. Does she have a bruise, a split lip, finger marks around her neck? Is there nothing there and he has just changed tack to mess with her mind even more? To confuse her maybe? Or give him another excuse to hit her for not listening to him?

A hundred questions race through my mind. None of them make me feel better and none of them seem to make time move any faster. I have spoken to Jean this morning. She sent a text to ask if she could call. I always find that weird, back in the pre mobile phone days you would just get a call, no one would ask if it was ok first yet now the etiquette seems to be a text message with a pre call warning. I kept it brief, though now think I should perhaps have conveyed some of the doubts I have about how this might end. It may have dampened her optimism but it may also have prepared her for the worst even if she was hoping for the best.

After what seems like an eternity the clock strikes midday. I gather my bag and my jacket while the butterflies flutter madly. I wish I was having the party they seem to be. I manage to catch Willow's eye but see that Charlotte still has her head firmly down.

Willow stops by my desk.

'Charlotte isn't coming.'

I hear the words but it takes me a while to comprehend what she's actually said.

'Did you hear me? Come on, let's walk and I'll tell you.' I feel the anticipation melt away and turn to despair.

'What do you mean?' I manage to say.

'She just messaged, says she doesn't feel very well so isn't coming. I asked if she wanted us to bring her anything and she said no.'

The anguish rises and threatens to choke the life out of me. How am I going to tell her mum? She has been clinging to the hope that a few magic words from me and the spell would be broken, returning Charlotte to her waiting arms. She is going to be crushed.

Damn it, what the hell do we do now?

CHAPTER 16

The mountain of work threatens to drown me. My concentration levels have not improved and B has noticed. It's funny how she never noticed when my desk was empty but manages to clock it when it isn't. I have had one of her snide e-mails asking if I was the 'wrong person for the job' and have responded assuring her that I am the right person and advised that a clear-out of some old campaigns was the reason for the mess on my desk. This is absolute rubbish but she won't know that unless she starts sifting through the mess. It's possible she may have already done that but she won't want me to know so for now my lie keeps her off my back.

I seriously need to get back to being focussed and productive. It's just over a week until I go on holiday and I need to go knowing that when I come back I won't be walking into a shit storm on account of something I've missed while on my #savecharlotte crusade.

When I confessed my failure to Jean she was desolate. She sobbed loudly on the phone, the sound went through me like chalk scraped down a blackboard. It was the kind of news that should have been delivered in person but I couldn't bear to see the look on her face when I confirmed Charlotte wouldn't be coming home anytime soon so. Willow and Nicky were both supportive in my chosen method of delivery and have rallied round but I still feel shit.

Nicky is coming over for dinner—for dinner think take-out. Will is going to the movies to see some comic book nonsense and Nicky thinks I need cheering up. A drink is what I need, not cheering up. Luckily her definition of cheering up is drinking copious amounts of alcohol so we're happy. We decide on curry tonight, I'm not in the mood for the stodge of pizza and we had Chinese last time so by process of elimination India is it.

Food has been ordered and will allegedly be here in half an hour. From experience I know that half an hour will more likely be an hour which is why I ordered a good hour before we'll be ready to eat it. We always like to sink at least one bottle of wine before it arrives then we can at least still taste it. After one bottle it matters not what it tastes like as it's purely being drunk for getting pissed's sake and no one gives a crap when they're drinking to get pissed. It could be Dettol and it would still be consumed. Some of that cheap stuff tastes like Dettol anyway. I don't know how Will and I used to drink it.

Back in the day when we had not long since met and were trying to be sophisticated we would go to the local off licence to purchase wine to drink while sat in one of our bedrooms. How very grown up of us. The trouble was at first that neither of us had a scooby doo about wine and all we knew (or we thought) was that there was sweet and dry varieties. I didn't fancy red as that doesn't go in the fridge so we set about being all culturally aware by buying the sweetest wine possible, Liebfraumilch. While all my mates were being Lambrini girls I was drinking that. My taste buds tingle at the thought and not in a good way. It's like drinking runny syrup and leaves a fur over your teeth that any dog would be proud of. I couldn't touch the stuff now.

The wine Nicky has provided is a far more sophisticated drop; a beautiful Semillon Sauvignon. I try to steer clear of wines that cost less than ten quid a bottle. Those ones are made from devil's piss, I'm sure of it. Without fail, after even just one glass of that stuff you wake up with wine mouth and a stonking headache. I suspect if you were to test it there would be more sulphur than sauvignon, cheap wine is only fun pre midnight. It seems that alcohol wasn't the only way Nicky thought of to cheer me up, she's gone assault mode via holiday chat.

'So, you packed then or what? You've not got long now, nine more sleeps,' she finishes the sentence with an 'eek'.

'I had some summer stuff packed away anyway but I haven't sorted through it or owt if that's what you're asking,' I reply.

'God that's not like you, you've usually packed three months in advance just for a one nighter. Do you want me to help you with it tonight? I can help you choose outfits.'

It might just be me but Nicky seems to be massively over-compensating for my miserable face.

'You hate packing, you turd, so why would you want to do it for someone else? Anyway, I haven't really been in holiday mode of late.' I shouldn't really have to spell out why.

'Packing someone else's stuff will be fun, I don't need to stress about the mess of clothes strewn across the bedroom or how much washing I'll have to do if I wear everything I take, the mess and washing will be yours.' Nicky says, making no attempt to address my last sentence.

'I'm just not in the mood Nik, it feels wrong to be honest,' It's the guilt again, how dare I feel excited and pack for a holiday with everything that's going on with Charlotte?

'You can't wallow forever, mate. I know it's a shit situation right now but you not living your life isn't going to make Charlotte's situation any better, is it?'

'But what if I leave her and something bad happens?' I ask. It's a thought that's been bothering me for days now.

'What if you stay and something bad happens? She's made it clear that you're not a part of her life anymore so you have to accept it but be prepared to be there for her if and when she needs you,' Nicky says in a tone that tells me she has had enough of trying to cheer me up.

'Well ok then, bring that bottle of wine and head to the wardrobe, I think we're going to need it'.

The wine got drunk and the packing got done, I attempted to do it in jolly, holiday mode but Nicky saw straight through me. I don't think she was particularly bothered that my heart wasn't in it, I wasn't talking about Charlotte and that was enough for her.

***

I have arrived at work early, determined to clear my desk (and my head) ready for a relaxing holiday. If nothing else, it is what Will deserves having listened to me drone on first about B and then about Charlotte for the best part of the last six months. I want to get on that plane and leave all of my worries at home.

A night of packing and faux happiness has left me shattered so the first call is the kitchen to make a strong coffee. I love being in work when no one else is around. The solitude is comforting and I am so much more productive than when the office is full. Then I spend too much time looking around to see what everyone else is up to, paranoid that B is watching my every move. At this time though I can relax safe in the knowledge that I am alone.

I walk into the kitchen and am momentarily lost for words as I find myself staring straight at Charlotte. She must have arrived just before me and had the same thought, hence the reason why I haven't seen her and thought I was alone. She says hi then goes back to making her coffee. She has her hair down and thick make up on again, the mask I believe she has taken to wearing when she has had a beating. I want to say something, I have to say something but although words start to form in my mouth I can't seem to make them pass my lips. I keep opening then closing my mouth like a goldfish and am relieved she isn't looking at me.

I have got to spit it out, this might be my last chance. If I don't say something I am going to spend all day, week, my holiday regretting it. Charlotte starts to walk out of the kitchen and I find my voice

'Charlotte.'

She turns and looks at me but says nothing. I'm trying to find the words, she's put her head down again and is starting to turn around

'Is everything alright?' I force the words out in an attempt to stop her leaving and engage her in conversation.

'Yes thank you,' she says and once again makes her way to the door.

'I mean is everything alright with Julian? It's just that I can't help notice that over these last few weeks you haven't really been yourself and you've, well, really changed. You're so quiet and unsociable and sometimes you seem to be covering your face like you are now and so I just wondered if there was something you might want to tell me, something you're maybe scared to say. You know you can tell me anything, I want to help you, Willow wants to help you. We're so worried about you.'

Once I start to speak I can't stop and the words tumble out along with a sense of relief. Charlotte is still stood there but the expression on her face hasn't changed. She starts to speak.

'Maybe I just don't want to be friends with you anymore, have you thought about that? I don't know what you're trying to suggest about Julian but you're wrong. He loves me and I love him. He was right about you. He said you were jealous of me and you would try to keep me away from him and that's what you've been trying to do all along.'

I am stunned. Julian has never met me so what the fuck gives him the right to make up lies about me being jealous? Jealous of what exactly? Getting a black eye every other day or not being able to breathe without him sanctioning how loud it is? I can tell by the look in her eyes that nothing I say is going to convince her of that.

'Charlotte, you're wrong. He's using you, controlling you even. He is distancing you from all of your friends. Why would he do that if he loves you? He's never even met any of us.'

'And he won't be doing that, ever! In fact you're not going to be seeing much of me anymore as I finish today. I resigned.'

The words cut me like a knife. When did this happen? We have to give notice so she must have known for a while. How are we going to be able to keep an eye on her if she isn't even here?

'What do you mean you finish today? You can't just leave like that, what about your notice?' I ask as the panic threatens to take over.

'I gave my notice four weeks ago. Julian says I don't need to work, so why should I? He says I don't need to be around your jealousy and negative energy and I agree.' With that she walks out of the kitchen.

I lean against the kitchen counter. I feel dizzy and my palms are sweaty. He stopped her contacting us socially and now he's stopped her from seeing us at work too. What a clever bastard. Now he really will have her all to himself. He will be able to do whatever the hell he wants to her and no one will know about it.

I want to run after her and tell her what a big mistake she is making but I know she won't listen. She is totally under his spell and if I push any further she will never speak to me again, I could see it in her eyes, defeat. What a sick, twisted prick. I wonder if his friends and work colleagues know what he is. One way or another, I will make sure everyone knows. If it's the last thing I do.

The rest of my work did not get done. It stayed firmly on my desk taunting me all day. B was out so I didn't have to worry about her beady eyes but I still ended the day feeling absolutely shit and defeated. One more week before I go on holiday and I have never felt less in holiday mode. Willow was as concerned as I when I told her Charlotte was leaving. We agonised over whether to make a fuss and have a leaving presentation and decided against it. Charlotte of old would have relished being the centre of attention and being lavished with praise but this Charlotte would like nothing of the sort.

In the end we settled on buying her a present from us (a handbag) and Willow offered to do the honours as after the morning's conversation I didn't feel Charlotte would be happy to see me hovering over her desk. She didn't come over and say goodbye when she left and I wonder whether I will ever see her again. Will she ever escape from the hell she has gotten herself into and if she does would she feel like she could come back into our lives? I need her to know that no matter how she feels about me I will always be here for her. I type 'I'm sorry if I upset you this morning. I need you to know I will always be here for you no matter what xxx' then I click send and burst into tears.

I have trouble sleeping over the following week. I lie awake replaying the last conversation I had with Charlotte. Was there something else I could have said, was there something I shouldn't have said? Does she realise I'm only saying anything at all because I love her and want the best for her? The constant questioning is like Chinese water torture. I wonder whether Charlotte is laid awake thinking about the same thing or whether I am just not on her radar at all now. Does she really love him and think he loves her or was that just what she's got used to telling herself. Does she secretly wish she could break free of him and just doesn't know how? She didn't reply to my text. Willow sent her a similar one and she didn't reply to that either.

Nicky suggested I put the whole thing to the back of my mind and just forget about it as I've done all I can, but I don't feel like I've done nearly enough and that by forgetting it I am condemning Charlotte to a fate so terrible that I don't even want to contemplate it. Will said much the same.

'You've done all you can Han, she's not your responsibility. She's made her own bed so let her lie in it.'

She hasn't made her own bed though, has she? He's made it for her. He wormed his way in with his flash car and his flash job. Gave her compliments to make her feel special and then when he had built her up he tore her back down again so that he could mould her into the person he wanted her to be. A mannequin. No thoughts or feelings of her own and now no family or friends either.

Surprisingly, I managed to get my act together where work is concerned. Despite thinking of nothing but Charlotte at home, my concentration at work has increased, possibly because I'm not spending my days gazing at her in the faint hope that she might reach out to me for saving. B has been ever present, watching me like a hawk, crowding my every move. She actually commented that I was much more productive without my friend. The word 'friend' emphasised as though it were a dirty word.

We have yet to see Charlotte's replacement. I expect her to be young and impressionable or old and miserable so that she can either be easily manipulated or is too old to get involved in office politics. I also expect her to be useless and available immediately as B will have spent the first three weeks of Charlotte's notice period in denial that she is daring to leave her bosom. The last week would have been spent speaking with HR about advertising for a replacement, which means she will take on the person who can start the soonest.

Management at its finest.

CHAPTER 17

Will is piling suitcases into the car. It's 4.30am. The only time of the year when getting up before the birds is thrilling. We clamber into the car all bleary eyed and freshly showered, which always seems odd, getting showered to sit in a car, an airport and on a plane for several hours then sitting in another car or a bus all hot and sweaty before arriving at your destination and promptly getting showered. Why do we just not leave out the shower bit and have fifteen minutes extra in bed?

'Have we got everything?' Will asks the same question he asks three minutes before we set off anywhere.

'We've got tickets, passport and money so yep we've got the lot.' I respond with the same answer I give whenever we're going away anywhere. I wonder whether every couple has the same pre-holiday conversation and if they don't whether any of them find themselves at the airport having left behind one of those important items. If they do what do they do? Do they drive back home for them?

We drive to the airport in relative silence, choosing instead to listen to Rag n Bone Man followed by Ed Sheeran. The look on Will's face when I fired up the *Matilda* soundtrack was not a happy holiday one so I swiftly turned it off. Best not start the week on a bad note even though I could really do with a *Matilda* style boost at the minute.

We've chosen one of those stop and drop car parks where you pay £70 to abandon the car and keys with some guy you've never met in exchange for only having to walk 100 metres to enter the terminal. We always have the same argument as to whether it's worth the extra twenty quid and always come up with the same conclusion, yes it is as it's all good and well having to walk three miles to the terminal when you're in excited holiday mode but it's not so fun when you're well into post-holiday blues mode and all you want to do is get home and get the washing done.

Check-in is already heaving. The flight information states that check-in opens two hours before so who are these in-breds who arrive at least four hours before with half a dozen kids each who spend the whole time in the queue screaming at said kids for running wild, pulling barriers down and generally causing chaos as they're knackered and bored out of their tiny minds having been dragged out of bed in the middle of the night so that mummy and daddy can ensure they're spot at the front of the check-in queue to secure the seats they have already paid £10 each to pre-book? They drive me crazy. I aim for the shortest queue but as usual the shortest queue seems to take the longest to move. This fact has already been worked out by many others before me hence why it is the shortest, no other fucker wants to join it.

I crane my neck to see what the tit on the desk is doing and why it's taking her so much longer than everyone else. I can see no reason other than her sloth like manoeuvres. My good holiday mood is dwindling fast. We need to ditch the cases and get coffee.

When we make it to the front we have to answer all the same questions we answered when we checked in online. I have yet to see how this makes things any quicker. You still have to speak to the bint on the desk, she stills asks about firearms and liquids, you still have to get a little tag for your cases AND you still get a boarding card. Perhaps they think they can catch out terrorists by asking safety questions in written and verbal form. Maybe they think a terrorist will slip up and answer one differently and if they do a silent alarm triggers the security forces that pounce and arrest them. Or perhaps it's just another way to wind holidaymakers up.

The people on those desks always look so bloody miserable. I get that they're at work and it might be annoying having to sit behind that desk while lots of happy souls beam with excitement for their week in Alicante but you would think that at the start of the day at least they could do their job with some enthusiasm and a hint of enjoyment. It's possible none of them are morning people. I don't think I've ever flown outwards on anything other than a morning flight so perhaps they all become animated the nearer it gets to lunchtime.

'Next time we go away, can we fly after lunch? Not too late after lunch though, as they might be tired and fed up by then but say elevenish.' I hadn't realised I said this out loud until Will responds.

'What the hell are you talking about, who might be tired and fed up by eleven?'

'Sorry, I was just thinking that the check-in people always look miserable and I wondered if that's because we always fly on a morning and they're not morning people so maybe if we fly later in the day they might be more cheerful,' I explain

'Can't say I've given it much thought Han, but now you've brought it to my attention I will be sure to add it to our non-negotiables list for our next hol.' Will replies, a look of pity on his face.

'Ok, don't take the piss I was just thinking that's all.'

'Well how about you think where to get breakfast then we can go and look at expensive shit and massive Toblerones that we're not going to buy.' Now he's talking, about the breakfast, not the Toblerones. Who the hell does buy those? Who is jetting off on a jolly to Spain or to find their long lost relatives in Australia with a metre long Toblerone for company? It's the same the world over too, every Duty Free has them and yet I have never seen a single soul purchase one. It's one of life's great mysteries.

Breakfast consumed and fully caffeinated we embark on window shopping. Will announces that he could do with some new sunglasses. This is a revelation. Will does not like spending money and here he is declaring that he needs something which requires the spending of money whilst in the vicinity of a place where they can be purchased. Ordinarily this is the kind of statement he makes only after the shops are far behind us and it's almost impossible to return and purchase anything. I force him into the shop. I realise within minutes that this is a big mistake, there are now only thirty minutes until boarding and Will couldn't make a decision if his life depended on it.

I am encouraging his purchase mainly because I too want to purchase something and now if he spends 300 quid on himself he can't say no to me spending anything. Genius, I know. He has picked up and put down again at least a dozen pair. I am going to have to take matters into my own hands. I start scooping up ones I think he'll like and I stand in front of him holding my arms out like one of those dodgy sellers of fake pairs on the beach. He tries them on as I mutter words of encouragement 'ooh, I like those, they make your jaw look squarer' and, 'I like those ones too but they look a bit big for your face compared to the last ones,' after another ten minutes we have it down to two pairs.

If one was more expensive than the other he would just opt for the cheapest. These cost exactly the same which means he has to make a decision purely on preference, something he is incapable of doing. After a further five minutes of procrastination I take matters into my own hands and march to the counter with both pairs.

'What are you doing? I'm not buying both!' Good, I have him where I want him.

'You're not buying both, I am. I can't stand here staring at them any longer so if you can't decide between them we'll just get both.' I start fishing my card from my purse.

'But we have the same account so it would be me buying both and I don't want to spend that much,' he says the panic rising in his voice.

'Well you don't have a choice. Actually, you do. You can choose one or the other but as you're incapable of making that decision I have taken it away from you.' I can see him squirming as he reaches out a hand.

'Ok, I'll have these ones then!'

Bingo! Worked like a charm. A minute later I am racing through the airport with Will trailing behind me.

I know they sell Jo Malone somewhere and I am hoping my nose will lead me to it as there is now less than fifteen minutes to boarding and Will wants to get to the Gate. At last, I find it. The Holy Grail of all that smells delicious. Will groans.

'You can groan off, you have what you wanted so now I get what I want,' I say with my face shoved into a very expensive, but very beautiful candle. I need at least one new perfume and a candle. They last forever, unlike those ones you buy in a supermarket that claim to burn for ten hours but are pretty much wickless and scent free within two. Alright so they cost ten times as much but they are worth every penny.

Will is on fully payback mode and is spraying everything on the little tester sticks and wafting it in front of my face. He knows full well that too much perfume smelling gives me a headache and I hiss at him to stop. I've already had to shut down the over-zealous shop assistant with a 'no thanks I know what I want' when really I have no idea. I get sick of them wafting smells asking what about this and what about that. I just want to be left to sniff in peace. I wonder if that's how a dog feels when it's out for a gentle walk and stops to sniff a lamppost but is rudely pulled along by its lead.

I finally find the smell that I like, English Pear and Freesia. I ask Will his opinion.

'It's alright,' is all he manages to muster, which is disappointing given how much I assisted with his sunglasses purchase. There is a 30ml for £40 or a 100ml for £100. It's a no brainer. I get more for my money with the bigger one. Now, candles! I don't like anything too floral as it gives me headache, I like fresh and vibrant. I go for Lime, Basil and Mandarin. It smells delicious and is a bargain at £50.

'Christ, you're not expecting me to lug that around with me, are you? Don't you think this bag is heavy enough?' Will has spotted the size of the candle and is less than thrilled. 'I thought you were getting a travel one,' he adds.

'They're not as good a value for money though are they, so I might as well get a big one,' I reason. He sighs but realises further resistance is useless. I pay and we run to gate twenty three, arriving just as they call our row. Phew!

The flight was torturous. I am elated when we touch down on Greek soil. We had the misfortune of sitting right in front of one of the 'first in the queue families' whose small children spent the entire flight kicking the back of our seats. I allowed it to continue for an hour before turning around and politely requesting that they keep their feet to themselves. Sadly it fell on deaf ears as the parents had cleverly sat elsewhere so when I spun around I was met with three very tiny faces who did not give one fuck about me or my whiplash. They continued to do it throughout the whole of the flight while Will miraculously slept through it. I was tempted to give him a bigger kick to the front of his person than I was getting to the back of mine particularly when he woke up declaring he hadn't slept a wink.

Our bags are the last off and I am at the very end of my tether. The little shits from the plane are running amok banging into everyone and everything while their parents ignore them and talk amongst themselves. From what I can gather there are four adults and six kids. They look like they may have starred on *Benefits Britain* and their language is a little more colourful than I would expect when talking to young children. Not that I blame them, I'd be swearing at the little fuckers as well. I am thankful that the parents weren't in earshot when I spoke to the little darlings as they don't look the type to take kindly to other people teaching their kids manners. Bullet dodged. I start to panic when we find our coach and see that the little shits and they're accompanying adults are sat on the same one. I find seats as far away as possible but fear they have the ability to annoy from very far away. I'm not wrong.

Once the coach sets off the tearaways ditch their seats and start running up and down the aisle. The poor holiday rep tasked with escorting us newly arrived holiday makers safely to our destination keeps asking nicely for them to sit down but they and their parents take no notice. The parents are busy swigging out of plastic bottles that purport to contain coke but I suspect contain a little extra. My suspicions are all but confirmed when the lower the liquid level gets, the more animated they become. They are raucous by the time we reach the first stop. I'm muttering under my breath 'please get off, please get off,' but they don't. I sigh loudly.

'What's up with you?' Will asks, clearly oblivious to the circus going on around us

'Are you kidding?' I reply. 'Have you not seen or heard the Nesbits? Kids running wild, parents getting smashed at the back of the bus. It's those kids you managed to ignore kicking hell out of our plane seats. I am praying they aren't getting off where we get off,' I put my hands together in mock prayer.

'God fun police, calm down, they're on holiday, they're entitled to be happy about it.'

'What do you think they're on holiday from? Collecting their dole? Because it sure as hell isn't work. Look at the state of them. Head to toe in designer gear yet they look like they've been thrown in a tumble dryer full of Primani.' I know I'm being mean and judgemental but I'm tired and anxious.

187

'You practically live in Primani so don't be such a snobby cow.' Will fires back

'Yes, but I wear it like it's designer and that dear husband is the difference between class and trash.'

In spite of himself Will laughs, 'if you say so.'

We have stopped at no fewer than four hotels. There are three groups remaining, us, the roughians and one other couple. My hope is fading fast. The parents are well pissed having downed at least two bottles of 'coke' each and all of the kids are complaining of feeling sick. We stop again, and to my delight it is our hotel so the chances of being puked on by feral kids are diminished.

I elbow Will, 'this is us,' I say and we start making our way down the aisle and off. Thankfully the Nesbits don't follow and I breathe a sigh of relief.

Let the holiday begin!

CHAPTER 18

Our room is every bit as nice as it looked in the brochure — crisp clean bedding, white washed walls and a balcony overlooking the pool with a slightly restricted view of the sea. Perfect. We start unpacking so that we can crack open the first alcoholic beverage of the holiday and set about relaxing. I asked as we passed the bar whether wine could be purchased by the bottle and I was assured that it could, so I have volunteered Will to go get some once we're done. Had I been thinking clearly I would have grabbed some there and then so we could drink as we unpacked but I am prepared to wait an extra ten minutes.

Will wants to do the obligatory exploration once we're sorted but I'd rather relax on the balcony until it no longer feels hotter than Venus. I hate the ritual of applying sunscreen so if I can avoid it for today by staying indoors until the sun is no longer a threat to my transparent skin then avoid it I shall. Will knows this. He also knows that going on and on about it will serve only to annoy me so his best plan of action is to indulge me and keep quiet. We have been on enough holidays over the years for him to know that no amount of cajoling, whining or cries of, 'you're not burning you've just put cream on' will convince me to surrender to the mercy of the big yellow ball in the sky until at least day two. Day one is all about the wine pour and the ahhh!

Clothes nicely put away I get to arranging toiletries on the smallest shelf in the world (why do hotels do that?) and send Will off in search of very cold alcohol. I quickly shower and change into cooler clothes. Optimum comfort is required if one is to relax on the balcony and watch the sun go down whilst not caring a jot about anything. I reach for my phone in order to update my Facebook status accompanied by a fantastic picture of our view. I am on the balcony adjusting the camera zoom when my peace (and world) is shattered by a familiar sound. It can't be, oh please god no tell me it isn't. Oh shit, shittity, shit, it is. The bastard Nesbits are here!

I am tempted to throw myself from the balcony and as I am contemplating the same Will walks in looking like he lost a tenner and found a penny. He walks towards me holding out the bottle and as he gets to the balcony he sees what I have seen (or rather heard).

'Oh, so you know then,' he says thrusting the bottle into my hands. I am torn between hitting him with it and removing the cap and downing the lot like a shot. I push him back into the room whilst frantically trying to remove the screw cap.

'It' a cork,' he says and I want to hurt him, I want to hurt him so bad.

'Why the fuck did you bring one with a cork. Every bastard winemaker in the world sticks screw tops on now but you manage to find the only one still brandishing a cork. Did you get it before or after you saw who the twatting hell was next door?' I ask as I wrestle with the cork.

Will has the good grace to remove the bottle from me and take it to the kitchenette to search for a corkscrew. 'I got it before. I saw them going into the room as I walked back. They were talking about going to the wrong hotel, what a bunch of idiots.'

'Is that all you can say?' I huff. 'Our holiday that I have been looking forward to for months, that I need badly after all that has happened lately lies in ruins and all you can say is they're idiots. You're the bleeding idiot around here.' I wail then promptly burst into tears of frustration.

'Come on Han, it's been a long day and we're both tired. Nothing is ruined. So their kids are a bit boisterous, that won't bother us. It's not like they're staying in our room is it? The parents seem like right piss heads anyway so I bet they'll spend eight hours by the pool and six in the bar. We won't even know they're here so let's get this wine drank and start as we mean to go on,' he hands me a glass.

I take a sip. Mmm it's pretty nice. Not too sweet, not too dry and doesn't taste of alcohol which generally means a fresh mouth in the morning. 'What do you think of it?' Will asks, his little face searching for hope in mine

'Yeah, it's not bad,' I say trying not to sound too enthusiastic. I don't want him to think he's brought me round that quickly.

'It was only four euros for the bottle too, we can get pissed for less than a tenner,' he says clearly pleased with himself.

I make my way back to the balcony with trepidation. It's 4pm and still baking hot. I can hear chatter from next door, mum is screeching at the kids telling them to, 'get your fucking towels will you' so it looks like Will was right and they are going to spend the remaining daylight hours in the pool leaving us to our planned relaxation.

'Cheers,' Will says with a smirk.

'Cheers big ears,' I reply, happy to feel the tension lift.

Wine finished, Will jumps in the shower then we head out to explore. The sun has started to go down but the air is still warm and it's a perfect summer's night. We discovered before we arrived that Skiathos has pretty much one long road that runs from the Harbour to the last beach on the stretch, Koukounaries, which is where we are staying. We decide to head in the direction of the beach, which is less than a mile away, and leave the Harbour for tomorrow. Information in the hotel says a bus runs up and down every ten minutes or so and the stops are in numerical order. Nice and easy for us tourists, but this evening we walk.

We walk around the pool, which is still heavily occupied by excited kids and pissed looking adults, including our neighbours. I hope that means they are planning an early night so that we can sit outside to finish off another bottle of wine. Within minutes we pass a cosy looking restaurant with a less than cosy name, The Big Bad Wolf. Interesting choice. It looks busy enough so the name mustn't put many off and a quick glance at the menu reveals the usual Greek fayre, tzatziki, Greek salad, souvlaki, moussaka, baklava etc etc.

We walk on despite starting to feel hungry. We haven't really eaten since breakfast (plane rubbish cannot be classed as actual food) and the consumption of even the tiniest amount of wine has a tendency to give me severe munchies.

'Are you hungry yet?' I ask, trying to gauge how long Will is likely to want to wander about for.

'A bit, but I'd rather get something on the way back rather than on the way out while it's still light. You know what these foreign places are like. Health and Safety isn't as rife and it's likely to be pitch dark as soon as the sun goes down.' Will clearly hasn't noticed the many lampposts we've walked by. 'Is the fact that you asked a hint that you are by any chance?' As perceptive as always.

'Well I am a bit, but I can wait, it's only six o'clock so if I eat now then walk, I'll be hungry again and go home the size of a house.' The inevitable side effect of drinking copious amounts of wine.

'You could just not eat again you know, go to bed and wait for breakfast,' he says.

'Then I'm likely to be sick as I wouldn't have had anything to soak up the alcohol.' I am surprised I need to point this out.

'Well you could just not drink so much then,' he replies.

'Well then I may as well be dead!' The look on my face and the tone of my voice should be enough to convince Will to accept he has lost the argument but he can't help but have the last word.

'Fine, stay hungry for a bit longer then but you know even if we don't have dinner until ten you'll still have your head in a bag of crisps at midnight.' I can't argue with that. Salt and carbs, the only choices when one has consumed her body weight in wine.

A steady twenty minute walk and we arrive at the beach. It's dusk now so it's difficult to tell whether the sea is blue or brown but with the sun shimmering on its surface it looks beautiful anyway. Will is keen to walk onto the beach to do some paddling, I'm not. I didn't come dressed for sand. I am quite happy to stand right where we are gazing out at the ocean.

'Come on, your feet will soon dry off. Don't you want to go and see how warm the water is?' Will asks pleading with puppy dog eyes.

'Not really, I can wait until tomorrow to find out, I like surprises. If you want to do it then go and do it I'm not stopping you.'

'A romantic stroll on the beach isn't the same when you do it by yourself.' Will sounds wounded.

'Well you never mentioned romance; I thought you wanted to see how warm the water was not my heart.'

In my book sand has never been synonymous with romance. All that frolicking Danny and Sandy do at the start of Grease is bollocks. As soon as the cameras stopped rolling they'd have been rubbing grains of sand out of places they didn't know existed. The evil little bastards that stick to everything and that you're still finding three days later even after nineteen showers.

'How about I pick you up and carry you to the water then?' Will is not giving up easily.

'How will that help? If you're just going to drop me in the water I'm still going to be wet and sandy.'

He picks me up before I can say anything else and starts walking towards the water. 'Fair enough, I won't put you down.'

I laugh. 'You better not or you'll regret it, I won't talk to you for the rest of the week.'

'Ooh promises, promises' he says, smiling.

Dry and sand free (me at least) we make our way hand in hand, back towards the Big Bad Wolf. The sea air has made me ravenous and although I didn't actually set foot in the water or on the beach I am feeling in a rather romantic mood too. I've also managed to get this far through the day without thinking of Charlotte, I haven't even checked my phone for messages. Why is it that when

I'm at home with a million distractions I can't bear not to check my phone at least once every ten minutes yet I come away with literally not a thing to do and I haven't given it a second thought? I resolve to be less phone dependant once we get home. I'll set myself a new rule whereby I am only allowed to check my phone once at night and the rest of the time it is tucked away in my handbag. I tell Will my plan and he scoffs.

'You'll never do it; the withdrawal symptoms will land you in the nut house.' His disdain makes me all the more determined.

'We'll see, and as you're so sure I'll fail how about we bet something on it.'

'Like what?' he asks.

I'm frantically thinking of something that either of us are that bothered about. 'I know,' I say. 'If I spend a full week only checking my phone once at night then you have to come with me to see *Matilda*.' It's the best I can come up with at short notice.

'Ok, I'm not worried as you won't do it so what do I get when you fail?' He is an arsehole and I am not going to fail.

'If I fail, which I won't, but if I do then I'll go to a footy match with you.' I have zero desire to do this so had really better hope I win.

'Well I don't see how that's a prize for me, having to listen to you moaning for two hours that your feet are cold, and you don't understand the rules.' He knows me so well, I would be complaining about both of those things, If I went, but as I won't be going, he doesn't need to worry his pretty little head about it.

The restaurant is much busier than it was when we walked by earlier. There are people gathered around the lectern, presumably waiting for a table, so I shove Will forward to put our name down. He has the good sense to ask if we can have a drink while we wait and we opt for a half carafe of house white. I don't know what a carafe is or what the house white tastes like, possibly paint stripper but at four euros it seems like a bargain.

I am relieved when the carafe arrives and seems to hold a good half a litre which is close enough to a full bottle of wine and even more relieved when the wine itself tastes delicious. I suspect more half carafes will be ordered. I wonder why they don't have full carafes. They'd save so much time on having to refill them. Will is in the process of ordering another one when we are beckoned to a table by a Waiter. I'm practically starving having consumed even more wine and I'm feeling a little tipsy so I set my sights on the starters.

I settle on bread and dips, they should come quickly and I'll get some all-important carbs. I opt for chicken souvlaki for main with rice and Will goes for the moussaka. We order more wine after a short discussion about whether we should order one or two and conclude that it is still on the warm side so one would be better as no one wants to drink lukewarm wine. They must have the wine already poured and sat waiting in a fridge as within about twelve seconds of ordering, a fresh one is delivered to our table and not 20 seconds after that the starter arrives.

The bread is warm and fresh and smells divine. I hoover it up as though I haven't eaten for a week. I devour four pieces without pausing.

'Steady on! Munchies set in early have they?' Will knows the post wine drill

'Just a bit but the wine is wearing off now.' I say.

'I'm not surprised! You've eaten almost a whole loaf of bread in about three minutes. You best get a doggy bag for your main.'

'I won't need a doggy bag, I'm still hungry.' I know full well that I will need a doggy bag though. We have no food in the apartment and no matter how much I eat now I will still want to eat anything in sight if we carry on drinking when we get back. If I don't, the morning will not look pretty and there is nothing worse than feeling hungover when it's 100 degrees outside. I should have been sensible and brought my anti-nausea pills just in case I get caught out (drink too much) but I left them at home in the misguided hope that knowing I didn't have them would make me more sensible.

The mains arrive almost at the same time as the wine runs out so we take the opportunity of ordering more while the waiter delivers our food. The food looks and smells amazing and there is enough to feed at least six people.

We dig in while the waiter pours wine from our fresh batch and neither of us speaks for several minutes. I start to feel full and then overfull within the space of about 90 seconds and have to stop eating.

I am pleased I have my elasticated waist pants on, even they feel like they're struggling to contain my bulging stomach. I take another sip of wine but it's a struggle.

'I think we might need to go for another walk to shift this food, once I can move that is.' I feel very uncomfortable. I burp and a little bit of sick creeps into my mouth. Oh god, there is so much food it hasn't even managed to make its way past my throat. I try to make myself as flat as possible in my chair as though leaning back will somehow aid in the digestion process.

I really had my eye on the yoghurt with honey and nuts for dessert but the thought of eating it now just adds to my urge to throw up.

'You ok?' Will asks. 'You've gone all red in the face.'

I am not rushing to answer as I feel as though my mouth being shut is the only thing stopping the food packed into my body from expelling itself. When I do respond I speak slowly and in monosyllables.

'Too full. Feel sick. Need to walk,' I start taking deep breaths

'Ha-ha, eyes bigger than yer belly. Thought you wanted dessert, that yogurt looked good, so did that chocolate ice-cream sundae, look they've got it over there. It's huge.'

I know full well he's winding me up.

'Fuck off. Finish, pay, then let's walk,' I say, still keeping conversation to a minimum.

'Jeez, no need to be so bossy.'

It pains me to let Will finish the wine off but the last thing my stomach needs right now is more acid. I feel massively uncomfortable and just want to lie down but I know doing that won't help.

We arrive back at the hotel in good spirits. After a slow walk back my waistband no longer feels under so much strain and the thought of drinking more wine is a pleasing one. We order a bottle. The bar is fairly busy, there is no sign of our neighbours or their holiday companions so I settle down in a comfy chair and let Will do the pouring.

'I know we've only been here a few hours, but I definitely like Skiathos,' Will says.

'What is it that you like about it so much, the cheap wine or large portions of food?' I reply.

'Both. The company isn't bad either.' He leans forward and gives me a kiss. I'm taken aback as he isn't ordinarily one for public displays of affection

'You've clearly had too much to drink,' I tease

'I don't have to be drunk to kiss you.'

'But it helps' I say.

'Very amusing. You could make a fortune selling those cheap wooden signs bearing that phrase, said no one ever!' Will is known for his sarcasm but isn't often accused of being witty with it so that's a good one for him. I laugh and tell him so.

'Maybe I have had too much to drink after all,' he replies.

'What's our plan for tomorrow?' I ask, changing the subject. I'm not good at spontaneity and like to know what's happening in advance so that I can plan my clothes (\and, if required, my mood.

'I thought we'd just have a lazy day, maybe get the bus into the town and wander around the Harbour.' I nod my approval at his suggestion and then it's his turn to change the subject.

'I know I've not exactly been the model husband these last couple of months,' he says.

I wonder where this is going. Has he been having an affair, one night stand, wants a divorce? Oh god is that why he's being so nice to me? He feels guilty.

'Err ok' I say, too scared to say anything else.

'I know you've been having a shit time what with work and Charlotte and I haven't been as supportive as I should have been. It's just that...'

This is it, he's going to say it's just that he's met someone else. How did I not see this coming? I've been neglecting him for weeks now. Doing my own thing, arranging nights out with the girls, talking on the phone with the girls, being busy working. What did I expect him to do, just sit around and wait until I could fit him into my busy schedule? Ok, if he's had a one night stand I can deal with that. I'm a grown up, I get how alcohol + flattery could = a drunken fumble or more. I'll absolutely make him pay for it for a while, I won't forgive easily but I will forgive him.

I notice that my cheeks feel wet and Will is staring at me with a concerned look on his face. 'Han, what's the matter, why are you crying?'

Oh no, I've daydreamed myself into a frenzy. I rack my brains for something to say that isn't, 'I just imagined that you've been having an affair' which will make me sound like a crazy person and finally say, 'Nothing, I was just thinking about Charlotte again that's all.' Good save but now I've probably ruined the mood.

'That's what I was trying to say.' Is he going to tell me he's been having an affair with Charlotte? I'm even more confused now. He carries on. 'You've had so much on your plate and I have been so worried about myself and work that I haven't stopped to think how you must be feeling or tried to do anything to make you feel better. I'm sorry for being shit. I will try much harder when we get home to be less shit and more supportive'.

I breathe a sigh of relief. 'Is that it?' I ask.

'Yeah. Why, what did you think I was going to say?' He looks baffled.

'Oh nothing, just that you looked really worried so I thought you had some big news to share.'

'No news, just the realisation that I've been letting you down and it's not ok.' He reaches over and holds my hand. I smile back at him.

'Thank you,' I say. 'Now let's get ratted.'

CHAPTER 19

We didn't actually stay up that late so that probably played a part in us both being wide awake at dawn. We consider going for a run but think better of it when we open the patio doors to discover it's already boiling hot. I look down over the pool and see there are fresh towels laid out on some of the lounges. Seriously, who are the people that do that? Are they perfectly reasonable human beings the other 364 days of the year or do they set off to work six hours early to get a parking spot and go for lunch at 10am to beat the queue?

My Nan used to say that bums save seats, not bags. I think the same should apply to towels. I'm tempted to sneak out and remove them all but I'm too scared in case the seat bagging swines also have rooms overlooking the pool. I tell Will of my displeasure.

'But we're not going to the pool today so it's no skin off your nose,' is his response. I should have known better than to tell him. He's useless when I'm on my high horse. He never joins me up there. In fact, more often than not he pushes me off with little effort and then I'm angrier at him than I was at whatever put me up there in the first place.

'Shall we go for a swim then?'

Will looks perplexed. 'You can't stand swimming.'

'Well it's too hot for a run and I definitely won't want to get in later when it's even hotter and full of little shits so we may as well have half an hour before brekkie.' I also really want to see who it is that has saved all the seats, though I expect they won't surface until well after we've left.

'Fine then, swimming it is,' he says reluctant.

Despite my usual misgivings about swimming I secretly enjoy myself. The water is fairly cool against the warm air and there isn't another soul around so I don't have to worry about little bastards splashing me in the face or crapping in the water. As we leave I have an overwhelming urge to do some seat saving of my own so I collect a pile of pool towels and start laying them on all of the empty beds.

'You're such a child,' Will says mock exasperated.

'Little things husband, little things,' I say and we both snigger all the way back to the room.

The Harbour is beautiful. It is surrounded by green hills dotted with little white houses and is every bit a picture postcard. The town is vibrant and packed with restaurants and shops selling furniture, paintings and artefacts, none of the usual tourist rubbish I'd expected to find. I haven't seen a single lilo and even though there are bars a plenty, not one of them looks remotely British. We have a lazy day meandering around the shops and trying cocktails in pretty much every bar we pass. We convince ourselves this is for health reasons, we need to keep hydrated in the searing heat and keep out of the midday sun so we are killing two birds with one stone. Although we're hot and sweaty and not really dressed for the evening I make an executive decision to say in town and have an early dinner so we can spend the rest of the evening on the balcony drinking cheap wine.

We've drunk a fair bit of it so far and have yet to feel drunk. We were slightly tipsy last night but no more than that so either they water it down or it's impossible to get drunk in Skiathos. I recall us having the conversation last night after working out we'd drank at least three litres between us yet could both still walk and see straight. What is this magic? We have vowed to experiment again this evening, though I fear that having changed one of the variables (i.e. spent all afternoon drinking cocktails) our findings tonight may be different. If that's the case we shall just have to try again tomorrow evening.

We eat dinner and head back by bus getting off two stops early to buy snacks and wine in the supermarket. 'What is the point dieting to go on holiday?' It's a question I've been thinking about since last night

'I give in, what is the point?' The tone of Will's voice says he isn't really interested in the answer and is just humouring me.

'I'm being serious, think about it. We, I mean us women, spend weeks, months even, eating half a cherry tomato a day and doing seventy-two different squat challenges, then we arrive on holiday and before we've had chance to wear a bikini we've eaten a tonne of bread and drank a gallon of wine so all the hard work has gone to waste and we're wobbly and riddled with cellulite again. I've eaten more since yesterday than I have in the last two weeks.'

Will says nothing.

'Seriously, why do we do it? I spent hours and hours trying on bikinis and finally found two that were the perfect cut so that when I breathed in I had no muffin top and they didn't cut my arse in half so that I had four cheeks. I practiced my poses and worked out exactly which limb to put where so that I could upload the obligatory 'oh no please don't take a photo of me in this bikini looking so fat and horrible (smoking hot)' Facebook pic.

It is my favourite pic of the year, the jealous bitches (like Emma) either totally ignore it or make a snotty comment like, 'wow you're brave' or, 'rather you than me' because they don't want to say, 'bravo you look amazing.' Their holiday photos consist of 3700 pictures of their kids each captioned with #myworld so that we don't forget how much they love their kids and don't think for a minute that they would rather be on a couples-only holiday doing nothing but getting shit-faced and suntanned. Pull the other one! Willow is a mum and a bloody damn good one but ask whether she would rather take the little angels to an all-inclusive five-star family resort in the sun for a week or take herself and the hubby off for a dirty weekend in Blackpool and she'll choose Blackpool every single time.

I'm so bloated from excessive carbs that I am going to be resigned to doing a legs only pic highlighting my beautifully pedicured trotters. I didn't need to practice that one; anyone can make a legs only pic look good. You just have to follow the rules of not allowing any part of your leg that's in shot to touch ANYTHING. The slightest bit of pressure and the jelly is spread further than a nasty rumour. Legs must remain airborne at all times. Knees up (but no calves touching back of thighs), feet pointed and a filter and anyone can have legs that Kendall Jenner would be proud of. Actually, I'll practice in the morning.

It's all quiet when we head to our room and I have to admit that my initial (over) reaction to the neighbours has been unfounded. We have heard not a peep from them. I grab the mozzie repellent and take my spot on the balcony while Will gets the glasses. A quick spray and I'm safe to be sat outside for at least three hours. I start working on my leg pose.

'Hello,' a female voice startles me. It's quite dark outside as the kitchenette is furthest from the balcony so there isn't much light coming from inside. I look around.

'I said hello.' I turn to my right and there leaning over the balcony is a girl who can be no more than seven or eight staring straight at me.

'Oh hello,' I say back regretting being so hasty in my belief that the neighbours had been no trouble.

'I'm Sarah, who are you?' The little girl asks. I am desperately trying to signal to Will not to come out with the wine so that I can pretend I was just going back inside but he has his back to me and is taking no notice.

'Shouldn't you be in bed?' I say, not wanting to tell her my name.

'I can go to bed when I want,' she replies. She's still leaning over onto our balcony and staring right at me.

'Lucky you, where is your mummy?' I ask quite loudly realising that I have been whispering and if her parents are to rescue me from her gaze they need to know she's outside talking to strangers.

'She's in bed and so is my step-dad but I don't have to go to bed yet.'

I'm really going to have to speak up to get their attention.

'Well I don't think they'd be happy if they knew you had opened the door and were outside talking to strangers, do you?' I all but shout.

'I didn't open the door. My step-dad did. He's called Colin. It's too hot and he doesn't want to pay for the air conditioner so we have to keep the door open.' She tells me, and that's a concern. We are only one floor up. Literally anyone could climb over the balcony and get into the room yet these idiots would rather risk a kidnap than pay 35 euros a week for air con.

Not wanting to scare the kid to death I say, 'Blimey, don't you get lot of mozzies in with the doors open?'

Will arrives on the balcony just as I'm asking. He looks from me to her, then back to me again. He rolls his eyes but sits down and places the drinks on the table. I shoot him a death stare. Christ, he could have assessed the situation then asked if I was coming to bed yet. Now we're both stuck outside.

'Yeah, we get hundreds. Look, I'll show you all my bites.' Sarah proceeds to point out bites all over her body, the poor kid looks like she's got measles. Her skin is so tanned that the bites look purple.

'Wow, you have got a lot. You've got a nice suntan though. I wish I got one of those.' I am genuinely envious of this little kid and her deep brown limbs.

'I always get tanned cos I don't wear sun cream. I'm used to it, this is my second holiday this month. We just came back from Egypt.'

Right, so not only are her parents slack, they're neglectful as well. Doors open all night and no sun cream worn. My initial instinct about them could not have been more right.

'No sun cream, don't you get burnt?' I ask, deciding it's probably not appropriate to talk to a kid I don't know about skin cancer.

'Yeah but it doesn't hurt, and it turns brown, so I don't care. I like being brown. Colin says this place is a right dump compared to

Egypt,' Sarah adds. I wish Colin would wake the fuck up and take her inside.

'Oh does he? Well I like it here but I've never been to Egypt.' Not only am I running out of things to say but I'm also running out of patience.

'We go every year, we've been twice this year.'

Well bully for you. Three holidays this year and we're not even halfway through it

'Gosh, your parents must get lots more days off work than we do then.' I give Will a knowing look.

'They don't work so we go on holiday whenever we like.'

Bingo! No jobs and three holidays every three months. How delightful for them.

'Sarah, get in here now!' A male voice booms from the room next door.

'Ok I better go now, see ya,' and with that she scurries inside but doesn't close the door. I point inside and nod my head in a, 'let's go in' mime and hope Will gets the message.

He does and we both go in closing the door firmly behind us.

'What the actual fuck, three bastard holidays and no jobs. What an absolute piss-take and don't even get me started on the door being open all night or the skin cancer they're going to let her get. Un-fucking believable.' I am livid but trying to keep a lid on my volume as I don't want next door to hear

'She might be lying about all the holidays Han, she's only a kid,' Will the voice of reason counters.

'Bollocks, have you seen how brown she is? You don't get that from an English school playground, so either they dipped her in wood stain before they came or she's telling the bloody truth. I knew they were no-good scroungers when I first clapped eyes on them.'

Will knows better than to try and stick up for them

'And to add insult to pissing injury we can't even sit on the balcony we paid extra to have because the tight bastard next door would rather have his step-daughter kidnapped and/or attacked by a million mozzies than pay for air con. Yet the knob head will pay for half a dozen holidays a year. What a cock.'

The mood totally ruined, Will downs his glass of wine and turns in. Being too wound up to sleep I stay to finish the wine and text Nicky who I know will be as outraged as I at the inhabitants next door.

***

The next morning I wake up feeling pretty rested, even though I stayed up longer than Will, it was before 10.30pm when I called it a night so I've had more sleep that I do when I'm at home. Today we have boating planned, so Will is in good spirits

'You all ready, Captain Pugwash?' I joke.

'It's Popeye actually, so off you go Olive and find me some spinach.' There is nothing that makes him happier than playing Captain. We talk about owning a boat whenever we're on holiday. The trouble is we live well over an hour from the nearest water and have no room for a boat at our house so it is merely a pipe dream.

I have to admit that although it's more his thing than mine I do love it when we go out on the water. I get a bit worried when we can't see any land at all but there is something glorious about being surrounded by only water and fish. The only downside is the lack of toilet. Drinking a gallon of water and being surrounded by gallons of water has a detrimental effect on my bladder. We never stop the boat and get in the water so there is no opportunity to relieve myself. I guess as I get older and definitely after I've had kids it will be harder to contain it. Willow has often said that she only has to clear her throat and she pisses herself.

As we have booked the boat for only a couple of hours we take bottles of water but no other food or refreshments. I did consider bringing a bottle of wine and a couple of glasses, but Will was concerned about the sea Police, so we opted to leave them behind. This was probably a good idea as the boat is tiny and resembles a tin can, the canopy looks like it might disintegrate any moment. I think Will was hoping for a James Bond-style speedboat but it looks more suited to Popeye.

We listen to the briefing which tells us where we can and can't go and what to look out for as we motor through the water. As long as there are no sharks or icebergs we should be all good. Will heads off in what he says is a North Easterly direction, to me it just looks like he turns the boat to the right but I know not to argue with him when he's in Captain mode, and in any event I was totally shit at geography so have no sense of direction.

There are a few other vessels about, pedalo's, jet skis and the like. I find it so weird that we slack holiday makers are let loose with all manner of modes of sea transport without so much as a single lesson provided we have a form of ID and 100 euros refundable deposit. I'm pretty sure the boat we're in and all of the jet skis are worth more than that and if I survived an accident which totalled a hired boat I think I would be more than happy with losing a few quid so I'm not really sure what the incentive is to return them in one piece (other than valuing one's own life I mean).

We've barely been out on the water for half an hour when the discussion turns inevitably to, 'when we have a boat'. It always follows the same pattern but I indulge Will as I quite like the sound of his dream.

'If we moved a bit nearer to the water we could own one of these you know and be out every weekend just cruising around the coast.' I've heard the same thing a million times before.

'Yeah but we don't exactly have the weather for it do we so it wouldn't exactly be like this would it.' I've said the same thing a million times before.

'It only needs to be calm though, it's not like it needs to be eighty degrees every weekend. We just wouldn't go out when it was too windy.' I wonder how windy too windy is but I don't ask as I want to stay awake.

'Ok but where would we move to? Would we move to the coast and get something to go out on the sea with or just move to where there is a big lake and get something smaller?' We have a lake ten minutes from where we live but it's tiny and I've never seen any boats on it so I'm thinking a much bigger lake, Windermere perhaps.

'No, I think it would have to be the sea then we can get something bigger that we can stay out all day on.' I enjoy our two hour a year boating expeditions but I'm not sure I'd enjoy a full day every weekend one, it does get boring after a while. Once you've seen the open sea…

'But what about when we have kids, they're not going to want to spend all day bobbing about, especially when they're little. They might wind up in the sea.' I am thinking about the last time Willow went abroad. They thought it would be fun to take the kids on one of those glass bottomed boats so they could see the fish. Unfortunately, one of them was absolutely petrified at the sight of the fish and spent the whole trip screaming and trying to throw herself over board and the other one was violently seasick.

'They'd be fine, the younger they start the more used to it they will be.' Did he just say they, twice? I can't let this go. We have talked about having kids, well we've touched on it enough to know that at some point we would both like to have one but that was one, not they which implies more than.

'What do you mean *they*? You said *they'd* get used to it?' I ask.

'Just a figure of speech I guess and nicer than saying *it.*'

I'd still like more clarity now that we're on the subject. We don't talk about it often enough and the more I think about it with how shit work is the more I like the idea of a year off.

'Oh, but do you think you would like *they* rather than *it*?' I press

'Yeah, I reckon I would. I don't want a football team full or anything but I think a couple would be nice, don't you?' I think about it for a few minutes.

'Maybe, but neither of us have any brothers or sisters so I guess I always thought we'd just have one as well.'

The more I think about it the more I think having at least two could be fun. I had a great upbringing but often times I was lonely and wanted someone to play with. My parents were dead against a sibling though and as I got older and pressed more they would joke that I was the reason I was an only child. At least I think they were joking. Will's parents desperately wanted him to have a brother or sister but after three miscarriages his mum couldn't cope with the emotional anguish and gave up trying. She dotes on Will (a little too much) and is desperate for grandchildren so she would be thrilled if we had several.

'Have you thought about when you might want to have them then?' I emphasise the *them* part.

'I don't know, it would be nice to have them fairly close together so we don't get too old to have number two and there is a small enough gap between them that they can be mates.' He seems to have given this far more thought that he's ever let on.

'Well maybe we should get cracking this afternoon then.' I joke.

'At least let's wait until we're home, no more drinking if you're with child.' I have no idea whether he is being serious or not and now I am absolutely dying for a wee so can no longer concentrate enough to continue such a serious conversation.

'I really need the loo.' I say, crossing my legs.

'Are you serious? You went just before we got on board and it's been less than an hour. You're going to be crossing your legs a long time.' Will scolds, as If I am a child.

'Well I can't wait that long, we'll have to go back now.' I've added a little bounce to my crossed legs stance.

'We've been heading in the same direction since we set off, Han, which means in order to get back we have to go in the opposite direction for the same amount of time. So you can hang on the extra half an hour. I'm not wasting money.' His attitude is not helping my situation.

'Will, if I don't get to a toilet now I am going to wet myself and I'm not joking.' I scream.

'What the hell do you want me to do? There's no toilet on here so you're going to have to get into the sea. I'll stop, there's no one around.' He has got to be kidding me and I tell him so.

'Get lost. I am not jumping into the sea, you don't know what's lurking in there and I'm not risking getting eaten by something so you'll have to think of something else.' Will is exasperated. He looks around the boat.

'Fine, I'll hold you.'

'What do you mean you'll hold me?' I ask, envisioning him holding my arse over the side of the boat like my dad used to do with me at the side of motorways whenever we went on a family jaunt. I could never pee straight and always ended up with it down my leg.

'You can crouch on the ladders at the back and I'll hold your hands so you don't fall off then you can pee straight into the sea. If it's good enough for the fish…' I think about it for a few seconds and decide I'd rather pee in the sea than in my pants.

'Ok, let me take my bottoms off.' I look around to make sure there is no one close to us, I don't want to see my white arse being shared around Facebook anytime soon. I take off my bottoms and stand on the ladder. I walk down a couple of rungs so I'm half a meter or so from the surface of the water. 'Now what do I do?' I ask, starting to panic a little.

'Give me your hands and then you can stick your backside right out and not piss on your feet.' Will moves towards me.

'What if you let go and I fall into the sea?' I ask, my grip firmly on the ladder.

'Han, I'm not going to let go. I'm not going to look either as frankly the sight of my wife pissing into the sea isn't exactly a turn on.'

Will grabs my hands. The indignity of the situation is not lost on me but rather this than pissy pants. I go for it. Oh the relief, and the freedom. Will might be grossed out but my bladder is happy and empty. There is the small issue of no tissue paper to contend with. I shake my backside as hard as I can while Will shakes his head in disgust. I climb back up and try and attempt to salvage some modesty by covering myself up.

'It's a good job I love you,' he says.

CHAPTER 20

We're still laughing about me being caught short while debating whether or not it's safe to sit on our balcony and enjoy the sunset. I swear I heard the neighbours go out but Will is not convinced.

'You go out there and try and look over into their window. If it's open they're in, if it's not they're out,' I say, not keen to be accosted by Sarah again. Ironically, although they are quite happy to have their window open all night at the risk of their daughter being kidnapped they have it closed all day as heaven forbid someone should get in and steal their phone chargers.

Will creeps out onto the balcony then gives me the thumbs up. I follow with our drinks. We're switching our routine to drinks first then dinner and bar later with strictly no balcony sitting.

'What did Nicky have to say last night?' I am surprised Will knows I called her, I'm sure I never mentioned it.

'How do you know I spoke to her?'

'I heard you. My head had barely hit the pillow before you were facetiming.' In my head he'd been in bed ages, I must have drunk more than I thought

'Oh right, not much really.'

We have only been gone a couple of days. I did ask if she'd been in touch with Willow and she said they met up for drinks. No one has seen anything of Charlotte though. It's not that I expected anyone to have been in touch with her in the short time we've been away but it would be nice to know she's ok.

'I might message Charlotte's mum just to check on her,' I say out loud.

'Is that wise while we're away? If she hasn't you're going to be upset and it will ruin what's left of the week.' Will says.

'I know, but if I find out it will put my mind at ease so I can fully relax,' I reason.

'I suppose. I'll support whatever you want to do,' he says squeezing my knee.

I have been thinking about Charlotte more today than I did yesterday or the day before. It's the not knowing what's happening that's getting to me. At least if she was at work I could ask Willow to keep me informed but with her no longer working there's no way of knowing what's going on with her. I wonder whether he has confiscated her phone now that she isn't leaving his sight. He must go out to work during the day and I can't imagine he would allow her to not be contactable to him 24/7. I have no doubt he checks it to see who she has been in contact with but she could reply then delete the messages so he doesn't see them, that's what I'd do.

I messaged her mum and wished I hadn't. She said she hadn't seen Charlotte but had a message from her saying she was fine and to stop fussing otherwise she won't message anymore. Stop fussing?? The woman is worried out of her mind and Charlotte's cold messages are doing nothing to alleviate her fears. I reply in as upbeat a way as possible but I know that when she reads it she won't believe a word. She knows full well that I am as worried as her.

Almost as soon as the sun had set Will went to bed. He is fast asleep and I am wide awake, my mind in overdrive torturing myself with what ifs. I choose to torture myself further by turning to Dr Google and asking him things like, 'what are the signs of domestic violence' and, 'how can I help someone who is being abused by their partner'. A list of warning signs pops up after my first search telling me that (among other things) warnings signs to look for are having low self-esteem and a drug/alcohol abuse problem.

I know she doesn't have a substance abuse problem so I rack my brains for any evidence of low self-esteem but I can't recall thinking she had an issue with it, even when Julian started dressing her she seemed happy, excited about it even, acting like she was some designers muse and I never felt that she was allowing it because she didn't feel capable of dressing herself. I read on dismissing other signs such as talking about suicide and start to wonder whether I have fabricated the whole thing and in fact Charlotte is happy, in love and just evolving as a woman. Perhaps she's chosen to change to be the kind of person Julian wants her to be and there is nothing sinister in it?

I read on and stop abruptly when I reach a list of 'other' signs. I read the list slowly shaking my head, I read it again and then again and any hope I had that my instincts were wrong have vanished. I am reading Charlotte's life: wearing make up to hide bruises, being isolated from friends, having to ask permission to do things with people, partner deciding what she wears, the list goes on. I sit stunned. I feel worse than I did when I first spoke to Jean and again I am faced with the stark reality that Charlotte is being abused. I have only re-affirmed what my heart already knew and yet it feels so raw. So raw and so real.

I have never known anything but loving relationships, my parents, my grandparents, my married friends, myself. Happy marriages, equal partnerships, strong women. Is that the key? I have only ever known strong women who wouldn't allow such a thing to happen to them? I chastise myself for thinking such a thing. Charlotte was a strong women, IS a strong women. In my wildest, darkest dreams I would never have imagined her to be in this situation. No one would. She had so many friends, she was gregarious, the life and soul of the party. If it can happen to her it can happen to anyone. I look at my watch, it's 11pm back home so it's too late to ring Willow and what would I tell her anyway? 'Hey you know how we think Charlotte is being abused, well she definitely is because Google says so.' She'd think I was crazy.

I put my phone down and lie on the bed, silently crying myself to sleep.

***

Our last few days are spent sunbathing, eating, drinking and avoiding the neighbours. I don't feel much like sight-seeing anymore and Will is quite happy to spend his days swimming in the sea while I pretend to read a book. He knows something has changed but I don't want it to be on his mind for the rest of the week so choose to keep it from him and he doesn't pry, just says his ears are always open. This almost has me in tears. He is trying to live up to the promise he made at the start of the week to be better but I feel so vulnerable that

I think the no nonsense Will would be more beneficial to me right now.

I called Willow when I'd had time to digest everything, she was gentle in her response but pretty much said what I thought she would, that it wasn't really a surprise but that she could understand why seeing it in black and white, even from Dr Google had shocked me. We chatted briefly and agreed to meet up when I got back. She told me to enjoy the rest of the week and I know I should, if only for Will's sake but the guilt has started to eat away at me, and I have barely slept at all the last two nights. I feel guilty for smiling, laughing, having a nice husband, being able to choose which bikini I wear. I know it's irrational when I have done nothing wrong yet no matter how I try to bury it I can't change the way I feel.

'All packed and ready to go?' Will has been packing since yesterday so if we weren't, I'd be concerned, but I smile and reply nicely, 'yep, time to get back to reality.'

I regret the words as soon as they leave my lips, for I am a prisoner of reality and have been ever since I made the foolish decision to ask a search engine for help. A reality that poisons my mind and threatens my sanity. A reality that isn't mine yet I can't escape from. Isn't that what people usually use their minds for, to escape from reality? If that's the case why does my mind insist on trapping me there, in reality? I want to close my eyes and forget all that I know, think good thoughts, feel happy and alive. Instead I close my eyes and imagine how Charlotte may be, alone, fragile and with fear in her eyes as he bears down on her with hate in his? The image haunts me and I don't know how to stop it.

'Right, let's get on the bus then.' Will's voice jolts me from my thoughts. I nod, smile and follow him, grateful for the moment's distraction. I find myself hoping he wants to talk, lots. Talk about anything and everything that means I have to think about something else and for just a short while be free of my thoughts.

Thankfully Will is in a chatty mood and we resume our conversation about children, specifically when we might have them. I'm on the pill which can easily be stopped so it's just a matter of timing.

'Yeah but there's never really a right time to have children is there?' Will surprises me with his philosophy.

'Where the hell have you heard that, because I know you didn't just make it up?!'

'Everyone who has kids says it don't they, it's true though. If you think about it, there's always a reason why not to, not saved up enough, house not big enough, not the right time to be off work, not spent enough time travelling. If you actually did all of those things and had all the ducks lined up you'd be retired before you had one.' He's got a point.

'Maybe that's why there are really old people like them in India who don't have a kid until they're seventy, they've just been waiting for the right time,' I say.

'Exactly, and then they're too old to do anything and too arthritic to kick a football about.' Will adds.

'Not really a problem this day and age though is it that, not being able to kick a football about. Kids would rather play FIFA on the X Box than kick an actual football so the oldies can join in.'

'Not with arthritic thumbs they can't.' Will does an impression of an arthritic thumb that has us both in stitches.

'Ok, back to the first question then, when?'

I don't know why I'm wanting Will to make the decision. The more I think about it the more excited I feel. I've got a lot going on at the minute and a baby might just be the distraction I need. Not that a baby should be used as a distraction but I think we're ready. We've been together and married long enough and although Will wanted to renovate the house before we started a family, but we never have enough money to do it. If we wait until we do we'll both be forty.

'Why don't you just come off the pill and we'll see what happens.' That takes me by surprise as it sounds more like a statement than a question. I thought he would say next year.

'But what about work and everything?' I ask.

'What about it? You hate work so I would have thought you'd be jumping at the chance to have a few weeks off,' he replies.

'A few weeks, you can piss off. If I'm going to be pushing a watermelon through a pinhole I'm having at least a year off.' The chances of me getting a year off are slim to none but I have nothing to lose by aiming high.

'A pin hole? More like a bleeding black hole and you can have six months off.'

I hit him for the black hole comment and say, 'nine months and you've got yourself a deal.' He ponders.

'Deal!'

We shake hands and exchange grins.

CHAPTER 21

We've only been home a few hours and the holiday blues have settled in. The laundry basket is overflowing and toiletries are scattered over our bed. It would take about six minutes to put them away but I just can't face it. I've sent Will out to get essentials which I'm hoping includes at least one bottle of wine and when he gets back, we'll order a curry. I don't know why it is that when I've been away on a foreign jaunt I don't return craving fish and chips or pie and mash but Indian or Chinese food? I have given it some thought and can't recall a single time we have landed and headed straight to the chippy. I wonder if it's because in all European destinations the accompanying staple of every main meal is chips and so having consumed at least 15kg of spuds over a seven-day period my stomach simply can't face any more?

I've told Will that after today I'm back on the healthy eating wagon as I'm 'sick of food'. I'm certain I only ate three meals a day whilst we were away which is exactly how many I would have eaten at home so why is it I look and feel as though I've eaten a mountain more?

There are so many people who claim not to be hungry when it's hot and I am not one of them. I'm thinking about lunch while eating breakfast and thinking about dinner before I've ordered lunch. All the sweating has me working up an enormous appetite. So, as of tomorrow, it's back to salad, veg, chicken and no alcohol until Friday.

I may have just hit on the reason for holiday blues. It's not the lack of sunshine or the abundance of washing, it's the severe restriction of food and alcohol. A drop in blood sugar must trigger a drop in mood. Perhaps I'll take it easy on the restriction and just cut out one thing every couple of days instead of going cold turkey. Yes, that's a far more sensible option. I'm feeling better already knowing I'll still be eating shit and drinking myself into oblivion for at least the next few days.

I've invited Nicky over for Sunday lunch and convinced Will to go for a pint with James afterwards so that I can fill her in on our baby chat. I should probably just keep it to myself as if things don't happen quickly and we start stressing I'll have the added stress of having to say every month, 'no not yet', but I'm excited and petrified all at the same time so need to tell someone else or I'll burst. I hope she'll be happy for us, she dotes on the devil child so I know she loves kids but sometimes, for several reasons, kids can change a friendship and not for the better.

Willow has a friend a few years older than her who doesn't have kids and who, according to Willow, for no reason whatsoever just stopped inviting her to stuff as soon as she had a baby. Her friend never asked her over for dinner or out for drinks with the girls and Willow has never broached the subject with her. She still sees her periodically and the friend always buys her kids birthdays and Christmas presents but they don't socialise anymore. Willow said her friend made the assumption totally of her own volition that mothers couldn't or shouldn't want to have fun anymore and should spend every waking hour with their little darlings. I might need to make it clear to Nicky over the Yorkshire puds today that I won't be accepting any such change.

Wow, that sounds really weird, me a mum! My mum is a mum, I'm a child. I don't feel any older than I did when I was a teenager. I look at other people my age and they seem so grown up compared to me. Maybe they just have more of their shit together or dress better. I'm not very sophisticated when it comes to dressing. I can dress up for a night out with the best of them but for everyday wear even for work I prefer a casual look. I like the thought of wearing the sexy skirt suit for work or nice pants and shirt combo for the weekend but all of that shit costs so much more than a Prim ani top and a pair of Hollister jeans.

I have fattened Nicky up and re-filled her empty glass. Will and James have been banished to the pub (we girls would have gone but Sunday pub drinking can get depressing when you realise you have work the next day so I'd rather be comfy in my own surroundings). I'm trying to start the baby conversation but I'm struggling with getting the words out and now Nicky has asked about Charlotte. I purposely refrained from mentioning her name at the dinner table as I didn't want to put a damper on our holiday chat but I can't avoid the question now.

'I've not heard anything from her and nor has her mum really, save for a couple of very brief texts.' I answer, hoping that will be the end of it.

'Oh, and how do you feel about that? Willow told me about you consulting Dr Google. That's never a good idea, I thought I'd taught you better.'

Great, Willow and her big mouth. I don't want to play it down because that wouldn't be right and yet I don't necessarily want to get into it all now. I'm trying to focus on something positive and if we talk about Charlotte and the hell she's in I can hardly end it on a high note with, 'oh by the way I'm planning to get up the duff.'

'I'd had a bit too much to drink and made the mistake of contacting her mum so it snowballed from there. I've processed it all now and Willow was right, It didn't tell me anything I didn't already know and it certainly didn't give me a better clue on how to deal with it so for now I am accepting that Charlotte doesn't want to admit what is happening to her.. I told her I'm here whenever she needs me so I'm leaving it at that.' I sound so convincing when I feel anything but.

'That's a healthy attitude. I know how much it's hurting you but trust me, if you hound her you will push her further away and she will never turn to you. Her mum is going to be the first to know if anything changes so she'll tell you what's happening.'

I worry what might happen if Charlotte finds out I'm in touch with her mum. Will she think I'm spying and cut me off completely, getting her mum to do the same? I'll call Jean at some point and ask her to keep the fact we communicate to herself so as not to cause any problems. Content that conversation is over I take a deep breath and dive straight in.

'So, we're having a baby!' I blurt it out then realise it doesn't sound as I intended.

'What the …? Omigod! Really? When? I can't believe it, how exciting. Eeek… but you've been drinking all day. Shit. Put that glass down, you don't know what damage you're causing.' Nicky snatches the glass from my hand. I snatch it back.

'Hold your horses, my fault. I meant to say that we've decided we're going to have a baby, I'm not actually preggo just yet.'

'Thank God for that.'

Not the reaction I was expecting.

'Sorry, I mean thank God you're not expecting when you've been drinking. But, oh wow, this is a revelation. Who, what, why, how did this come about? You were only gone a week!' She seems genuinely excited and interested and I relax a little

'I know, it must have been the combination of sun, sea air and wine. We got to chatting one night and to my surprise, well shock, Will said he was ready to get on with it now. It was pretty clear that he'd been giving it quite a bit of thought and he'd come to the conclusion that waiting until we could afford it would be the equivalent of waiting for the twelfth of never so now was as good a time as any. I finish this month's pills and then I am a contraception-free zone.'

Nicky is grinning from ear to ear. She reaches over and gives me a massive hug. 'Well I thought I was the one with the news today,' she says cryptically.

'What, you're not pregnant are you?' I ask excitement building at the thought of being pregnant at the same time as my best friend. We'd be able to go to the coffee shop every day and be exercise buddies so that at least under our sick-stained, creased clothes we'd have something our fellas might want to look at. Ooh and we wouldn't have to avoid baby classes just to avoid meeting new people who delighted in telling everyone how much better at the whole mum thing they are than everyone else (us). Bleurgh, no thank you.

'Am I hell! We're getting married!' Nicky's face has literally lit up. I instinctively look down at her hand but see it is ring free. She sees me.

'It was too big so it's being altered. I have a picture of it though, here look.' Nicky thrusts her phone at me and I see the most beautiful, brilliantly dazzling, round diamond I have ever seen. It's set in a platinum band with tiny diamonds down each arm.

'Oh, wow Nik, it's the most beautiful ring I've ever seen!' Now it's my turn to do the hugging.

'I know, I can't stop looking at it. I can't wait to get it back. It's even prettier in actual life. I never even thought we'd get married. He has never even mentioned it before and then out of the blue last weekend he hits me with it. For the first time in my whole life I was speechless.' For Nicky that is a pretty big thing.

'I can't believe you've kept it from me for a whole week. Why didn't you tell me?' Some good news on holiday would have been welcome.

'I didn't want to impose on your holiday and after what you've just told me about baby news, I'm glad I didn't'.

Oh shit. What if I'm pregnant when she gets married, I'll be the fat Bridesmaid. There's always one and I never thought it would be me.

'So when is the big date then?' I ask. 'Do I need to put baby plans on hold? I'm not being the fat bridesmaid. Assuming you were going to ask me, of course. Actually, whether you ask me or not I'm being one, so when is it?'

Nicky laughs. 'You would never be a fat anything and don't panic, it isn't going to be until the end of next year so you've got at least eighteen months to get pregnant, give birth then lose all of your baby fat.'

I give her a shove. 'No pressure then.' I say it in a jokey way but secretly I mean it. What if I don't get pregnant right away and it takes us a year and I put on loads of weight so I can't lose it in time.

My mind is in turmoil. Right, Hannah, have a word with yourself. Your best friend has just given you some totally amazing news. This is not about you right now, so focus. Ok I am back in the room.

'What did the fam say? I bet devil child is super excited, isn't she? A fancy frock so she can look like a Princess as well as acting like one.' This sounds mean but Nicky knows I mean it in good humour.

'Ha-ha yes she is, but when I rang and told her she said she had hoped I was going to find a richer boyfriend than James, who could buy her a horse and take her horse riding. She's such a brat.' I don't argue with that.

'So why so long away, don't you older brides usually go for sooner rather than later weddings?' It's true. Every other person over thirty that I have known get married announces their engagement then walks down the aisle within six months. It's like, 'we've got him we're keeping him so let's get this shit over with.'

'We want to move house first. Our house isn't really our house, is it? It's my house, so we want to have our house first. We're going to have a painting party in a few weeks and get it on the market so make sure you're available. Alcohol will be provided for unfertilised folk.'

CHAPTER 22

After all the excitement of the weekend, work is an even more daunting prospect. I am not relishing the idea of seeing B at all. Turning up an hour earlier than usual wasn't one of my best ideas either. I wanted to get some extra time so I could feel comfortable with being back before everyone else showed up. I don't feel very comfortable. I consciously refrained from checking any emails while I was away and had every intention of going through some at the weekend but I simply could not face it. I'm glad I didn't.

While I have been away Emma has been handed one of my campaigns (the one she was incapable of dealing with the first time of trying) on the basis that, 'the client needed someone who was always available, putting their needs before their own.' It seems that taking five days of the twenty-five days holiday I am entitled to each year means I am not that person. Never mind the fact I haven't used any other holiday entitlement this year, or for the last nine months or so for that matter means they owe me days in lieu. I should have known that holiday entitlement didn't actually mean you were entitled to take them. How silly of me. I have a good mind to throw a sickie and head home. No one would even know I'd been in.

Just as I'm giving serious consideration to that option I hear familiar footsteps behind me. The unmistakable sound of B. Perhaps if I don't look at her she won't notice I'm here. I try to make myself as invisible as possible. Had I been quicker I could have pretended to take a call but it would look too obvious now and in any event that would only prolong the agony. She's going to want to rub my nose in it at some time so I may as well get it over with.

I clear my throat and look to the side of me.

'Morning,' I squeak.

B looks in my direction and does a double take as though she wasn't expecting me and isn't quite sure what I'm doing here.

'Oh, it's you. Feeling better I take it?' It's a statement and not a question.

Feeling better? I haven't been ill.

'I wasn't ill, I was on leave,' I say, with as much authority as I can muster. The derision in her eyes is clear for all to see, unfortunately the only person seeing it is me.

'On leave? Well that's news to me. I don't expect leave to be taken during our busiest period so I assumed you must be sick. It doesn't really matter why you were absent. The fact is that your absence put us in a tricky spot with clients who were expecting you to be readily available. In order to appease the situation I had to give them a new executive who could guarantee their fullest attention at all times. You have an e-mail.' And with that she walks away and sits at her desk.

Didn't know I was on leave? Is she on fucking drugs or something? We can't take leave without it being authorised by her and what the hell is she on about 'busiest time'? This time of year is our quietest time, has been for the whole time I have been here, which is why I knew she would authorise it with only a couple of months' notice when usually she claims she needs a minimum of three months, despite the one month it says in my contract. She is so full of shit her eyes are brown. She's got some knob in a suit making demands so rather than stand up to them she throws me under the bus and gives my account away. An account I gave blood, sweat and tears for, metaphorically speaking. I should never have come back. I should have stayed in Skiathos forever.

I message Will. 'Bollocks to finishing that pack of pills. As of today I am no longer taking anything. Let's get this baby shit going xx.'

He replies immediately, 'Good first day back then?'

He knows me too well. I am serious though. This is my get out of jail card, leave the bitch in the lurch and get paid to sit at home while all the other mugs spend their days sucking up to her miserable face in the hope she'll throw them a bone. It's a no brainer. BTW I don't include Willow in the suckers category, she isn't trying to climb any ladder here and certainly does not want one of B's mangy bones. She gets to do the hours/days she wants, gets paid a decent wage for doing them and doesn't give the place a second thought when she finishes for the day.

Common sense tells me I ought to consult my favourite internet Dr before being too hasty. There might be side effects or disastrous consequences to getting pregnant so close to stopping the pill. I should be going through the rest of my e-mails or the pile of folders on my desk but this is more important. I type 'should I have a break between stopping the pill and getting pregnant' I choose the first result that comes up and get the answer I want. Nope. No need to wait at all. You can wait until you've had one natural period as it makes it easier to try and work out when you're fertile and to date the conception, but no harm to the baby so it's game on.

Tonight we try!

***

It seems trying isn't working! We have officially been 'trying' for six weeks and nothing is happening. How do those poor women do this month after month, year after year? I would be a nervous wreck. I have spent about fifty quid on tests believing the more expensive will be accurate and every single one has said 'not pregnant'. I have been sounding off to Willow on account of the fact she has two children so would get how I felt. She's less sympathetic than I was hoping for.

'Mate that's no time at all, the average time is a year. Only a few people get pregnant straight away, you know.'

'But we have literally been doing it like four times a week which is about four times more than usual and still nothing,' I am so frustrated. Our usual once a week has quadrupled (much to Will's delight) so I had hoped our odds were better than a year!

'Yes but there are only two or three days a month when it is even possible to get pregnant so unless you're doing it on those days it doesn't matter how many times a week you do it. Have you tried to work out when you're fertile?' Willow has turned all statistician on me.

'Eh, I didn't know I had to or know you could, I don't think anyway,' I say, feeling stupid.

'Well you can, and you should, ask your favourite doctor and she'll help you figure it out. Interestingly, I figured it out from my discharge.'

I wince and put a hand over my mouth like I'm trying to prevent myself from vomiting everywhere.

'Yeah I know, TMI, but honestly look it up. Worked for me, both times!'

It can't hurt, I suppose. Having some clue about how and when it is likely to happen would be preferable to keep trying and failing. It is abundantly clear that I have no clue currently.

'Ok, I'll get right onto it after lunch then and make a little chart.' I like planning so this is right up my street.

'Well, don't take it that far. If you get caught up in plotting and planning you'll be obsessed before you know it and then *it* won't happen because you're so stressed about it.' God, work this out but don't work that out, spend time doing this but not too much time. It's so confusing.

'How the hell do teenage girls manage to get pregnant their very first time having sex and how come so many one night stands lead to pregnancies when it's so damn difficult to get pregnant?' I ask.

'I don't know but I guess if someone has four one-night stands in a month it's possible one of them could do the trick. As for teenagers, I've no idea. Maybe they're extra fertile.'

'I'll google that as well then.'

Armed with a wealth of the internet's finest tips on maximising the chances of conception I set about making a chart. In my head. When I mentioned our conversation to Will a dark look crept over his face and I could tell he wasn't exactly keen on turning our baby-making efforts into a pie chart. I assured him that wasn't what I had in mind and that I wasn't going to base when we did it around my body temperature but secretly that's exactly what I have in mind. I worked out that this month I should be at my most fertile at the end of the week and so I am hoping to keep him at bay at bedtime for the time being. It's exhausting trying to seem interested every night when all I want to do is sleep, untouched.

I'm not going to scare him by telling him the exact days – Thursday to Saturday. I'm merely going to mention that I am very tired tonight and over the next few nights and if he gets suspicious and starts questioning me about charts I shall simply say I have not made a chart (scout's honour) but that from my discharge last month I think it will be 'sometime' next week. Hopefully he will be so grossed out that he won't ask another thing but he won't be so grossed out that he doesn't want to touch me as that would defeat the whole purpose.

Now that both Nicky and Willow know our plans I am desperate for Charlotte to know too. Contact has been non-existent though and it isn't really something I want to say in a text. She is apparently a lady of leisure now so it would be safe to assume she has lots of time on her hands to see friends and socialise and yet no one has seen a thing of her. Not even her mum. I know how excited she would be if I had given her this news six months ago, she would have been straight to Next buying baby clothes. Now though, I don't think she'd give a shit or at least she would act like she didn't and that makes me beyond sad.

CHAPTER 23

We have Nicky's engagement do this weekend, which might put a spanner in the Thursday-Saturday plan. I think alcohol has a weird effect on sperm or something. I'll do further research, although it won't make a difference as Will won't spend the night tea total even if it reduces our chances.

There wasn't going to be a party but I talked her into it, James didn't take much talking to as he quite liked the idea of getting lot of presents to fill their new house. Theirs (Nicky's) sold to first-time buyers within a couple of weeks of going up for sale, which is pretty impressive. You could still smell the fresh paint! The buyers are happy to wait to move which is a good thing as Nicky has yet to find anything she likes. They have looked at approximately seventy-two places and they've all had something not quite right with them. Fingers crossed that one of the three they are seeing this weekend is 'the one'. Even I don't know what she wants as I'm sure she changes one of her very important criteria every time I speak to her. In reality I don't think she is quite used to the idea of leaving her very first home. I did dare to suggest that may be the reason she was struggling recently but she bit my head off and said that was a stupid thing to say as, if she didn't want to leave it why had she agreed to sell it. I got the impression I'd touched a nerve so have said no more about it.

The do is at a local pub with a function room. They've invited around fifty people, most of whom I know so I am looking forward to a good night. Charlotte was invited but declined claiming she had something else on. It's been over two months since I last heard from her. I hear from Jean at least once a week so know nothing has changed. Charlotte is still keeping in minimal contact and making no effort to instigate. She sporadically replies to texts but never sends any and hasn't called her family in forever.

Her parents have had their work cut out preventing her brother from getting involved. He is younger than her and hot headed and, like me, just wants to fix it. They tried to keep it from him but he got suspicious when he realised he hadn't seen or heard from Charlotte for weeks. Jean took the blame and said that she and Charlotte had had words and that was why she wasn't getting in touch but either she isn't a very good liar or he is just smarter than he looks and he refused to accept what he was being told. She had no choice but to tell him the truth. He did not take it well and in the end she threatened to call the Police on him if he went over to Julian's house. Things have been tense for her to say the least.

It's a pretty good party, Willow has only just arrived and is clutching two presents. It turns out Charlotte delivered one to her house and asked her to pass it on to Nicky with her apologies. She didn't turn up on the doorstep in person, she had it couriered there and when Willow called to ask her about it she claimed she was ill and didn't know Nicky's address to send it direct. The thing is, Nicky is my friend, well she is Willow and Charlotte's friend now also but that's only as a result of them being my friends and meeting Nicky through me, so if she was going to ask anyone to pass on a present I would expect her to ask me to do it. She knows where I live. I voice this to Willow.

'I thought it was odd but I didn't want to make an awkward conversation even more awkward by asking her why she hadn't sent it to you.' she explains.

'Fair enough, let's get drunk then.' I say.

'Steady on there you, I thought you were baby making.' She eyes me suspiciously.

'Not until next weekend I'm not.' I give her a wink and drag her to the bar. Everyone is in good spirits; the DJ is not half bad either. He's spinning some decent tracks so we hit the dance floor. I have no idea where our men have got to but as dancing isn't really Will's thing I don't bother searching for him. Cheryl Cole's/Fernandez-Versini's/just Cheryl's Fight for this Love comes on and the three of us bust out our best hand clenching/ boxing moves.

I spot Will on the other side of the room. He catches my eye and shakes his head in mock disgust. 'Have you seen him?' I try and shout above the music. 'He loves watching me doing a bit of twerking really.' They laugh and we exaggerate our choreography for Will's benefit. The song finishes and is followed by some shitty house track. I drag them both in the direction of the toilets.

After re-applying lipstick and adjusting strands of hair I look at my phone, 'oh shit!' I say out loud.

'What's up?' Willow and Nicky are both preening themselves in the mirror and I have no idea who asked the question.

'I've had three missed calls from Jean, Charlotte's mum. Oh Christ, and a text.' This cannot be good, and my blood runs cold as I read what she's written. 'She's asked me to call as soon as I can because Charlotte's in hospital.'

My legs give way beneath me. Willow grabs me by the elbow and steadies me.

'Ok, let's not panic. Let's go outside where it's quiet and we'll call her, ok?'

I nod but I don't think I really heard what she said. Hospital? Nicky and Willow hold an arm each as they steer us through the crowd and outside. My mouth has gone dry and my heart is thumping.

'I don't think I can ring her, my hands are shaking.' I say as we get out onto the pavement.

'Do you want me to do it?'

I'm handing over my phone before Willow has finished the sentence. It seems to take forever for her to start speaking, she tells whoever answers who she is and why she is ringing instead of me. Time stands still as I process the side of the conversation I can hear, broken arm, cracked ribs, stairs, fall, ambulance. Has she fallen down the stairs, has she been pushed? How did she get to hospital? Which hospital is she in? Can we go see her? Willow hangs up.

'Well?' Nicky speaks before I am able.

'She's fine, that's the main thing,' Willow starts. 'She claims she was carrying something down the stairs and she missed her footing and fell. Julian found her when he got home from work and called an ambulance. She's at North Shore and will be there overnight but should be out in a day or two. She's got a badly broken arm which they've pinned and a couple of cracked ribs.' Willow's voice fades. I find mine.

'Wait a minute. You said he found her when he came home and called the ambulance. Why didn't she call the ambulance herself?

241

You didn't say she was knocked out, even with a badly broken arm she should have been able to get to a phone. How long was she lying there? Has anyone called the police, is anyone asking more questions?'

I can feel the anger building. 'He's pushed her, hasn't he? Pushed her or beat her and he hasn't called an ambulance straight away because he didn't want anyone to know. Then when he's realised how bad her arm is he's made up a story. I'm right, aren't I? You're thinking the same thing, aren't you? Well, aren't you?' I am practically screaming now and I am aware of passers-by staring at us.

Willow looks from me to Nicky and back again. She shrugs.

'Right, I'm getting a taxi and I'm going to see her.' I look around for one.

'I don't think that's very wise, Han. Not when you've been drinking. He'll be there and you're not going to be able to keep your cool.' Nicky is looking straight at me.

'Damn right I won't be able to keep my cool, I'm going to stab the son of a bitch. See how he likes it.' I mean every word.

'And how will that help Charlotte, you being banged up?' Willow has waded in as voice of reason number two.

'It won't, but it will make me feel a hell of a lot better. So are you coming with me or not?' I'm asking both of them and neither of them at the same time.

'No,' they chorus.

'Fine, I'll go by myself then.' I turn on my heel and start to walk away but Nicky grabs me by the arm.

'It's really not a good idea, Han. You're going to cause more trouble for Charlotte and trouble for yourself. You need to leave it tonight and go and see her in the morning. You know I'm talking sense.'

I know she is but it doesn't make me less inclined to jump in a taxi.

'Let her get some rest tonight, and see about visiting her tomorrow. We'll all go then, right Nik?' Willow looks at Nicky pleadingly.

'Yeah right, we'll all go tomorrow. She's safe in the hospital so let's get back inside and we'll figure out a plan, ok?'

Nicky gently touches my arm. I'm feeling slightly less murderous and after a short stand-off agree to go back inside with them.

CHAPTER 24

The visit to Charlotte isn't particularly pleasant. She's on her own when we arrive and puts on the fakest smile I have ever seen. We greet her with hugs and chocolates but the hugs are awkward and feel forced from her end. She is halfway through telling us what happened when in walks a guy I presume to be Julian.

He smiles stiffly and plonks himself on the bed taking Charlotte's hand in his. I'm sure I see her wince at his touch.

'You must be Nicky, Hannah and Willow then,' he says, 'nice to finally meet you.'

I would give anything to wipe the smug grin off his face. 'Is it?' I practically spit back.

Nicky shakes her head at me and mouths, 'don't'.

I look at Charlotte, the fake grin is slipping and there's a strange look in her eyes —fear, she looks frightened. I don't say anything else.

'So, has this clumsy cow filled you in on what happened?' The same smug look. 'I can't trust her to be on her own. She's forever walking into furniture and tripping over her own feet, aren't you?' He looks at Charlotte who nods in agreement. 'I don't know what would have happened if I hadn't come home early,' he concludes.

'What do you mean?' I ask, genuinely curious.

'If I hadn't come home and found her on the floor,' he adds.

'About that.' If I don't say it, I will kick myself later. 'How come you couldn't call an ambulance? I mean, I know you had some nasty injuries but couldn't you get up to get to the phone or next door to get help?' I aim the question at Charlotte but it's him who answers.

'She was in shock from the pain. Weren't you, angel?' She nods again. 'So she just lay there stunned until I rescued her. It makes me so sad to think of her lying there all alone for so long.' He kisses her hand for effect. He's a bloody good actor I'll give him that.

Neither Willow nor Nicky have said a word since he walked in. There's an oppressive atmosphere and it's making me feel claustrophobic. I want to leave but at the same time I want to stay and ask Charlotte what really happened. I can see I am not going to get that chance because he isn't going to leave while we're here.

'Well girls, thanks for visiting but she really needs her rest.' The smug bastard.

'But we've only just got here. Do you want us to stay?' I ask, looking straight at Charlotte.

She looks at him and says, 'I am tired actually.'

He grins and says, 'well there you are, straight from the horse's mouth.'

It's taking every bit of my strength to refrain from kicking him in the bollocks. We exchange more awkward hugs and make our way out of the room. I look back and swear I see tears in her eyes. I blink away my own.

We go to the café outside the hospital for coffee and cake, which seems an odd thing to do having just visited our abused friend, but it's comforting.

'What did you think of him?' I'm sure they thought the same as me but I need that validation.

'I thought he was a smug arsehole and I have no idea what she ever saw in him,' Nicky says without hesitation.

'I second that,' Willow adds. It's reassuring to know I'm not the only one wondering how she ever fell for him in the first place.

'I really don't know what she was thinking,' Nicky says through a mouthful of chocolate cake.

'Do you think he's always been like that? I hope not. I can't imagine Charlotte falling for such a knob,' Willow asks

'I doubt it,' Nicky says. 'He was probably charm personified at the start. His mask has well and truly slipped now. There was something creepy about him, the way he was stroking her hand but appeared to be holding it way too tight. She looked frightened to death of him and…' She stops mid-sentence and looks over at me, suddenly aware of her words and the effect they may be having on me.

'It's fine,' I say. 'I noticed it too, and the look in her eyes broke my heart. I understand now the hold he has on her. Well I don't really understand but I understand if you get what I mean.' I know what I mean but can't seem to get the right words out

'I understand. You don't know how she got to the point but you understand now why she isn't asking or taking help when offered, right?' Nicky always gets me.

'Exactly. I saw it today though, the fear factor. She's scared of what he will do to her if she told anyone what was happening. He's a nobody but to her he's the most powerful man in the world and I guess she doesn't feel like anyone can defeat him.' I'm still struggling to understand how she got to this point though. From, 'omigod I've met this totally amazing guy,' to sitting in a hospital room battered and bruised because the 'totally amazing' guy is anything but.

I fill Will in when I get home. True to his word he was super supportive last night. He wondered what the hell had gone on when I flung myself at him in floods of tears as ten minutes previous I'd been busting some pretty big moves on the dance floor. He was wrestling with his phone attempting to secure an Uber the minute I'd told him what had happened thinking I'd just want to go home but I convinced him I was happy to stay. I wasn't really happy to stay but it was Nicky's night and it was practically ruined, I didn't want to add to it even more by being the arsehole who ran out on her best mate's engagement party.

We stayed until the bitter end and I was sober as a judge. I was worried that if I carried on drinking I wouldn't stop and I needed to be fully with-it for this morning so I stuck to tonic water.

'I wish I'd gone with you, I'd have knocked his fucking head off.' He couldn't knock the skin off a rice pudding but I love him for suggesting he might.

'It wouldn't have helped matters. She's terrified of him, it was written all over her face. You'd have only got yourself in trouble and probably caused more for Charlotte and that's the last thing she needs.' There's no denying there would have been a momentary feeling of satisfaction had he hit him, though.

'Yeah well, he deserves it, the fucking coward.'

I don't disagree.

CHAPTER 25

I've felt as though I've been living in a parallel universe for the last couple of months. Everything has been exactly the same yet somehow different. Work has been as shit as ever, B is still taking great delight in making my life miserable and although I so want to tell her to stick her job, at the same time I feel as though I should be grateful that the worst thing in my life is having a total bitch for a boss. A situation I could easily change by finding a new job.

We're still trying to get pregnant but my heart isn't really in it. Having a baby is another thing that would add happiness to my life and I don't feel like I deserve to have extra happiness when my life currently is sunshine and roses compared to Charlotte's. I imagine her sat at home, wishing she could escape but feeling as though she never will and that what she has is as good as it's ever going to be for her. Will is overcompensating for my misery by being annoyingly cheerful at all times. It's obvious he has run out of things to say to try and make me feel better and I'm trying so hard to not appear miserable all of the time but the guilt of carrying on life as normal and the fear of what might happen to her consumes me.

I haven't seen or heard from Charlotte since visiting her in hospital. I tried to visit her again but Julian turned me away at the door saying she was sleeping. I called to speak to her too but she didn't answer the hospital phone or her own. Every time my phone pings I grab at it, half hoping it's her and half terrified it's her mum with bad news.

Willow bumped into Jean a few days ago and said she was barely recognisable, that she'd lost weight and aged ten years. They spoke just long enough for Willow to find out that Charlotte was still in contact, albeit sporadically, and that Jean had been to the police, who advised her they could do nothing unless Charlotte was prepared to report him. I was enraged and spent hours online researching as I was sure there had been a change in the law to protect people who were being abused but too scared to admit it. Seems I was wrong. Something can only be done if the police have enough evidence of the abuse to prosecute without the victim's statement. There isn't any evidence though, he's a bit too clever for that. Our assumptions and what we 'know' isn't enough either, even with the hospital records. They clearly state she fell down the stairs and not that her psycho boyfriend used her as a punch bag.

'Han, you coming or what? It's like talking to a brick frigging wall.'

I hadn't realised Willow had been stood at my desk so deep was I in my daydreaming (day-nightmaring would be more apt).

'Sorry, what, where are you going?' I reply, snapping out of my daze.

'It's lunchtime, where do you think I'm going? B is out for the day so I thought we may as well take advantage and have a longer than usual lunch. I didn't envisage spending half of it trying to get an answer out of you though.' She smiles.

'Why not? I can't concentrate on this shit anyway; a long lunch may help with my focus.' It won't at all.

'Well shift your backside then and let's get gone.'

We don't bother with our usual place and instead opt for the pub, which is dangerous on two counts. The first being it sells alcohol and I'm in the mood to drink, and the second being that it doesn't look all that sanitary so food poisoning is high on the menu's list of extras. With this in mind we both cautiously order Scampi and chips then hope for the best.

We've had a heatwave over the last few days, which suggests that once again spring is the new summer and there won't be a summer. We order a cider telling ourselves it will be refreshing and less intoxicating than wine. Obviously this is not true as the first thing you learn as a teenager new to alcohol is that compared to other drinks cider is inexpensive and gets you shit-faced in half the time of any other drink. I think back to when I was at school and drinking in the park with my mates. We just wanted to get pissed as cheaply as possible. I never needed more than four gulps before the grass started spinning which is probably how my parents never had a clue what I was doing.

'Did you hear a word I said?' Once again I am snapped out of my daydream by Willow's dulcet tones.

'Sorry, I was just thinking about when I first drank cider.' I tell her with a smile

'I don't know why I bother talking to you these days, I may as well just talk to myself in the mirror for all the notice you take. Where is your head at?'

Will's said the same thing to me on more than one occasion recently. 'I've got a lot on my mind, that's all.'

'Haven't we all. I've got two sick kids, an unhelpful husband, a Nazi boss and a mate who ignores me and yet I still manage to listen to you!' Her husband isn't unhelpful. He's one of the good ones, he's just not very good when the kids are sick. He's a fun dad, not clean up sick and bleach surfaces dad.

'They no better? You should have stayed at home and then at least you wouldn't have had to bother with the Nazi boss.' I say. Well, it would be one thing off the list.

'Yes, but if I stay home I have to clean sick up all night and day, so it's only fair I make him stay home and do it. He hates me for it. I can see it all over his face when I get home and he thrusts a vomiting child at me. He can't get away fast enough. Have you not noticed I've been staying late purposely? I decided an extra hour with the Nazi was worth it so that he has to do an extra hour on puke watch.'

I can see Willow is very pleased with herself. 'Crafty,' I say.

The scampi arrives and doesn't look too bad, no obvious signs of salmonella and after a pint of cider the carbs are most welcome. We talk through mouthfuls, mostly slagging off colleagues and without a single mention of Charlotte. It's the first time I've felt 'normal' in months. Maybe this is what I need to do in future, not talk about her. If I don't talk about her she might not enter my head as much and I might just be able to go about my own life without feeling guilty.

'How is your coffee shop plan coming along?' Willow asks draining the last of her drink.

'It's not.' I say huffily.

'I've told you, you'll never do it if you don't plan it.'

She is referring to a conversation we had with Nicky a while back. She told me that plans need to be on paper not in minds. She believes that writing things down makes them real and once you put it out there you can focus on making it happen. Trouble is, I haven't yet got around to writing it down. I've had so much other stuff going on what with Charlotte and trying to make a baby and, to be honest, I don't know how writing 'I want to own a coffee shop' on a piece of paper is going to help.

'I'll get around to it, I've been busy,' is all the excuse I have.

'Mate, you spend hours a day scrolling through Facebook and you're telling me you don't have time to write a few words? Pull the other one.' She has a point.

'If you ask me, you're all talk. You want a coffee shop but you don't WANT a coffee shop. It's the idea that you love. If it wasn't, you'd find time and make it happen.'

She's right about the idea, I do like it. I like it very much but I can't deny it just feels that it will never be a reality.

Lunch with Willow gave me a new perspective. We talked about us and I didn't feel guilty. I felt like a weight has lifted. I realised that for such a long time my thoughts have been dominated by an oppressive darkness and it's been exhausting. I am allowed to carry on with my life, I am entitled to feel happy without being guilt ridden. My mood shouldn't be determined by something that is outside of my control. I've tried to help Charlotte, tried to make things better and I haven't been able to. I shouldn't beat myself up about that, everyone else has been right all along.

I'm not going to stop trying to help but I am going to stop being consumed by the situation and letting it overshadow my every thought. Charlotte would be mortified if she knew, the old Charlotte anyway. She would be the first person to tell me to get a grip and stop being a martyr, so that's what I'm going to do.

Will was the first to benefit from my new-found freedom. I whisked him upstairs as soon as he stepped foot in the front door and demanded that we make a baby. He didn't quite know what to make of the smiling, domineering me but he duly obliged.

Afterwards I nestled in the crook of his arm and fell asleep. Despite waking up ravenous after having had no dinner, it was the best night's sleep I've had in weeks.

CHAPTER 26

Saturday afternoon, Will is at the pub playing pool with his mates and I'm eating my body weight in cheesecake. I didn't even bother to cut a slice, I just sat at the kitchen table with the whole thing and a fork staring at a piece of paper upon which I've written down my dream. It says, 'I want to own a coffee shop.'

I giggled when I wrote it. It felt silly and yet thrilling at the same time. I sent a picture to Willow and Nicky, 'about bleeding time,' was Willow's response. Nicky was less enthused, 'and I want to marry Channing Tatum but what's that got to do with the price of fish?'

I call her. 'Stop pissing on my parade, it's taken me months to write that.'

Nicky isn't fazed, 'well for Christ's sake don't give up your day job to become an author, you'll starve to death.' Always the joker.

'I'm serious. Willow said I needed to get the dream from my head and onto a piece of paper as it would make it seem real. It does feel quite exciting.'

'I should have known it was one of Willow's in touch with the universe ideas. Alright, so now it's written down how exactly do you turn it into reality,' she asks

'I have no idea, it's taken me forever to get to this point. I just thought I'd enjoy that for a while.' I genuinely don't know what to do next.

'Well I don't reckon a bank is going to throw money at you because you have a dream. I would have thought a business plan might be a good place to start. You can get template ones on the internet.'

A business plan sounds scary. I've never even seen one let alone written one. What kind of shit do you have to put in them and how do you find all the shit? What am I supposed to do, go speak to a Costa Manager? 'Excuse me, teenage girl, but could you please give me an idea of how much it costs to run this franchise you seem to be managing?' I wish I hadn't written it down.

'Thanks for your support.' The words are dripping in sarcasm. I don't care, she can take it.

'I just don't want you going in half arsed, if you're going to do something...'

'I know, do it properly. I want to, I just don't know how and I haven't really had much time lately to look into it.' I've had physical time, just not mental time.

'Well now you have your new attitude you should have time and if you don't then damn well make some. I'm not going to spend the next ten years listening to you whining on about how much you hate your job and wished you had a coffee shop. Wishing doesn't make things happen, doing does.'

'You wouldn't make a very good life coach you know, you're far too bossy and judgmental.' I say in jest.

'That's why you love me,' she replies. 'How about I come over and we do some brainstorming? Can't accuse me of not being helpful then, can you?'

Our brainstorming isn't going too great. The three of us (Willow included) have been staring at a tiny whiteboard I borrowed from work ages ago and never returned, and so far all that's written on it is 'coffee shop'. We've spent more time pouring wine than thinking. Perhaps this wasn't a great idea after all.

'Right bitches, focus.' Willow has nominated herself as team leader. 'What's the first thing you need to set up a new business?'

I want to say a clue but instead I say, 'cold, hard, cash.' Willow writes it down.

'Depending on the business, a building,' is Nicky's contribution.

'That's a start, so how do we get the cash and the building?' Willow barks, it feels more like an interrogation than a brainstorm.

'Bank,' Nicky answers, 'for the money not the building but I suppose you'd buy the building with the money.' She clarifies.

'Good, then how do we get the money from the bank?' She sounds like a school teacher.

'Rob it!' I answer laughing.

Willow is not in a laughing mood, she is taking this very seriously. 'If you don't want my help Han, I don't have to be here.'

Wow, very serious indeed. 'Sorry,' I mumble.' I'm expecting the cane if I say anything else out of line.

'Business plan,' shouts Nicky.

'I'm pleased to see one of you is taking this seriously.' I stifle a giggle. 'So Nicky, what do we need on that business plan?' Willow asks, her eyes burning into mine with an intensity that I haven't seen before and which is actually scaring me a little bit.

'Err, ideas,' I say. That's the wrong answer.

'If you're not going to say anything sensible then don't say anything at all.' I was being serious, Willow clearly does not agree.

'Projections!' Nicky (teacher's pet) shouts. 'Ooh and detail about your business,' she adds for extra brownie points.

Willow looks impressed. I am not, this was supposed to be fun but all it's doing is making it blatantly obvious that I don't have the necessary skills to run my own business.

'If I can't even come up with a single thing to go in a business plan then how the hell am I going to run a business?' I ask, deflated.

'That's why we're doing this, to help you.' Willow says.

'Well you're not helping me, Willow. You're making me feel stupid and getting annoyed with me. Maybe you should open the coffee shop.' I nod over at Nicky so she knows the last bit was aimed at her.

'I think we need more wine.' Nicky responds, sensing the tension and removing herself from harm's way.

Willow looks hurt. 'I'm sorry, I didn't mean to upset you. I just want you to get to where you want to be that's all and for someone who says they really want this you don't put too much effort into trying to get it.'

She's right, I don't. Not because I don't want it, but because I don't have the first idea how to get it and shouting words at a white board is not helping.

'I get it, and I appreciate your help, I really do. I just wonder how I will cope in the big wide world of self-employment when I can't even come up with a plan on my own.' I sound pathetic.

'But you don't need to do it on your own, we're here and we want to help. Three brains are better than one even if they're pickled in sav, so stop wallowing and start thinking.' She smiles sincerely and I get to thinking.

Having put together what we felt was a good basis for a business plan we went about trying to find suitable premises, while fully aware of the fact that those premises are unlikely to be available by the time I get the cash to purchase one. We discovered a couple of little gems on the south coast; small but perfectly formed. Neither were kitted out as coffee shops – one being a former art studio and the other being a shell, but they looked to be about the right size and are in nice little spots. The art studio is a stone's throw from the beach in an elevated position so it has the views. Both places are in the five-figure region, with the beach one slightly more expensive. They're literally a dream come true.

***

The next morning I wake in a positive mood. Despite the alcohol it took me forever to get to sleep, I was overwhelmed with excitement at what might be. I was buzzing when Will came home and I insisted on telling him every part of the plan we had come up with. I'm pretty certain he fell asleep about two sentences in but I kept on anyway. I'm willing him to wake now so that I can tell him again, after all it won't just be a big change for me.

He needs to wake up sans hangover. I'm keen to discuss the lightbulb moment I had after my mini breakdown last night. The girls thought it was a brilliant idea. I'm not sure he will agree but it's my job to convince him. It might just be the best idea I've ever had, I don't even know how I thought of it. It won't be easy and it will take us out of our comfort zone but in business you have to speculate to accumulate.

'Have you actually gone mad?' Not the response I was hoping for. 'No, seriously Han, have you? Has all that wine finally addled your brain cells or are you just trying to wind me up?'

I had to wait almost two hours before Will woke up. In all my excitement I had woken at 6.30am. It's a good job I realised before waking him if this is the mood he's in. He should be grateful that I had enough self-control to not do it earlier.

'What do you mean? It's a brilliant idea! Everyone has to start somewhere and if you don't take risks in life you never get anywhere.' I'm trying to sound like a well-informed business women and not a whiney wife.

'I agree, but risking our house on a business you know nothing about isn't what I had in mind.' That's harsh but fair, I suppose.

My fabulous idea, and I still think that despite Will's misgivings, is to re-mortgage our house to buy premises. We bought it years ago and the house prices have shot up. We are cash poor but in assets less poor, and could easily secure £50,000 by re-mortgaging. That way when I went to the bank I would only need business set-up costs for fit-out and stock buying and I would have an asset against which the loan could be secured. Genius!

'I've thought it through you know and I really think this is it, a way to get what I've always dreamed about,' I say, still trying to sound businesslike and convince him I can do this.

'Right, and what about my dream, Han? You know, that one where we extend the house so it's big enough to house that kid we're trying to make. When I mentioned doing the exact same thing to release cash for that you were having none of it and said we couldn't afford increased payments and yet, now it's for something you want increased payments aren't a problem. I need a coffee.'

Oh, so that's where I got it from. I thought it was too good to have just come from my brain. God, he never forgets anything! That argument was well over a year ago and I didn't think we could pay the increased payments. Well, we would have managed but we wouldn't be able to have a life. He's just not getting it, though. If we got the money to buy a business then we would lease the premises to the business, which would pay the rent and cover the increased mortgage payments. It wouldn't cost us anything. So Nicky says, anyway. Obviously we might have to do some jiggery pokery initially if I'm going to secure a business loan on those premises but we can cross that bridge when we come to it. I'm not giving up, not when I can almost taste it.

'So he's not convinced then!' Nicky says when I call her to convey the bad news.

'Is he fuck. He's stopped listening to me and says he doesn't want to hear another word about it. Maybe you could convince him for me.'

As far as Will is concerned it is the most ridiculous idea I've ever had. Considering, 'risking everything we've worked for on a bloody whim and a pipe dream,' is not what sensible people do and is apparently proof that I do not have a business head on my shoulders. Arsehole.

'He's not going to listen to me, he already thinks I'm a bad influence.'

'I'll have to think of something else then, because this is happening. Trust me.' I say.

CHAPTER 27

I'm not altogether stupid so I keep my mouth shut for the remainder of the day and don't say another word about re-mortgaging the house. If there is one thing I have learnt in all our years together, it's that Will says no a lot but, as a thinker often reconsiders and says yes. I'm hoping this is what is going to happen on this occasion. I'm going to find time at work to create a visual aid. After all, selling is what I do. I need something that convinces him it's a good idea. I just haven't thought what yet.

The following morning I amble into the office full of Monday blues and am stopped in my tracks when I notice a woman I don't recognise but who looks spookily like Charlotte sat at her old desk. That space has been occupied since Charlotte left by a guy who I presumed was her replacement. In true B style she never actually introduced him to anyone but the logical explanation was that he was our new teammate and I was ok with that. I am not ok with this. Her hair colour, her clothes, her features – she's her doppelganger!

Willow is just as taken aback when she walks in. I see her do a double take. B is already in so she doesn't stop by my desk but we make eye contact. I'd been doing so well since Willow and I had lunch. I've been thinking of mine and Will's future and very little else, but now I can feel the familiar gnawing feeling in the pit of my stomach. Although not sensible I call Jean and arrange to meet for coffee, she sounds pleased to hear from me but I feel worse afterwards. A wave of nausea suddenly descends and I run to the toilet and promptly throw up. I'm rinsing my mouth when Willow walks in.

'You ok, you look pale as?'

I shake my head. 'I've been sick. I knew calling Jean wasn't a good idea but I didn't know it would make me ill.' I carry on wiping my face bemoaning the fact I have no toothpaste, only floss which will be fine for the caught lumps of carrot but not so great for my vomit-covered tongue.

'Why did you ring her? You know being in touch with her is not going to help you, it just adds to your worries and reminds you of everything that's happened and is happening.' Willow says sympathetically.

'I know and I've been feeling so upbeat lately but seeing Charlotte's double has made me realise that I haven't really come to terms with her leaving yet. I thought I had but I was wrong. I can't talk to her so her mum is the next best thing.' I say.

'Just be sensible yeah. You were so fired up last week about your own dreams, don't let yourself get distracted and it be put on the back burner again, okay?' Willow strokes my arm and walks out. She has a point but concentrating on me is harder said than done.

Jean looks better than she did the last time I saw her which can only be a good thing. She smiles emphatically when she sees me walking towards her. She stands and embraces me which takes me a little by surprise.

'It's lovely to see you,' I say as I sit down.

'You too,' she answers, 'it seems to have been a while'. I rack my brain, I last saw her when Charlotte was in hospital so it's been a few weeks now.

'How have you been?' I ask as I glance down at the menu realising I still feel quite sick and not at all like eating or drinking coffee. Green tea and toast seems the sensible option.

'Oh I'm doing ok love, some days are better than others. I've come around to the fact that none of this is Charlotte's fault. I was so angry with her for choosing him over us but I'm not now because I know that isn't what she did, not really.

She does seem much brighter so I'm prepared to believe her. 'I'm happy to hear that, you can't blame yourself for something you can't control.'

'No, I suppose I can't.' She smiles.

We order but I regret my choice when Jean starts to look all worried and question why I'm not eating properly. I tell her I've been a little under the weather and am just getting over it. It's a little white lie but I'd rather tell her one of those than the truth and risk upsetting her. She asks what I've been up to and I tell her all about my business idea. She listens, nodding enthusiastically. I always feel on edge when I speak to her but as I tell her everything I feel myself relax and become more animated.

'Well, I think that sounds like a marvellous idea. You're very clever to think of it.'

It was actually a group effort but I'm happy to take the credit. 'Thank you, I think so but unfortunately Will isn't quite so convinced.'

'I haven't ever met him but I am sure you can bring him round to the idea. He'd be silly to not let you try. If you don't follow your dreams now when you're young enough to, you'll live to regret it.' She says it with the understanding of someone who has been there.

'You sound like you're talking from experience,' I say.

She takes a deep breath and smiles wistfully. 'That's because I am'.

She tells me how once upon a time she was a bit of a singer on the pub and club circuit. She got offered a gig on the cruise ships but turned it down as she had just started seeing her boyfriend (her now husband) and she would have been away from him for weeks at a time. She didn't think their relationship could stand it so she said no.

'I've regretted it ever since,' she tells me with conviction. 'Oh don't get me wrong, I don't regret being married to him or having the kids but I regret not having that experience. Maybe had I been a little more mature I would have seen that our relationship could work but I was only nineteen. Mind you, he didn't help telling me we'd probably split up as I'd be too busy for him and have loads of fancy pieces on the boat.' She starts to laugh. 'Fancy pieces, I don't think I've heard those words since that day! So you see I do know what it's like and that's why I'm telling you to do it'.

Against the norm, I feel much better after seeing Jean, I am even more convinced about the coffee shop, though I am no nearer working out how I am going to get Will on board. Me telling him Jean's story of regret isn't going to help as he's never even met the woman but perhaps I can twist it into my own story of how I could end up feeling in twenty years if he doesn't let me do it. Maybe I should make him feel bad for not trusting or believing in me.

A bit below the belt, but desperate times call for desperate measures.

CHAPTER 28

I've spent the remainder of the week dropping hints to Will about all the regrets I'll have in the future if I am prevented from at least trying to follow my dreams. My tactic hasn't exactly worked but I can see that it has softened him a little. At first he was annoyed that I had dared suggest he did not have my best interests at heart. 'How is not wanting us to lose every penny we have, me not having your best interests at heart exactly?' were his actual words. He was smart enough to use the word 'us' instead of 'you', just to show we were in this together. I was smart enough to twist his words and suggest that although he was using the right words he wasn't feeling the sentiment as if this was about us he would not dismiss my idea out of fear but would consider it in a fair and balanced way, removing all sentiment. I told him to imagine this was the idea of someone he didn't know, what would he think of it then?

Sometimes I am too clever for my own good. He agreed to look at the business plan with a more open mind and not to be so dismissive. Now I just need to make it perfect. I've managed to pen a simple one using all the tips I found online and I just need to make it look more professional. It may take a while to perfect so I need to spend every spare second on it, which will be a bind as I have 6 episodes of Kardashians to catch up on and Will is out playing pool which seems to have become his new Sunday afternoon habit.

I spent the night mostly awake, tossing and turning trying to come up with the perfect plan. I decide I may as well go into work early, not to work obviously, as no one would choose to do that. Besides, I have very little work to do currently. A fact which I am sure is not lost on B. She'll simply be biding her time before she makes an issue out of it and an idiot out of me.

I'm going in to crack on with my big plan. I might be able to have it finished by tonight and have Will's final decision by tomorrow. I need to strike while the iron is hot.

Disappointingly, I am not alone when I enter the office. It is only just after 6.30 and B is already there. This cannot be a good sign. I consider turning and walking back out but she has already seen me.

'And to what do I owe this pleasure? I was expecting to be alone at this time.' Oh shit, now I have to come up with a lie.

'Err I just thought I'd get in early and deal with some e-mails.'

'Really? I wouldn't have thought you had enough e-mails to warrant being here this many hours early given how little work you currently have to do.'

I knew it. I knew that she knew and just hadn't said anything yet. Now she's got me. At least there is no one else around to witness my humiliation.

'It's just a couple,' I lie again, 'but they're ones that needed some careful consideration so I wanted to deal with them while the office was quiet and there were no distractions.' I don't sound at all convincing.

'I don't pay you to be distracted. If you can't get work done in office hours because you're so easily distracted then perhaps you shouldn't be working in an office full of people.' Great, now I need to back-pedal.

'Oh no, it's not that I'm distracted as such, it's just the general office background noise that makes it hard to concentrate sometimes.' I am not getting any more convincing,

'Or, perhaps it's the fact that Willow woman spends as much time at your desk as she does at her own.'

I can see the delight in her face as she taunts me and waits for me to play. She's like a kitten playing with a ball of string.

'Well I don't agree with that,' the words are out before I can stop them and now I need to do some damage limitation as it is way too early in the day for a war with B. 'I mean yes, she does sometimes stop by and say hello but it's generally only a couple of times a day and she's never there more than a few minutes.'

This is actually true. We're very careful not to spend too much time together in the office so we can avoid precisely what is happening now.

'And what about Skype, e-mail etc?' She is enjoying every minute. Does she really know about those, does she see them even? Oh god, if she's seen them I might be sacked on the spot.

'What about them?' I mumble, sounding far less confident than I did a few minutes ago.

'I'm talking about all the time you spend sending each other messages. Did you think I didn't know? I know everything that happens in this building, in fact I know most things that happen outside of it too, so don't ever think otherwise. I may or may not have seen some of those messages and you may or may not have thought you were being clever using "that manipulative bitch" among others instead of actual names but do not think you are clever enough to pull the wool over my eyes. I may not be able to fire you for talking shit when I have no proof it was me you were talking about, but I could easily make a case against you for violating the internet policy.'

Wow, so she does spy on us. How can that be allowed? Surely she has to have good grounds to obtain access to our e-mails? I wouldn't mind but I delete the Skype conversation history daily because I'm so worried about her looking at them but I didn't really think she did! It's always been a bit of a joke that she knows our every move and has cameras in the office to watch us when she is not there but this takes spying to a whole other level. She has actually read the Skype messages between Willow and I. Does she do that with everyone or has she specifically picked on us? Why would she even do it? The paranoid bitch. I find some courage.

'If you were going to do that you would have done it by now so if you don't mind I really need to get some work done.' I scurry to my desk before she has time to answer.

I haven't moved from my desk all day. Willow has been sending me messages that at first I tried to ignore but I felt dreadful about it so I replied whenever B seemed to be otherwise distracted. I kept the replies almost monosyllabic to refrain from giving B anymore ammo should she be reading them. Now that I'm leaving for home I can text Willow and tell her what the hell has been going on and warn her not to Skype anymore, not about B anyway.

I arrive home and realise I haven't eaten all day. I felt a bit sick again this morning and by lunchtime, although I felt better I then had a huge knot in my stomach from that cow so I didn't eat then either. I am now starving. The problem with being starving is I have no food. I forgot that I needed to go to the supermarket and I really can't be bothered going back out. I rummage around in the cupboard and find a breakfast bar, which will have to do. I'm ravenously tearing at the wrapper when my phone rings. It's Willow.

I give her all the grisly details having only given her a snippet by text and she laughs albeit in a slightly uncomfortable manner. 'So you see, we have been rumbled.' It does seem pretty funny now. Two grown women not daring to speak to each other because their boss knows they speak to each other!

'Haven't we just. So what do we do now? Just avoid each other or work out some special code so that we can still message but she won't know what we're saying?'

I don't think Willow's idea is actually a bad one, it could be quite amusing if only I had the time or inclination to make up a language.

'What about Klingon? I bet Will is fluent in that so I could get him to write it for us.' He does love his Trekking, much to my distaste. He has been a massive fan ever since I've known him. Until *The Next Generation* ended he would sit poised every Monday night eager for the next instalment. I tried to watch it a couple of times but it just reminded me too much of *Lost in Space* from when I was a kid and I hated that show.

'Jason's probably pretty good at it as well, he loves that shit. I'll ask him to do some as well.' I forgot that Willow was also *Star Trek* widow. We didn't know each other back in the day when it was actually on, it was just one of the many things we discovered we had in common.

'Cool, that's sorted then, we're going to speak in Klingon. Now it's settled I need to go shove this breakfast bar in my gob. I haven't eaten all day and my stomach thinks my throat's been cut,' I say, taking a bite.

'You haven't eaten all day,' Willow says in surprise, 'did B wind you up that much?'

I finish chewing before answering and filling her in on why not a single morsel of food had been consumed up to this point. She's silent for several seconds.

'Willow, are you there?'

'Yeah, I'm just thinking.' I didn't realise me not having any breakfast or lunch would provoke such thought.

'So you were throwing up yesterday, you couldn't eat this morning because you felt sick AND you've been trying for a baby. Do you think there might be a connection?'

I let her words sink in slowly. Do I think there might be a connection? Well, I wasn't thinking that but now I am.

'Err, I don't know, not really,' I mumble.

'God, you really are an idiot. Go out and get some tests and call me later, yeah?'

She hangs up leaving me a little stunned, breakfast bar in one hand, phone in the other. Will walks in as I'm still processing the information. I grab his hand, 'we need to go back out.'

'Where's the fire, Han?' He asks as I drag him towards the car, 'don't I even get a hello or a welcome home kiss?'

The answer is no he doesn't, my mind is too busy swirling with the suggestion Willow just not-so-subtly made. Could I be pregnant? No, I can't be, we haven't really tried much lately. She's probably wrong, it's probably just stress, feeling sick for two days doesn't mean anything.

The supermarket is less than five minutes away and I drive in silence. Will spent the first few minutes asking what was going on but I couldn't concentrate to answer him. I pull into the carpark.

'Oh I get it, you're hangry. That explains things. What we getting, chicken ding? I'm guessing you can't be arsed cooking anything fresh at this time. Let's just get a curry thing, they're not bad.'

I have managed to find my way to the relevant aisle in the time Will has been prattling on about microwave bloody meals. I look up and down until I see it. Clear Blue. I grab a couple. Shit they're expensive. There's some own brand ones for less than half the price. Will they be as accurate though? I can buy three of them and it will still be cheaper than two of the others, best of three works for me.

As I ponder I realise Will has finally shut up. I look up at him and he's starting right at me.

'Oh,' is all he manages to say.

CHAPTER 29

It's the longest two minutes of my life. I've seen movies where they do a test then walk around with the stick in their hand looking at it every few seconds. I opt for the leave it on the toilet lid method, as I have no desire to flick piss all over the bathroom, Will does that enough as it is. He did not shut up all the way back to the house, bombarding me with questions about how I knew, how long I'd known, why I hadn't mentioned anything. I answered as best I could given I'd only 'known' for about five minutes longer than he had. He's now wildly pacing around the bedroom waiting for results.

Time up, I pick up the stick and walk into the bedroom where I promptly burst into tears. Will looks disappointed.

'Don't worry babe, we'll keep trying and it will happen eventually. At least we get longer to save up.'

I wipe my tears on his shirt. 'It's positive,' I mumble into his shoulder.

'It's what? Positive? Are you, err positive?' he asks.

I nod my head and hold the stick up for him to see. Plain as day, two blue lines.

'Holy shit! We're going to have a baby.' He picks me up and spins me around. 'We're going to have an actual baby,' he repeats. The last time he was this excited we had just had a new bathroom tap fitted.

I can hardly believe it, all the months of trying and hoping then the second I forget about it, it happens so I have no idea how pregnant I am. I try to work it out, I don't actually think I had a period last month which means I've missed two and would be two months pregnant, doesn't it? I'm sure that's how these things work. So If I'm two months that means I'm almost a third of the way there already. Holy crap, six more months and I can leave that bitch B and never look back. I throw myself back onto the bed, no more work for a year. This deserves a celebration, a nice cold glass of ... nothing.

I can't drink now, can I? Oh balls, I didn't think of that. Oh god and even worse I have drunk, been drinking I mean. I haven't really stopped. Shit, what if I've damaged the baby? I'm a terrible mum already and the baby isn't even here.

***

We've been sat on the sofa googling for the last half an hour. For every page we find accusing me of damaging my unborn baby by drinking alcohol we find another that says moderate drinking in the first couple of months won't harm it at all. I'm more confused than I was when we started looking but for the sake of sanity (and until I can see an actual Dr or Midwife or whoever you see at this stage) I'm going to go with the ones that say no harm has been done.

I'm desperate to ring the girls and tell them, they'll all be so excited. Willow will be sensible aunt, Nicky will be do-whatever-you-want aunt and Charlotte will be cool aunt. Actually, Charlotte won't be anything. She'll just be a person I mention now and again, a person I have photos of, memories of. I want to tell her anyway, maybe it will help us reconnect in some way. It can't hurt. Will tells me not to tell anyone until we've been to the doctor and made sure the test was right and everything is ok. I nod in agreement but I'm telling them. What he doesn't know won't hurt him.

I want to tell Nicky and Willow in person. I know I told Willow I would let her know as soon as I knew but a few hours won't make a difference. I'll sneakily call Nicky while Will is in the shower or out collecting dinner. We decided to celebrate with take out which is the next best thing to Champagne. I'm going to text Charlotte. I'm trying to come up with the right words, I don't want to sound like I'm showing off or rubbing her face in it. I just want her to know. I type words, delete them, then type some more. I finally decide on, 'Hi, I hope you're ok. I really miss you and wanted you to be the first to know that Will and I are having a baby. I sure hope baby gets to know Auntie Charlotte like I know her xxx.'

Nicky screamed for a good six minutes. In the end I hung up and called her back as you can't converse with a screaming women and I needed to talk quickly while Will was out. I told her I had messaged Charlotte, she approved. I swore her to secrecy advising that Will didn't want me letting the cat out of the bag just yet so she hadn't to tell James. She promised she wouldn't breathe a word to him or anyone else.

I feel emotional again when I hang up. I can't really believe it. There's no bump and I don't feel pregnant, yet apparently I am. Wow!

Will was surprisingly quiet through dinner, he must have exhausted himself with his three million questions before he went out. Perhaps the excitement has given way to the reality, we are going to be parents. No more spontaneity, no more weekend lie-ins, no more quiz nights at the pub (unless we get a babysitter and we won't be able to afford one of those) no more relaxing holidays. What have we done? Why would anybody do this, give up their freedom for another human being who has done nothing to earn being the recipient of such selflessness? It can't be all bad though, can it? There are people who have loads of kids and they can't all be insane. There must be some good things about parenting as well. I'll need to start buying some parenting guides and magazines to find out.

In bed that night I can't get to sleep. All I can think about is having a baby in my belly. I'm not really thinking of anything else just, literally, there's a baby in there. I wonder what flavour it will be, what colour hair it will have, what we'll call it? It won't be any of Will's stupid sensible names that's for certain. I want something different, not ridiculous different but slightly unusual different. I need another wee.

It's 2am and this is the second time I've been since climbing into bed four hours ago. Is this what pregnant women mean when they go on about having to pee all the time? Surely it can't be because I'm pregnant, the baby will be a tiny bean-sized blob at the minute, not big enough to make we want to wee. God, if it is big enough, I am in for a rough ride. I cannot pee every two hours until it pops out.

When I climb back in bed I notice my phone is flashing. It's on silent. I grab it to get rid of the light and see that I've had a missed call. It's Charlotte! Why is she ringing me at this time? I'm happy that she is but she hasn't rung me for months and now she's ringing me in the middle of the night. Do I call her back? I wouldn't usually call someone at this time but if they called me first then surely it isn't a problem. I press call. My heart is beating so fast I think it might beat out of my chest, the phone rings and immediately is answered.

'Hello,' I whisper, not wanting to wake up Will.

'Hi,' she whispers back. 'I got your message and I just wanted to …' There's some loud rustling and a sharp intake of breath and then the line goes dead. I try to call again but the phone is switched off. Maybe her battery went dead, but what about the noise and the deep breath? Maybe she was ringing me at that time so he didn't know and he woke up and heard her. The rustling could have been him wrestling the phone from her and the deep breath her surprise.

I wonder what he's doing to her now and the image of her in the hospital bed. The look on her face is vivid in my mind. Should I call someone? Who would I call? I can't call her mum she'll be worried sick. I could call the police, but what would I say to them? 'I rang my friend and she hung up on me so I think she's getting beaten.'

I consider ringing Nicky or Willow but think better of it. It's too late to be waking other people up no matter how worried I am. I lie awake struggling to get back to sleep, but the image refuses to leave. I get out of bed and throw on come clothes. I'm going to drive over there, to where Charlotte lives.

I sneak out of the house and hope Will doesn't hear the engine. It's pitch black and there isn't another soul around. They live about twenty minutes away. I speed all the way there, my hands shaking on the wheel.

The apartment is on a quiet street. I slow down just before their block. There are only nine units in it so they can all be seen from the front. There are no lights on in any windows. I get out of the car and creep towards the front door. How am I going to get in? I don't know the apartment number and it's unlikely anyone is going to come out at this time. I walk around the side of the block. It's eerily quiet. I can't hear a single thing. I lean back against the building and cry silent tears.

What was I thinking coming here? I trudge back to the car.

CHAPTER 30

In the following few weeks I don't get any more early morning calls from Charlotte. I have to assume that whatever I imagined was happening to her was just that, imagination. I thought about it non-stop for the first few days and told Willow and Nicky about it as soon as I got out of bed the following day. They were relieved I hadn't called her mum and assured me everything would be fine. I didn't tell them about my middle of the night drive to her house. They would not approve.

The day after my midnight drive I had arranged to take a pee sample into the doctors so they could confirm I am indeed pregnant. Taking into account the hormone levels and my last period they reckoned I was around nine weeks, which means I am now almost twelve weeks and heading into the second trimester. Apparently the second trimester is supposed to be the good one where I will feel at my best, so I am looking forward to that because I have felt shit during this one.

I've lost count of how many things I can't eat because the aftertaste makes me want to vomit, anything with tomatoes, tea, curry, Chinese. I'm mostly surviving on white toast, which is also the only thing that stops me feeling sick. I'm like a junkie rushing to the toaster for my next fix and then for three glorious minutes the sick feeling leaves me. I don't know about no carbs before Marbs, it's more like more carbs for Marbs as I reckon I'm consuming enough to sustain the whole of Essex.

I'm not going to tell B until I have to. I've been reading up on it and I have to have some form or other signed by my employer by week twenty in order to get maternity pay, which means I have at least nine more weeks before I have to say something. I'm planning to tell her just before the nine weeks is up, unless the little pod starts showing beforehand. It's summer, so wearing big jumpers is out of the question. I suppose I could turn all bohemian and start wearing big flowery floaty frocks. That would cover it up. She might get suspicious though, as that look is so far removed from my usual wear. The thought of telling her fills me with equal measures of dread and delight. Dread as I know she'll be furious so will make my life even more miserable, but delight at the fact she will only do so for a maximum of twenty four weeks.

It's been so hard at work having to avoid speaking to Willow while being desperate to talk all things baby. We go out to lunch every day so I'm certain B suspects something is going on. We've stopped trying to pretend we're not going out together by leaving at different times, it was exhausting trying to co-ordinate around phone calls and meetings and B not looking. Today will be no different, I'll just wait until I see her picking up her bag and I'll do the same.

We head to our usual spot and when we walk in I'm taken aback. Jean is sat at a table all by herself and she's watching the door. I think she must be waiting for me. We walk over as she stands up. She looks upset and my stomach does a somersault.

'Is everything ok?' I ask giving her a hug. 'This is Willow,' I add.

I let go of her and she looks at Willow. 'Yes, I know. Hello dear and thank you so much for asking me to lunch,' she says, touching Willow's arm. Willow smiles back.

Jean turns back to me and says, 'Charlotte came to see me. She had bruises on the side of her face and on both wrists. They were faded but they were there. She saw me looking at them and said she'd been clumsy and had walked into the corner of an opened cupboard but you don't get bruises on your wrists from walking into a cupboard, do you?' Her voice trails off. I wonder whether I should tell her about the phone call but I can see Willow shaking her head. She knows what I want to say and is telling me not to.

'When was this?' I ask, hoping and praying it has nothing to do with the call.

'Oh, a week or so ago I suppose, they didn't look fresh either.'

My skin turns cold. The timing of it could easily mean it happened on the night she called me, BECAUSE she called me. If I had thought for a minute he would do that just because she was speaking to me I would never have called her back.

'Well it must have been nice to see her even so,' Willow says, filling in the silence so that I don't spill the beans.

'I suppose. She came to bring her dad's birthday present but HE was sat outside. He stayed in the car so she didn't stay above five minutes. Scared to death of him she is, scared to death.' She shakes her head.

'Has Hannah told you her news?' Willow is determined to steer the conversation away from the direction she thinks it's heading in.

'No dear, what news?' she asks staring straight at me.

'Err, I'm pregnant.' Saying it to her makes me feel sick again. What will she think? I've purposely not told her because she is worried to death about her own baby.

'Oh Hannah! What wonderful, wonderful news.' She reaches out and hugs me tightly. 'You will be a fantastic mum, you're such a kind, caring person. That baby is lucky to have you. Now I'm looking at you properly I see there is a glow about you, the kind you only get when you're in the family way. I bet you're ecstatic, aren't you?'

Much of lunch was spent on baby talk. Jean reminiscing about when her two were babies and asking what my parents thought, what my husband thought, if I wanted a boy or girl etc, etc. I think she was as relieved as I that we had something else to talk about for once, something more positive. For the first time in a long time she was smiling when we said goodbye. Willow was right to stick her nose in. The rest of the afternoon dragged as it always does when B is in. I have become quite obsessed with checking her diary weeks in advance in the hope of a B free day. It doesn't even have to be a day, just an hour or two respite is more than enough. She has a very nasty habit of having appointments in her diary that she fails to attend, leaving me desolate. I haven't decided whether she's plain rude and accepts invites for events she has no intention of attending, or whether she makes herself phantom appointments purely to inflate my hopes (knowing how much I look forward to her not being there) and have the pleasure of knowing she has dashed them. Knowing how scheming she is, I plump for the latter.

I'm even more excited about going home than usual, firstly to escape B and also because Nicky is coming over. As usual we'll have a lot to talk about. Sadly, one of the key ingredients to our relationship –wine, will be missing. For me, at least. Although I said she was welcome to bring her own if she placed so little value on our friendship and was willing to rub my face in abstinence.

I answer the door to Nicky holding up two bottles of wine, as suspected. On further inspection it transpires that one is alcohol free.

'You do love me after all,' I say feigning shock.

'You haven't tasted it yet, I bet it tastes like piss.'

'Not unlike Chardonnay then. I can't wait to try it.' I drag her and her bottles in. She's looking me up and down quizzically.

'You're making me nervous, will you stop doing that.'

'I'm merely checking for signs of life, I mean signs of extra life growing inside you.' She's not right in the head.

'It's a bit early for that, though I have been told I'm glowing.'

'Interesting, I'd say you emanated more of a dull than a glow to be fair.' Who needs enemies?

'Piss off. You try having a belly full of arms and legs and let's see how dull you are.' Insults exchanged Nicky squeezes me. She squeezes so tight I feel like I might pop.

'Ok crank, let me go, the baby can't breathe.'

She looks like she might burst into tears. 'I'm just so freaking excited for you. I never even thought you were grown up enough to have a baby and yet you're going to be in charge of raising a tiny human. How scary and awesome is that?'

Now that she has said it I feel more scared than awesome. Me, being responsible for a tiny little person, it could go so horribly wrong. I could make them as screwed up as B or as anal as Will or as paranoid as me. Oh shit, this is a big deal. I'm not sure I can cope with such responsibility.

'How are you really feeling then, are you shitting yourself? I reckon I would be.' She has such a delightful way with words.

'Well I wasn't until you turned up, I was leaning towards excitement. Admittedly that was more to do with finishing work and seeing the back of that bitch but now you've ruined it.' I turn my head away in mock disgust.

'Does Willow know you call her a bitch?' We both crack up.

'Speaking of Willow, we had lunch with Jean.'

'Bumped into or arranged to meet? You know I'm not super comfortable with this co-dependency thing you both have going on.' This is not the first time she's said that. She likens me and Jean to addicts, needing to get a fix from each other. To 'satisfy our souls', is how she put it last time she brought it up.

'She was the same as always and I'm going to ignore your last comment. She said Charlotte had visited, with her bodyguard who sat outside in the car the whole time. She had faded bruises on her wrists and face that she claimed came from walking into a cupboard. Do you really think she believes we are all falling for this shit?'

It's more of a rhetorical question but Nicky answers anyway. 'In her frame of mind, I'm not sure what she believes, maybe she doesn't even know she's lying, maybe she's so programmed now that she believes what she says is true. Who knows what you think in her situation.'

I take my first sip of the non-alcoholic 'wine'. It's so sweet it's like drinking honey. My liver might be happy to see the back of actual alcohol for a while but my teeth aren't going to thank me for drinking this crap.

'Well, what do you think?' Nicky is waiting for my critique.

'Licking a sugar cube would taste less sweet,' I answer truthfully.

'Well you can't please all of the people all of the time. You got yourself up the duff so you'll just have to suck it up for the next six months.'

I think I'll just not bother for the next six months, to be honest.

'So what's the big coffee shop plan now that you're up the duff?'

Will and I have discussed this and both agreed that the timing actually couldn't be better. I can use my maternity leave wisely to source possible premises and really work on the business plan, maybe make some appointments with banks and who knows, maybe just never go back to work and get the shop all up and running by the baby's first birthday. I tell all of this to Nicky.

'Sounds like you've got it all worked out, we'll make a businesswoman of you yet!'

CHAPTER 31

I spent much of the night thinking about Nicky saying that Charlotte was being programmed. Is she really or is it just a survival instinct that's kicked in and she's in self-preservation mode? I suppose when you lose so much control over your life you have to try and get it back somewhere. Perhaps she thinks she's doing everyone else a favour trying to protect them from the truth, when in reality the truth is so glaringly obvious there is no protection from it.

It's 6am and the morning light is seeping through the curtains making it impossible to sleep in. I climb carefully out of bed so as not to wake Will and look down at my stomach. Holy shit! There's a bump. It's little but definite. It's not the result of last night's dinner either – it's an actual, teeny baby bump. I shake Will, he wakes quickly looking confused then, as he realises I have woken him he looks a little annoyed.

'Look, it's started. I've got a bump!' I say, barely able to contain my excitement.

Had I not been pregnant and had a bump I would be mortified but today a bump seems like the best thing anyone ever had. Will beams at me and reaches out his hand to stroke my stomach. Now it's real, there is definitely a baby in there and we are definitely going to be a mummy and daddy. I disappear from the room to collect the baby books. We have two: an amusing yet factual one and a factual yet not amusing one. We read the 'your baby' bit of each every Saturday morning which tells us how big baby is and what body parts it's grown this week.

According to both books, at thirteen weeks our baby is the size of a pea and is developing its unique fingerprints. It has started to suck its thumb and if it's a boy his testicles have developed and his penis has started to grow. If it's a girl her ovaries have formed. How weird to think I might have an actual dick growing inside me. I say the same to Will.

'It's not like it's the first time, you've had plenty of dicks inside you,' he replies. Charmer.

I have lost count of how many times I have lifted my top up today to look at the bump. It gets bigger when I eat but I suspect that's bloating and not the baby growing at a rate of knots. I've sent pictures of it to Willow and Nicky. Willow responded with enthusiasm, Nicky said she has a bigger bump when she's constipated. It's a good job I love her.

During the day's excitement I realised that now I had a bump I was going to have to consider telling B. I know I don't have to for several more weeks yet, even if I had a massive bump I wouldn't be obligated to tell her but I don't have the brass neck to waltz around clearly pregnant without actually saying the words to her. I have scoured my wardrobe to see if I have anything slightly looser fitting that doesn't make it look obvious and I have nothing.

None of my trousers will fasten. The zip will go up but the button doesn't meet. I did force on one pair but the waistband cut off my circulation and I was worried it was squashing the baby so I whipped them off again. I'm going to have to go shopping tomorrow and get kitted out. At most I will be at work for another twenty-one weeks. So I'll try and keep the spending to a minimum. It's not like we're rolling in it and Willow says maternity clothes are extortionate.

Will is uncharacteristically excited about our shopping trip. Ordinarily If I mention clothes shopping he comes out in a cold sweat and tries to think of a reason not to come. However, when I mentioned my plans for today he was noticeably eager. I suspect he just wants to keep a handle on the spending but when I say this to him he looks hurt.

'Well thanks, Han. I'll not bother then. I just thought it would be a nice thing to do together as it will be the first baby thing we've bought. Well I know they're not for the baby but you get what I mean.' Now I feel guilty.

We give the fancy new shopping centre a whirl, although it has some high end stores it also has an H & M, which to me is like Primani's flashier sister. It has a maternity section, which has got to be cheaper than Debenhams, so if I cannot find normal clothes that are suitable I'll rummage around in there.

Parking is abysmal. It seems this is the place to be on a warm summer's day. There is little wonder the people in this country are so damn miserable, they could be out in the fresh air enjoying the lesser spotted sun and instead they are trudging around indoors trying to forget that tomorrow is Monday.

Having driven around the carpark for at least twenty minutes we finally get a spot. It's definitely coffee time. It's probably cake time as well (and I wondered why I couldn't fit into my clothes even when I wasn't growing a person).

'Coffee first?' asks Will expectantly.

'You betcha!'

We scurry inside hoping that the gazillion people whose cars are outside are busy milling around the shops and are not busy stuffing their faces with cake while getting a caffeine hit. We pass a couple of overfilled places and my heart sinks. At this rate it will be coffee and cake to go.

Not wanting to be defeated we change floors and our luck is in. We find a solitary empty table. It's in a shit position, right by the entrance but I'll take knocked elbows over a paper cup any day. Will doesn't look impressed when I take a seat, he looks around for a better option.

Seeing a better option isn't available and noting the look on my face which clearly says I'm not fucking moving, he goes off to order. I want coffee and a big fat piece of cake. With a bit of luck the ensuing bloating will make me look six months pregnant and I'll be able to measure the give in the non-maternity, maternity clothes. It takes almost fifteen minutes for Will to return with coffee. I have kept myself amused scrolling through Facebook. The usual Sunday morning posts about hangovers and shit men. Luckily I have not been afflicted with either and I feel relatively smug about the hangover bit at least. It would be nice to abstain long past baby bean's arrival but I am only setting myself up for disappointment if I kid myself that it will continue. Best I just play it by ear.

I'm busy filling my face when I spot a familiar figure. I do a double take as the familiar figure appears to be with a child so my instinct is that it can't be her. As it gets nearer I see with horror that it is her and she has seen me. She stops at the table. We exchange pleasantries and she introduces her niece. For an awful minute I thought she had a secret child. She tells her niece that I am one of her 'friends' from work. Nothing could be further from the truth but the coffee shop on a Sunday morning isn't the place for a reality check. She tells me their plans for the day and then waltzes off advising she'll see me tomorrow. I'm too stunned to speak and go back to eating.

'She seems nice,' says Will. I almost choke on my cheesecake.

'Nice! Are you being serious? Do you know who that was? It was B! The master manipulator who inflicts pain and misery like no other. She is the polar opposite of nice'.

'She hides it well then.'

I refrain from throwing the cheesecake at him but I glare and snarl at him through gritted teeth.

'She is not fucking nice. A two-minute chat with her and you think you're an expert. Try fucking working with the crazy, evil bitch and see how nice you think she is then.'

I'm no longer in the mood to shop.

***

When the morning rolls around I'm slightly giddy to be dressing in my new clothes as despite Will's best efforts at sabotage I did purchase some that fit and am now in full-on comfy mode heading to work. I don't think anyone can tell but then I look at myself every day. Will said he couldn't tell, but then he's trying to get back in my good books after forming the B Appreciation Society.

I take a selfie and send it to the usual suspects with one word: 'Obvious?' Nicky replies immediately with, 'totally you fat bastard.'

291

Willow is more reserved, 'Can't really tell on that, I'll tell you when I see you in person.'

I walk to my desk holding my bag at waist height like pregnant celebs do and sit down sharpish. B doesn't move a muscle. Success! As soon as my bum hits the seat I get a text from Willow. When I look across at her she is shaking her head.

'How the fuck am I supposed to see if you can tell when you sneak in like a member of the SAS?' I suppose she has a point but I'm not really comfortable with standing back up again so that she can observe me like a zoo exhibit.

'B has a meeting in ten mins, we'll go to the loo then,' I reply.

I watch the clock tick down and B rise from her desk. Good we can convene in the bogs soon. To my surprise, actually horror, B has left her desk but is stood at mine. I don't know what to say so I say nothing.

'Do you have a minute?' I look around to make sure she is talking to me. There is no one else around.

'Err yes,' I say, wondering what the hell she wants and how I'm going to disguise anything if I have to stand up.

'It wasn't really a question. I've booked room four so follow me.'

What the hell is this all about? Rooms booked for meetings I know nothing about. She is up to something and I'm not sure I want to find out what it is. I follow her to the room like a sheep.

'Sit down.' She points to a chair. 'Do you have something to tell me?'

I am trying to work out of this is a rhetorical question or if she actually wants an answer. If she wants an answer what the hell do I say? Obviously I have something I need to tell her but it isn't something I had planned on telling her for another two weeks at least. If I don't tell her now and she knows it really isn't going to look good, if I do tell her now that's an extra two weeks of hell she'll subject me to. I'm in a quandary.

'No, I don't think so.'

'Really?' She isn't surprised, she's just saying it for effect.

Now that I have dug the hole I can't clamber out (not in my current state anyway) so I have no choice but to let her have her fun. I say nothing.

'For someone who thinks I have the office bugged it's astonishing how little you think I know.' I still say nothing.

'I believe congratulations are in order,' she continues.

Nope, I'm not speaking.

'Well I must say I am surprised you're not shouting it from the rooftops, I would have thought any reason to be away from here for any length of time and you'd be telling anyone who would listen.'

That gets me. 'I don't know what you mean?' I say, knowing exactly what she means.

'Oh, so you can speak. I have no idea why you have been keeping it secret and I don't really care. What I do care about is you trying to sabotage me by leaving and not allowing me any time to find a replacement. That's borderline gross misconduct.' I'm pregnant and she still wants to make my life hell. Well I am not standing for it.

'Actually B, I think you will find I am well within my rights to hold off telling you anything until I am twenty-one weeks pregnant. Anything could go wrong up to that point and I didn't want the stress of telling everyone I was pregnant and then having to tell them I wasn't any longer if something happened.' It's a lie but a plausible one. 'I wouldn't expect you to know or understand that as you've never been in this position. So you're wrong, it isn't gross misconduct and you can stop trying to threaten me.'

The look on B's face is a picture. I'm quite pleased with myself.

'You can tell yourself whatever you like but I know you have kept this to yourself out of pure spite and nothing else.' She turns on her heel and marches off.

All of a sudden I start to shake and appear to be having a hot flush. I run to the toilets and swill my face in cold water over the sink. When I look up I have mascara all down my cheeks, great. So now it looks like I've been crying and I know for a fact everyone will have seen me walk off with B so they'll put two and two together and make five. Emma will be delighted to think I've had a doing.

When I get to my desk I have to send a message to Willow advising the mission has been aborted. B knows so I don't really need Willow to evaluate the size of my bump anymore. Her response is, 'I'm not surprised, I just clocked it when you walked back in and you'd have to be stupid not to know you were smuggling a belly full of arms and legs.'

Sometimes I wish I had friends who lied.

CHAPTER 32

The weeks slide by, the bump grows and before I know it it's huge and I'm in my third trimester. There has been much chatter over the last few weeks about a baby shower. I'm not keen as I just can't be arsed and hate being the centre of attention. Will loves the idea as he says we'll get loads of stuff for the baby that we can't afford and Willow (who came up with the idea) and Nicky (her partner in crime) think it's an excellent idea to get pissed one afternoon and eat lots of cake. They have been badgering me constantly about it. I have started to come around slightly as apparently I don't have to do anything. Now that's my kind of party.

I am assured that the party will not be held at my home, so I will have no setting up or clearing away to do and I'm not even expected to contribute anything for eating or drinking, I simply turn up. I have no idea who they would invite, I don't have a massive circle of friends and neither does Will. I only like three people in the office and one of them is a bloke, so it's going to be a small party and I fear Will may be disappointed by the present count. I express my concerns to Nicky who tells me there are lots of people on the guest list she and Willow have compiled so I've not to worry about a single thing. She adds, 'in your condition' like the thought of a lack-lustre party may send me into early labour.

I can't quite believe I am in my final trimester. I quite enjoyed the second, but I'm not feeling the same about the third. I feel huge.

My arse has spread and looks purple due to the myriad of thread veins that have appeared. My legs rub together when I walk and I can only eat paleo-sized portions of food as anything more than that feels like it sticks in my throat and will be ejected if I speak. I sit uncomfortably on the sofa each night trying to push baby down from under my chin in order to eat dinner. Baby is a little shit and does not budge.

I wanted to be one of those glamorous and glowing pregnant women. I am not. I don't wear bump skimming, trendy maternity clothes as they also skim my arse making it look even bigger than it is, so instead I wear baggy stuff which probably makes all of me look massive but as long as they cover my arse I don't care. Will has not touched me in months. Four to be exact. He kisses me good morning and good night but that's about it. You get those blokes on tv shows who are so overcome with love for their pregnant wives that they can't leave them alone. Will is not one of those husbands.

I read that sex when pregnant is fine and although I don't much feel like it now I wouldn't have minded a few weeks ago. When I told Will it was ok his response was that he didn't want to poke baby in the head. What a load of bollocks. What he actually means is that I am fat and turning his stomach so until I've slimmed down again I am a no-go area. It does little to boost my confidence. All those women who 'celebrate' their stretch marks and mummy tummy because they're 'warriors' are talking shit. If there was a cream that got rid of them overnight they would use it. Thankfully, so far I have been spared the stretch marks at least. Only time will tell re the mummy tummy.

On the day of the baby shower, I have been instructed to turn up to a little restaurant in town at 2pm. Apparently Nicky didn't want to hold it at her house as she's no host and Willow didn't want to do it at hers as it's a shit tip (her words). It's one of those little bistro-type places with furniture that doesn't match but yet looks good. I notice some very comfy-looking sofas and resolve to be on one before the afternoon is through. I am ushered into a little room towards the back.

Inside are around a dozen women, all of whom I recognise. Thank fuck for that. The room has been very tastefully decorated (which means Nicky didn't do it) with pastel pink and blue bunting and table settings, there are pink and blue bows around the chairs and pink and blue flowers dotted around in cute vases. I imagine if kids got married this is what their reception would look like. I'm impressed. The group have noticed I'm here and one by one they stand up to greet me, besides Nicky and Willow there is Katie and Sophie (from work), my mum, Will's mum, my cousins Toni and Lucy, Ella, Claire, Jo and Lyndsey (old friends I love dearly but barely get to see) and Jean.

I'm surprised to see Jean and feel a lump in my throat that Charlotte isn't here. I regain my composure quickly and continue to hug everyone in turn. Before long, greetings are done and the games begin. I don't yet know whose idea they were but suspect they were Willow's (too much thought for them to be Nicky's). We have guess the sex, pin the dummy on the baby (rather disturbingly the baby has B's head super-imposed onto its body), dirty nappies (which is disgusting and quite possibly was Nicky's idea) and drink up baby, which I refused to participate in as if I can't down wine out of a baby bottle then I ain't playing. Apple juice is not the same. It's hilarious to watch though. Unsurprisingly Nicky and Willow are well in the lead as they won't let a little thing like a pin hole prevent them from consuming the most alcohol in the least amount of time. Nicky almost passes out she's sucking that hard. Just watching brings tears to my eyes.

Having guffawed our way through games and food it's gift time. Looking at the pile of presents I can see why people do this shit. By the looks of things I won't have to spend a penny until baby is three. Will is going to be beside himself. I take my time unwrapping and inspecting each item, many of which are alien to me, apparently Gro Bags don't make baby grow, they just keep them toasty while they sleep. I am stopped in my tracks by the breast pump, which looks like a form of mediaeval torture. I wonder whether Will insisted someone buy it to aid his breast feeding agenda and it isn't a surprise when I realise it's from his mother. My mother-in-law buying me a present that is breast related frankly feels weird and I'll be flogging it on eBay as soon as I get home.

Nicky has bought me a massive basket of smellies and lotions and bubble bath, it smells divine. Willow pisses herself when she sees it. 'Only someone without kids would buy a mum to be that. She'll barely have time to wipe her arse when junior comes never mind wallow in a bubble bath and lather herself in lotion.' Nicky tells her to piss of as not all mothers, 'let themselves go like you have.' Willow, ever practical, has gifted a bottle sterilisation centre. It looks very complicated but she assures me it's simple to use and will make my life easier. I suspect a full-time nanny would make my life easier but no one appears to have got me one of those.

Jean hands me two gifts and I notice that one is from Charlotte. I'm touched but also suspicious as to whether it came from her or from Jean on her behalf. I open Jean's first, it's a large bundle of baby clothes. I thank her for being so generous. I hesitate before opening Charlotte's, turning it over and over in my hands. Those in the group who don't know the story are urging me to open it, those that do are looking at me sympathetically. I start to slowly remove the paper and reveal a Baby's First book. I open it and on the first page are the words, 'Love from Auntie Charlotte.' It's her handwriting.

The baby shower was a roaring success, I thoroughly enjoyed myself and didn't have to lift a single finger. Willow and Nicky outdid themselves and were fully deserving of the copious amount of champagne they drank. Will was like a kid at Christmas when I came home with my haul of presents. He wasn't quite so thrilled with the book mum had bought him on how to be the perfect dad but I did catch him thumbing through it after threatening to throw it in the recycling.

Jean hung around after everyone had left, she told me Charlotte had actually posted the present to her with a note asking her to pass it on as she wouldn't be able to make it. I told her I was touched that she'd even thought of me. She said Charlotte seemed to be getting in contact more often of late. Jean felt like she was reaching out, trying to reconnect maybe, but that things were still strained and she wouldn't hear a word against the twat she was living with. I suppose more contact is better than no contact even if her living arrangements are still the same.

I text her afterwards to say thank you and to my surprise she replied, what's more it wasn't just with one word. She said she was sorry she couldn't make it and hoped we could meet up for a coffee sometime. I wasn't expecting that! I said I would love to. She hasn't replied to that one yet but I'm hopeful of seeing her soon. Willow said she'd heard from her too and we wonder whether she is starting to take some power back.

I'm going to message her daily even if she doesn't respond, just to let her know I'm here for her.

CHAPTER 33

I've been having those Braxton Hicks things a lot lately. I have consulted my Dr (Google) and apparently it is very common at this late stage and nothing to worry about. Could have fooled me, some of them are freaking painful and they are not helping me feel any better about getting this baby out. This is the third night in a row I have laid awake watching my stomach tighten and release like the alien in there has it on a piece of string. I consider waking Will, after all he put the little twat in there but I know if I do he will be miserable as sin all day tomorrow and I can do without that.

I'm trying to get myself into a comfortable position when my phone starts to vibrate. Someone must be calling. It's 3am. It isn't a weekend so it can't be a pissed up Nicky. There is only one person who would call me at this hour. I turn the phone over and freeze. It's Jean. With trembling voice I answer.

Forty-five minutes later I am in ICU starting at the battered face of my beautiful friend. Jean is inconsolable and it's been difficult trying to get any information out of her. From the few words she has managed to say I determine that Charlotte was trying to leave him. She was sneaking out with her bag in the middle of the night when he woke up. A neighbour heard her screams and called the police and now she is here and he is on the run.

Willow has arrived. I meet her in the corridor as only two visitors are allowed at once. I hug her then wait outside while she goes into the room. Her usual stiff upper lip dissolves as soon as she walks in and I struggle to work out whose sobs are loudest. I haven't shed a tear and I wonder if I'm in shock or denial. I see a nurse walking down the corridor and stop her. Jean hasn't told me anything of Charlotte's condition and I need to know how bad it is.

'She's in a serious but stable condition,' is the first thing she tells me. 'She has several fractured ribs, a punctured lung, a broken wrist, fractured eye socket and a ruptured spleen. There is some internal bleeding also, so the next twenty-four hours are critical.'

I thank her and sit down stunned. How can a human do that to another human, not just any human, one they're supposed to love? She was leaving him, she'd had enough and finally plucked up the courage to get the hell out of there. I wish she had confided in me. I could have been waiting outside to drive her away and this wouldn't have happened.

I say this to Willow when she emerges from Charlotte's room.

'Or maybe he would have done the same to you too and you'd both be in a hospital bed,' she replies.

'Maybe …'

We sit outside the room making small talk. It's light outside now and I remember I left without saying a word to Will. I reach into my bag for my phone and sure enough there are two missed calls and a text asking where the hell I am. I go outside to call him.

The cold air seems to awaken my senses. The reality of the situation hits me and my legs turn to jelly. I manage to stumble to a nearby bench where the tears come, big heaving sobs. I call Will and tell him I'm at the hospital. He immediately thinks there is something wrong with the baby and goes into panic mode. I scream at him, 'It's not the baby, it's Charlotte. Will you fucking listen to me? Charlotte, Charlotte, Charlotte!'

I start telling him what I know. 'No, I don't know how long I'll be staying, I know I need to think of the baby but have you heard a word I have said? She's in a serious condition and I'm not leaving her until I know she is going to be alright.' I hang up on him.

After much resistance, Jean has gone home to have a shower and get some fresh clothes. Willow's gone to sort the kids and I'm sat holding Charlotte's hand silent tears staining my cheeks. I tell her how sorry I am that I didn't save her, that I didn't do more to get her away from him and above all how ashamed I am of how I all but washed my hands of her because she chose him instead of me for Sunday lunch once. I may be imagining it, I probably am, but I swear she squeezes my hand, it's the tiniest of squeezes but I call for a nurse. One comes running in and I tell her what I felt.

She speaks gently, rubbing my shoulder.

'It's quite common in coma victims for them to make involuntary movements but that doesn't mean she can't hear you.'

She leaves the room and I cry some more, then remember Charlotte can hear me and I pull myself together. I don't want her listening to me sobbing. Instead I reminisce, asking her if she remembers this or that like the time we went to a music festival tent in hand all prepared for camping but barely lasted an hour in the less than satisfactory conditions and wound up staying in the most expensive hotel known to man when they saw us coming and increased their price by 50 per cent. Or the time she got so drunk in a restaurant that Willow and I had to escort her out before our main meals after she stumbled into a waitress sending the plates full of food she was carrying flying.

I talk about the plans we had but never followed to go on a girls' holiday and I promise her that once she's recovered and baby is old enough we'll go away somewhere hot and spend our days drinking, eating and sleeping and our nights drinking and dancing. She loves dancing. Whenever we go out and 'Dancing Queen' comes on she screams at the top of her lungs and throws herself about like it's an ode to her. She just changes the 'only seventeen' part to whatever age she is at the time. I pray I get to see it again.

Jean returns and I realise I have been talking for around two hours, It's almost 10am.

'Any change, love?' she asks. 'I've spoken to the nurses a few times while I've been gone and they say not but they haven't been sat with her like you have they so how would they know?'

I hear the desperation in her voice and consider telling her about the hand squeeze but think better of it. I don't want to get her hopes up. I shake my head.

'You should go get some rest, it can't be good for the baby with you sitting here all night.' She takes hold of Charlotte's other hand.

'I'm fine,' I tell her. 'It's not like I sleep much these days anyway.'

'Ooh got to that stage, have you? It's not much fun, is it? I remember feeling like I'd never sleep again with this one. As soon as I lay down it was like having a washing machine inside me. Not much change when she came out either. She still kept me up all hours but then on a morning I'd look at that beautiful little face smiling up at me and all was forgiven. She was the most beautiful baby.' She starts to cry again.

I can feel my phone vibrating in my pocket and see that Willow is calling, so I excuse myself and go and take the call. I tell her about the squeezed hand and she tells me not to get my hopes up. She suggests I come into work as B is pissed at not only my absence but the lack of call to say I won't be in. She's making a big song and dance about it to anyone who will listen despite Willow telling her where I am and with whom. She really is the pits. I tell her I'll call B but I am not going in until I know Charlotte is going to be ok.

Willow returns after work and both she and Jean insist that I go home if only to get something decent to eat. I am quite hungry, I've only had a vending machine sandwich since I arrived and I'm not convinced that was good for the baby at all, limp lettuce and rock-hard bread. I agree to go but insist they call me if anything changes. Jean assures me she will and makes me promise I won't come back until morning. I don't want to make that promise, I don't want to leave at all let alone leave for the night. She says it's bad enough having one daughter in a hospital bed, she doesn't want the other one in one as well. I give her a big hug and promise I'll rest.

***

We have sat in shifts for three days and nights but today I am back at work. Not because I want to be but because I have no choice. I had a call from B and HR advising that unless I returned they would put me down as ill and start my maternity leave. I was quite happy for them to do so, but Will wasn't. We had a huge argument about it, where I called him selfish and uncaring, and he told me I wasn't thinking straight. He pointed out that we couldn't afford for me to be at home unpaid and that if I didn't go back to work now I would miss out on time at home with the baby as I'd have to go back sooner than planned after maternity leave.

I didn't want to back down but both Nicky and Willow said he had a point and that although I didn't think so now, when it came to it I'd be gutted I finished early and regret being so hasty. So here I am, back in the hell hole feeling guilty as sin for not being by Charlotte's bed and wondering what the hell all this shit is about anyway. Really, in the grand scheme of things, what does it all actually mean?

Willow is waiting in the carpark for me so I don't have to walk in alone. I shuffle through the building as slowly as humanly possible. When we arrive at our office B is hovering.

'Oh, it's nice of you to finally join us,' she says.

Neither of us responds.

I take my seat and mutter, 'Strike 1,' under my breath. If she says anything else I'm going to blow.

Throughout the morning I have numerous people stop by my desk to tell me how sorry they are to hear about Charlotte. and I'm fighting hard not to cry. I check my phone every couple of minutes just in case there's news. They say no news is good news but is that true when you're in a coma? Are you more likely to come out of it the longer you're in it or not? I look it up and the answer is no. The longer you're in the less likely recovery is. How long is too long, though? I start another search and fail to notice that B is stood right behind me.

'Thinking of becoming a doctor, are you?'

I jump in surprise but compose myself immediately. 'No, I'm just making sure I'm as informed as possible about what's going on that's all.' I carry on reading hoping she'll skulk off but she doesn't.

'You've had plenty of time to research while you've been away so I suggest you get some actual work done,' she sneers.

I'm counting to ten before I answer, I get to six and my phone starts ringing. Jean's name is flashing on the screen. I grab it and answer it not giving a shit about B. Jean simply says, 'Come now.' I try to answer but my mouth is so dry that my lips stick to my teeth. She has hung up before a single word escapes my mouth.

Like a robot I start packing stuff into my bag.

'It's barely twelve o'clock, would you care to tell me where you think you're going?' B growls under her breath.

It takes me a minute to compose myself. 'I'm going back to the hospital,' I say much louder than I intended.

Willow rushes to my side. 'What's going on?'

'Jean called. I need to go to the hospital,' I answer, putting my bag over my shoulder.

'I'll drive you,' she says without hesitation.

'No it's ok, I'll be ok,' I reply, feeling anything but ok.

'I'm driving you and that's the end of it.'

Willow rushes to get her stuff together. B, who has been stood at the side of me the whole time, grits her teeth and says, 'I'm sorry to burst your bubble but I'm in charge here and you don't get to come and go as you please so put that bag down and get back to work!'

I look at her defiantly and start walking towards the exit.

'I am warning you, if you step one foot outside of this office you will not be coming back again.' That is it. I've had enough.

I find my voice and scream at her, 'Do you know what you are? You're an evil, spiteful, manipulative bitch. You are miserable and lonely, so you treat everyone like shit to make them feel as bad as you do. Well you can fuck off and shove your job up your arse. My friend needs me so I'm leaving and the fact that you happen to know that friend yet are still trying to blackmail me into staying here instead of being by her side shows exactly how fucked up you are. Screw you and your job.'

Trembling, I turn on my heel and run towards the door.

The hospital is only fifteen minutes away but it's been raining all morning so the traffic is heavier than usual. I have tried to call Jean several times but each time it goes straight to voicemail. Willow has asked me twice if I'm sure Jean didn't say anything else. I've told her I'm positive. She said two words and only two words that were as clear as day.

We're halfway there when I notice a rainbow has appeared in the sky. The grey clouds have parted and there it is right above us and at once I know. She's gone. She hasn't woken up, she isn't getting better, she's gone.

A wave of nausea hits me and I let out a piercing scream.

EPILOGUE

Charlie James Eccles is four months old and the love of our lives. We have no idea what the hell we're doing but so far he seems happy and healthy so we must be doing something right. He has the most beautiful blue eyes and chubby cheeks and he smells divine, which is odd as I expected him to smell of sick and shit given that's mostly what he does. He's such a happy little thing who barely cries and has slept through the night since he was eight weeks old.

Jean was one of the first people to visit me in hospital. She cried when I told her his name and said Charlotte would have been honoured. I hope so. I think of her every single day. I wonder what she would make of all that has happened in the short time that she has been gone. The guilt has eased but it hasn't gone completely and I'm not sure it ever really will. I still think there is more I/we could have done but I guess I'll never know.

At least HE had the good grace to spare us all a trial by pleading guilty. We still had to face him in court and my god what a weak, pathetic, snivelling excuse for a human he is. He's where he belongs now and I hope he wakes every day in a living nightmare, just like we do. I also hope Karma comes calling and one of his new neighbours gives him the same treatment he used to dish out to Charlotte.

The door opens making Charlie jump. Two of my builders walk in with their bacon butties and brew in polystyrene cups. Every day they call at the burger van a couple of miles down the road and every day they tell me they can't wait until I'm open to get 'a decent cuppa'. I tell them that they need to do less bacon butty munching and more building if they expect me to be ready any time soon. I've also told them that the idea of a coffee shop is that people buy coffee so I'm not expecting to sell too much Tetleys.

I still can't believe it's happening and that in the end it was Will pushing for it and not me. He said losing Charlotte and made him see that life was too short to spend saving for the future. Tomorrow and the next day and the next were also the future and we were more likely to see those than twenty years ahead. He wound up taking my plan to the bank and securing the funding.

While Will was on paternity leave we scoured the country for potential properties. We were lucky as it was just before the start of spring when the property market suddenly gets hectic so we got this place for an absolute bargain and it's now full steam ahead. It's right by the coast which is what I wanted and every day I pinch myself that it's mine and I'm finally doing it!

I managed to get a payout from work. I needed somewhere to channel my anger and sued the bitch for constructive dismissal. Willow said her face was a picture when she found out. Many secret meetings were conducted and the company was denying it until I produced my secret weapon, Emma! We may not have seen eye to eye but she was one of the first people to contact me when I left and she was very genuine in her sympathy. She also put the constructive dismissal idea in my head and said she would back me all the way. Having spent so long up B's arse she was the last person B would have expected to be on my side.

When B found out, she caved like a wet cardboard box. We settled out of court for forty thousand quid and although part of me feels like it's B's money, so I don't want to touch it, the rest of me thinks I deserve every single penny.

Will is still working back home but has secured a transfer, which happens next month. I got a cheap apartment online and stay here with Charlie Monday to Thursday before Will joins us on a Friday. We have a full house this weekend with Willow and Nicky paying us a visit. I told them I didn't want visitors until everything was finished but they insisted on the basis that as godparents they have a spiritual right to see Charlie whenever they like. Not true, but it's pointless arguing with them. In any event they're helping me spend my settlement. There is lots of planning still to do for Nicky's wedding too (I still can't believe it's happening) and with only three months to go it's getting pretty close.

Nicky is so stressed. She is ordinarily the least stressed person I know, so when I mentioned I was considering trying to set up a charity to help people like Charlotte, to give them hope so they don't feel so alone and a place to stay when they think they have nowhere, I wasn't expecting her to offer to help. But offer she did, so she also has that on her plate. Willow is helping too and between us we're hoping we can get the charity up and running in as little time as possible in order to help as many people as we can.

I never thought being so busy would be so much fun let alone so rewarding, but I suppose the difference is I've chosen it. Working for B was a necessity, the things I'm doing now aren't. They're choices. Choices I've made and choices that Charlotte will never get the chance to.

She didn't even have the chance when she was here. Control of her life was taken away from her. I gave mine away to a woman I hated and a job I despised. Now I've taken control back.

I might fail. I've never run a business before, I've never even worked in a coffee shop, let alone owned one. I've never set up a charity and I don't know the first thing about it but I know this: there will be a greater sense of pride in failing at something I chose to do than there would be in succeeding at something I had to do.

Printed by Amazon Italia Logistica S.r.l.
Torrazza Piemonte (TO), Italy

17110170R00180